For my father, Raymond Wills, a proper hero.

FOOTNOTES[1]

WITHDRAWN

1. Footnotes are what writers use when they want to share something interesting with you but don't want to hold up the story. Instead, they put a little number next to a word so that you know there's a gripping bit down here, at the foot of the page. Personally, I call this the bottom of the page and think footnotes should be called bottom-notes. However, try as I might, publishers simply refuse to talk about bottoms.

❋ I ❋
A Star is Shorn

Our story begins in the Greek Underworld.

And yes, I do know Greek Underworld sounds a bit like Greek underwear, but let me assure you that our story has nothing to do with pants. In fact, the ghosts who haunt this Underworld don't even wear pants because pants hadn't been invented by the time they died. So, please, do stop talking about pants and let me get on.

Now, where was I?

Ah, yes, the Greek Underworld.

It lies many miles beneath our feet and nestles at the centre of the Earth like the stone in a peach. Brimming with sun-dappled waterfalls and forests, it's home to every potter, poet, thinker, soldier, slave, actor, dog, cat, goat and olive tree who ever lived in ancient Greece, including Aries, the ghost ram of the Golden Fleece and the hero of our story.

Now a ram, for those non-shepherds amongst you, is a male sheep and a fleece is his coat. Usually a fleece is made of wool, snagged with twigs and leaves and is quite often dribbly with dung. But not this one. The Golden Fleece, as its name suggests, was made of pure glittering gold, dazzling to look at and absolutely priceless.

On the afternoon our story begins, Aries was hiding in a bank of Underworld laurels that encircled a special building called the Heroes' Pavilion. Carved from the creamiest marble, it looked like an ancient Greek temple. A row of columns topped by swirls of stone leaves ran all the way around its sides whilst the panels beneath its roof had been carved to show several Greek heroes, their hair and armour picked out in gold and silver paints – which made Aries want to wee on it.

And I know what you're thinking.

Ghosts aren't supposed to wee, are they? They're not supposed to burp or blow their noses either, but let me assure you that the ghosts in the Greek Underworld do, and plenty of other much ruder things besides. And while we're on the topic – of Underworld ghosts that is, not ruder things – I might as well mention that Aries, like all the Underworld spirits, wasn't invisible either.

He didn't shimmer.

He didn't waver like a heat haze.

He didn't leave glowing hoof-prints where he'd trotted.

And he most certainly didn't vanish like fog. In fact, he was just as bulky as the rams you see up here standing in fields on Earth.

Only bigger.

Much bigger.

Wide as an overstuffed armchair, Aries rippled with muscles. Brawn quivered up his legs and thickened his back, tendons stood taut as ships' cables along his chest and strained around his wide neck. His face was handsome, and some (Aries mostly) said it was noble, lit by treacle-coloured eyes and glittery with gold dust. On either side of his head, gilded horns looped out, like twisty handlebars on a bicycle.

And since by now I'm sure you're imagining the most awesome and handsome of rams, I ought to mention one other thing.

Quite a big thing, actually.

The ram of the Golden Fleece was bald.

That's right:

BALD

As bald as a grape, as bald as an artificial eye, as bald as an ice cube, as bald as the world's baldest crab whose shell has been polished to a blinding baldness by the tide. Not one gilded knot, curl, cowlick or twirl remained on his body. Gone were the ringlets that had fronded his brow and the blaze had that dazzled down his neck. Gone was the fiery thatch across his back and the shimmering coils of gold over his shanks because, before he'd been sacrificed to the gods, his fleece had been sheared off first[2]. And since ghost rams can't regrow their wool, Aries' ghost had remained the colour of three-day-old porridge and bulged like a cheap duvet.

Which brings me to why the most famous ram in history was hiding in a bush in the first place. The problem was that, without his magnificent coat, everyone treated him like any other ordinary sheep.

Can you imagine?

The ram of the Golden Fleece reduced to the sort of sheep you might see bouncing about in a field on a wet hillside? The sort of sheep banned from all the important places, like the Heroes' Pavilion, because he might eat the dahlias or leave warm, smelly 'presents' on the lawns? Worse still, the sort of sheep that ancient Greek ghosts loved to chase and pick on because he was bald and funny looking? All of which made Aries furious enough to hide in

---

2. *Not wishing to dwell on such an unpleasant subject, let's just say they didn't want any messy drips spoiling the golden wool.*

the laurels every day to wait for the chance to sneak out and wee down the pavilion's gleaming walls.

Except today he couldn't.

Today the place was busier than the **agora** on Buy One Get One Free day. Ghost slaves had been tottering past for most of the afternoon, carrying tables, stools and benches, pots of lilies and jugs slopping with red wine. Serving women in white dresses had picked their way through the honking, flapping swans specially coloured gold and silver for the party to take in platters of pork and beef or bowls dripping with grapes, plums and olives.

Crossing his legs, Aries wondered at the ivory-coloured ribbons and swags of pink roses that had been tied to the pavilion's columns. Clearly, he realised, something important was happening today.

But what?

As if in answer, two slaves scrambled up onto the tall urns either side of the pavilion door and tied a banner above it, which read:

THE ANNIVERSARY OF JASON AND THE ARGONAUTS! OUR HEROES!

"Jason and the Argonauts?" snorted Aries in disgust. "Heroes?" The words buzzed around his brain like flies around a cowpat in summer.

I'd better explain.

Jason was an ancient Greek prince and the Argonauts were the men who'd sailed with him on a ship called **the *Argo*** many years ago, when they'd all been alive. Together they'd journeyed to the island of Kolkis where Jason had stolen Aries' Fleece. Yes, stolen it. Snitched, snaffled, swiped it from where it hung high in a treetop in the middle of an enchanted forest, protected by an enormous snake called Drako[3].

Luckily for Jason, the king's daughter, **Medea**, who was a sorceress, had fallen in love with him and helped him. However, to tell you the truth, she was a rather unpleasant person and I don't like talking about her unless I really, *really* have to. So, I won't. (But, if you really must know what she did, take a look in the back of this book. I wouldn't.)

Now, glaring at the banner, Aries found his four stomachs knitted with anger as he remembered that terrible night back in the forest at Kolkis. That's right, *remembered*, because what the old books of Greek myths never mention – because the old Greek writers, such as **Apollonius,** preferred to write about

---

3. *Don't ask me why locking it up in a vault wouldn't have been far more sensible. Ancient Greek kings were clearly barmy.*

glamorous people like Jason and Medea rather than bald rams – was that Aries was there.

Actually *there* that night.

As a matter of fact, Aries had been there haunting the forest for years before Jason turned up because he'd been unable to leave his beloved fleece behind. Even with only Drako the snake, twenty metres of slither, slime and stinky breath to talk to, he'd been happy, because every so often, Drako would lift the fleece down from the branches, and lay it over Aries' back. And then, comforted beneath its sparkling weight, Aries felt special again. It didn't matter that in reality he was hock-deep in the stink-mud of the forest, because in his mind he was the ram of the Golden Fleece again, handsome and majestic, flying (because his coat was not only beautiful but magical too) over the blue Aegean sea. Screwing his eyes tight shut, he'd tilt his shoulders, imagining himself shooting like a golden comet across a cloudless sky, the claps and whoops of the crowds below ringing in his ears.

And then Jason had arrived.

Even now, a lump rose in Aries' throat as he recalled scrambling to the top of the cliffs around Kolkis Harbour that moonlit night to catch a last glimpse of his fleece, glittering over the **prow** of the

Argo as it sailed towards the horizon. He'd never seen it again. No, because after Jason returned home and married Medea, he'd only gone and lost it. Lost it like an umbrella on a bus. But unlike Jason, the fleece had never turned up in the Underworld, which made Aries' horns twitch to butt Jason into the lake every time he thought about it.

Which was all the time.

At last the lawns fell quiet. Aries stuck his nose through the leaves and peered round. Only a few dancing women were left, practising steps on the far side of the lawn. This was his chance. Uncrossing his back legs, he shuffled forwards.

Only to be stopped by a familiar and extremely annoying voice.

"Hello, ladies!" it said.

Aries ducked back into the greenery as Jason strutted out along the top of the pavilion steps. Dressed in his best white **chiton**, his famous leopard-skin draped over his right shoulder, he tossed back his shoulder-length blonde hair and stroked his beard, smiling. A moment later the women raced over the grass to him, and stood around him, their faces upturned, flushed and pink.

Jason nodded towards the banner. "Wonderful, isn't it?" he said. "All this? Just for me?"

The women giggled prettily and Aries felt his heart clench.

Snatching a mouthful of laurel leaves, he watched a dancer with long black hair threaded with lilies hurry up the steps and link arms with Jason.

"They say you've been in secret training," she cooed, the silver bells on her belt jingling as she led him towards the others.

Training for what? Aries thought sourly. *Getting his tunic on the right way round?*

"We know you can beat the others!" said a willowy fair-headed woman. She stroked his muscled shoulder. "But we'll miss you so much when you're up there!"

Aries' jaw fell open, the chewed laurel leaves forgotten in his mouth.

Up there?

There was only one place that was *up there*.

Earth! And no ordinary ghost from the Underworld had ever been allowed to return there. The gods only knew he'd begged King Hades often enough to let him go back, just once to search for his fleece, but no, it was absolutely forbidden by Underworld law.

He stared at the fair-headed woman, willing her to say more, to explain, but instead she began clapping her hands and singing some rubbish about brave heroes on quests, whilst the others joined hands and skipped around Jason.

Questions galloped through his mind: Who was going back to Earth? How would they be chosen? Why did no one ever tell him anything down here? How in the name of Olympus was he going to find out? They were questions, he raged, that clearly wouldn't be answered by a group of women jingling their bells.

And then the answer struck him.

Like a hail ball from the skies, it was so big and obvious; he wondered why it hadn't hit him before. Of course there was someone who'd know, he realised, someone who always knew everything, from what the gods were planning to what the pavilion cat had dragged in the night before. Someone who was at this very moment quite alone in the otherwise deserted pavilion.

Ignoring the scratch and jab of the branches, Aries bustled backwards out of the laurels, hunched down, tippy-hoofed to the back of the pavilion and…

Oh dear! Hold on a moment would you… and do try to ignore that splashy noise…

Right, where was I? Oh yes, now that Aries had relieved himself he hurried over to the servants' door to the pavilion.

He pressed his forehead against the sun-warmed wood and began to push. Of course, a full frontal charge would have been much quicker, but it would also have been much noisier and Aries couldn't afford to be discovered before he'd had the chance to ask his questions. Taking a deep breath, Aries stuck his hooves into the ground, stiffened his legs and forced his full weight against the door. There was a keening sound followed by a sharp crack and splintering as the wood gave way. Aries nosed the shards out of the way and squeezed quickly through the hole into the pavilion kitchen.

On either side of him wooden tables stretched away, piled high with food and hundreds of goblets that twinkled in the sunlight. A gloomy-looking stuffed peacock, set on a heap of glazed reeds, stared blindly down at him from a shelf as he clattered through into the Grand Hall.

Tall and airy, the hall was dominated by rows of looming white pillars with the statues of each of the fifty Argonauts set between them. Whenever he'd crept in before, he'd blown raspberries at Tiphys, the helmsman of the *Argo* and the Argonauts' getaway driver that night, and waggled his bottom at Pollux, supposedly the son of the west wind but who Aries thought was more like an annoying draught under the door. But he didn't have time today. Instead he clattered quickly down the hall, his hooves squealing against the mosaic floor, and skidded around the corner.

There she was!

The bowsprit from the *Argo* hung above the door to the Dining Hall, snoozing. A bowsprit, in case you don't know, is a wooden figurehead that decorates the prow of a ship, and is often carved to look like the head and shoulders of a woman. And, being made of a clump of wood, they don't usually know that much. However, this bowsprit was different. Hewn from an oak tree that grew in the magical woodland of Dordona, and enchanted by **Athena**, goddess of wisdom, this bowsprit had answered all the Argonauts' questions. Wise and thoughtful, she had guided the *Argo* to Kolkis, with tips such as, "Turn right at the Pole Star," "Take a left after the Clashing Rocks," and, "Turn around where possible."

"Psst!" hissed Aries.

The bowsprit's eyes flicked open.

"Danger all shipping!" she announced. "Major obstacle in the water!"

"Do you mind?" hissed Aries.

The bowsprit shrugged, her shoulders creaking

like old floorboards. Once her cherrywood face had been polished to a toffee-coloured sheen, her lips painted rose red, her eyes inlaid with ebony, but over the years she'd become infested with woodworm. Far from her life of sea adventures she now spent most of her time moaning about where the cleaners stuck their feather dusters.

"What do you want?" she muttered, raising a sea-stained eyebrow.

"I want to know what's happening tonight," said Aries breathlessly, putting on his most engaging smile, which, to be honest, was rather frightening[4].

The bowsprit regarded him for a moment, blinking her creaking eyelashes. "What's in it for me?"

"Linseed oil? Pot of beeswax?" said Aries. "It'll work wonders for your wrinkles."

"They're not wrinkles," snipped the bowsprit. "They're laughter lines."

"Really?" Aries frowned. "That must have been some joke!"

The bowsprit stuck her nose in the air.

"I'm sorry," soothed Aries, quickly realising his mistake. "I really didn't mean that."

---

4. With no top teeth and a bottom row like wonky gravestones, rams look like four-legged granddads when they smile, all gummy.

The bowsprit sniffed.

"However," said Aries, "I have heard that beeswax made from the hives of Elysium can work wonders even on wood that's already beautiful."

"Already beautiful?"

Aries nodded. "Obviously you don't need it, but if you're curious I could bring you some. Probably turn you back into a sapling, a mere twig of a girl."

The bowsprit tilted her head, interested. "And you'll throw in a muslin duster?"

"Certainly," said Aries, who'd be quite prepared to throw in his grandmother if it meant getting some answers.

"Done!" The bowsprit licked her splintered lips. "There's a party tonight."

"And?" prompted Aries.

"It's going to be amazing!" the bowsprit continued. "Athena's celebrating the Argonauts' anniversary by holding a competition! What's more, they've made me a crown of laurels, just like they put on the statues in the Olympics!"

"What's it for?" said Aries.

"To accentuate my good looks, of course."

"No!" Aries shook his head impatiently. "I meant the competition!"

"Oh, that," the bowsprit smiled coolly. "It's a

special assault course to decide who'll be allowed back to Earth on a quest."

Aries stared speechless.

"Oh, I know," the bowsprit continued, "there's never been a competition like it before, and it'll be tough. But Athena wanted something memorable to mark the occasion. Mind you, everyone knows that Jason'll win. I mean, he's just totally awesome."

"Awesome, my hoof!" spluttered Aries. "You were stuck on the boat that night! You didn't see him in the forest at Kolkis. Shivering like a swamp rat in the shadows whilst a teenage girl did all his dirty work!"

"So you keep saying," sniffed the bowsprit. "As if Jason would hide when there was a giant snake to fight!" Her face grew soft and dreamy. "Oh, Jason," she sighed. "Those glorious days we spent at sea together."

But Aries had heard enough.

Swinging his head round he turned back towards the Great Hall and began clomping out.

"Jason, is it?" he muttered, looking back over his massive shoulders at the bowsprit's contented face. "Win the quest? And return to Earth where *my* fleece is still hidden?" He harrumphed loudly. "We'll see about that!"

❊ II ❊

A WALK ON THE WILD SIDE

Well, I don't know about you, but after all that excitement I could do with a decent cup of tea. However, I'll soldier on without a brew, quite parched, so that I can tell you about Aries' best friend, Alex.

Alex was a thirteen-year-old Athenian boy, or at least that's what he'd been when he died in ancient Greece and come down to the Underworld. Strictly speaking, he was now two thousand, nine hundred and seventy-two years old. But have you ever seen a birthday cake with that many candles? Gangly and with hair as black as ripe olives, he loved being dead. Up on Earth he'd been a potter, spending his days in his grandfather's cool, white workshop, painting pot after pot after pot. Round pots, squat pots, pots with bulbous middles, pots with long necks, pots with curly handles that snapped off just as you finished painting the picture on them. But down here he was a keeper in the Underworld Zoo, the home to all the old Greek monsters and fabulous animals.

A kind and thoughtful boy, Alex's choosing to work in the zoo had been a surprise to his parents, especially to his father Lykos. During his lifetime Lykos had been a **hoplite** in the Athenian Army and had nursed hopes that his only son might follow in his footsteps one day, into a glorious military career. But Alex, who'd even been named after the greatest army leader of them all, **Alexander the Great**, couldn't see anything remotely glorious about tramping off on pointless wars, and despite his father's insistence that his son learn to box and throw javelins, Alex had remained uninterested. Alex, you see, was a thinker, not a thumper.

Now, as you might imagine, the Underworld Zoo wasn't like any zoo you or I have ever visited: no penguins skidded down ice slides, no hippopotamuses slapped about in mud and absolutely no sea lions ever leaped through a hoop for fish. Instead, the arcades rang with hisses and roars, the slap of tentacles and the clang of bronze beaks. Even that familiar eye-watering whiff you get in Earth zoos was here mingled with the stench of burning earth and vomited bile.

One enclosure held the ghost of the **Minotaur**,

the half-man half-bull creature who prowled within a high-walled maze beneath a viewing balcony. Another held the spectre of the **Ceryneian Hind**, a deer with golden antlers and hooves made of brass that shot sparks into the air as she scrambled over the rocks. The many-headed **Hydra** swam in a mesh-covered tank. Wild **man-eating horses** galloped around paddocks ringed with high bronze fences. The three **gorgons**, women with snakes for hair, bickered behind special one-way screens to stop their glances turning ghost visitors to stone.

What's that?

You're surprised that *ghost* gorgons could still turn spectators into statues? Or that *ghost* monsters needed locking up at all? I suppose that's because someone's told you that a ghost's just a ghost. It's dead, so it can't be harmed? Well, Greek ghosts are rather different. In fact, they're more like candles. Bright and brilliant they can spend an eternity in the Underworld. But, if they're killed a second time, they're snuffed out. POOF! Like an extinguished flame they vanish in a smoky smudge and become nothing. So the ghost monsters had to be locked up to protect the ghost visitors. Or more importantly, as Alex saw it, to protect the monsters. You see, Alex was not a typical Greek hero. He's certainly one of the heroes of our story and it is a Greek story, but that's not the same thing at all. This is because Greek heroes were famous for two things:

1. Not liking monsters.
2. Killing them.

Alex couldn't have been more different.

He wouldn't have given you last week's stale sardines from the bottom of Hydra's tank for a Greek hero. Even now, he couldn't understand why people admired them so much. Of course, it'd been the same old story when he was alive. He remembered how the customers loved pots showing Jason sneaking up on Drako or **Herakles** firing arrows at the **harpies**. It was stupid, Alex thought, how people swooned over biceps and shiny armour and never once stopped to think what the heroes actually did. Like attacking monsters that'd simply been minding their own business. It made him sad to think that every one of zoo's exhibits was the victim of one hero or another's handiwork with a sword or a spear or a magic shield. He could imagine the monsters' surprise and terror at being attacked and tried to make up for it with kindness now.

Which isn't to say he would ever step into one

of their enclosures. Oh, no. He understood the monsters and their habits too well to do anything so foolish. After all, habits like tearing people's legs off with your fangs or goring them through with the spikes on your tail are harder than most to break.

Not that he had to imagine anything when it came to Aries, who told him his opinions on a daily, no hourly, basis. He smiled, wondering what was taking the ram so long at the pavilion this afternoon, and collected the long ladder from the store. Neither a monster, nor in the zoo bosses' eyes a particularly fabulous animal any more, Aries hadn't fitted in and, but for Alex's insistence, he would have been abandoned on some Elysian hillside, anonymous in a shepherd's flock. It was Alex who had stepped in and demanded that he become his assistant. More than that, he'd built him a small white-walled barn in the courtyard of his family's house, despite the protests of his mother and two sisters. Now they too had grown used to sharing their sunlit spot with a ram that they loved even when he chewed the heads off the sunflowers or knocked the arms off the statues with his horns.

Late afternoon was Alex's favourite time of the day, the time after the tourists had gone home and he could be alone and feed the monsters. And so, at about the time Aries was splintering the back door of the pavilion, Alex was climbing a ladder propped up against the side of **Scylla**'s tank. Scraping away the green weed that floated on the surface of the water with a long pole, he peered down through the iron mesh that covered its surface, just able to make out the sea monster's dark shape against the tiled floor. She looked like a giant backwards squid with women's heads fanned out on six tentacles that led into a pair of women's shoulders. Further down, several dogs' heads on stalks sprouted from her waist and from then on she was a silvery fish tail. Pretty she wasn't, but that didn't matter at all, because when Greek sailors saw her rise frothing out of the sea, good looks were the last thing on their minds. Wet knees, splintered ships, rows and rows of gleaming teeth were all much higher up the list because, furious and terrifying, Scylla had sunk hundreds of ships and drowned more men than Aries had eaten fresh nettles. Today, however, she lay listless on the pool floor, her tail coiled around her, the dogs' heads snoring out bubbles.

"Scylla!" Alex called down, splashing at the water and tipping in a bucket of sapphire-blue fish and dog bones. "I've brought your favourites!"

He willed the women's eyes to open, for those heads to snake out of the water, for the dogs to bark and snap and keen as she twisted her body into the air before arching down like a **trireme** in a storm, sending walls of water over the edges.

But she didn't.

She didn't do a thing and the treats sank onto the floor.

Feeling worried, Alex slid down the ladder and hurried along the walkway to the stairs leading to an underground glass-fronted viewing tank for a better look. Squashing his face against the glass, he looked at Scylla's downturned mouth and closed eyes. She hadn't looked as miserable as this since the day Herakles had killed her.

Hurrying to the next tank of water, which would have appeared uninhabited to you and me, he finally spotted a patch of gently rippling water. **Charybdis**, the whirlpool, was neither whirling nor pooling. On Earth she'd kept Scylla company, forcing unlucky sailors to choose between being dragged down into her black spinning waters or being eaten alive by Scylla[5]. However, now she lay as still as a puddle.

Alex rapped the glass.

Not a ripple.

---

5. *What a charming choice and not one that would have had me rushing to join the Greek Navy.*

Sea monsters, by the way, cannot talk. They can blow bubbles and froth, but they're not great conversationalists. Neither are **fire-breathing bulls**. They do, of course, love a good scorch of the grass, and can often be seen snorting jets of flame that leave black trails across the meadow. But today, as Alex squinted against the sulphur that wafted from their paddock, he saw the bulls lying silently, their bronze hooves dull in the sunshine, their tails still despite the buzz of ghost flies around them.

Alex felt a stab of panic.

Even the **Stymphalian** birds had stopped dragging their bronze beaks over the iron bars of their enclosure for once. Usually their cage clanged like a giant glockenspiel, a jangle of metal that could be heard all over the zoo. Now they sat huddled with their backs towards the viewing gallery, a sulky wall of oil-black wings, silent save for the occasional tinkle-edged whisper.

What was the matter with everyone today? For the monsters to be this upset, something big must be happening. Alex bit his lip, wondering what it could possibly be and, feeling more worried than ever at the eerie quiet, turned and ran in the direction of the biggest gossips he knew, the loosest-jawed inhabitants of the zoo, the Skeleton Soldiers.

❊III❊
ORACLES PORACLES!

Despite their grand name, the Skeleton Soldiers were little more than muddles of bones planted in beds of yellow roses in a garden close to the Tropical House. Grown from dragons' teeth[6] centuries ago on Kolkis, they had burst out of the ground, six-foot-tall skeletons in armour, soil spilling from their helmets and cascading through their rib cages, swishing their swords to kill Jason before he could snatch the fleece. And they would have. Except that Medea had snitched and told Jason how to destroy them. (Look, I've told you before. I am *not* going to talk about her until I absolutely have to. You know where to look if you're going to be so nosy.)

Unlike the rest of the zoo, the Skeleton Soldiers were anything but subdued. In fact, even before Alex

---

6. *The most common ancient Greek method of creating monsters and one reason why you'll never find packets of dragons' teeth in garden centres.*

turned the corner of the Avenue of Arcadia into the garden he could hear them chattering wildly, the sound of their clacking jawbones punctuated by the wild ringing of swords.

"No wonder it's all anyone can think about," muttered one as Alex skidded into the garden.

"What is?" said Alex.

He looked down at the skull, which was perched on a criss-cross of hipbones and set on a ribcage planted in the soil. The other bone warriors turned their skulls to look at Alex. Not one was higher than Alex's waist and most were only knee high. This was because, after Jason's handiwork, the soldiers had turned up at the zoo in three boxes of bones. And despite Alex's and Aries' best efforts to put them back together again, it'd been rather like doing a jigsaw puzzle with pieces missing and no picture on a box lid to help.

"Tonight's competition, of course," replied a skull attached to a rib cage. To make up for the lack of legs, Alex had given him four arms, each of which now whirled a sword in the air, lopping off roses and sending them spiralling over the grass. "It's outrageous! Sending another hero swaggering back to Earth! No doubt some poor unsuspecting monster's number will be up. Is it any wonder everyone's in such a terrible mood?"

For the next few minutes, teeth rattled, finger bones clenched and knuckles cracked as the bony warriors told him all about Athena's planned festivities and the competition.

"As if Jason's lot didn't do enough damage the first time round!" grumbled a skull on shoulder bones with fingers where his arms used to be. "Why, if I had my legs back, I'd enter the assault course myself!"

"Have one of mine," muttered a ribcage flexing up and down on three legs, with a skull where one of his kneecaps had been. "Thanks to him I have to hide every time someone mentions playing cricket!"

"We'd have beaten him if his girlfriend hadn't helped him!" said the four-armed skull, spinning his swords even faster.

"Don't talk about Medea," said a little skull set on a lone foot, peeking out from under a nearby branch of rose leaves.

(See? It's not just me.)

Alex leaned forwards on the sun-warmed bench and rubbed the cranium of the frightened skull.

"Don't worry about her," he soothed. "The gods will never let her into the Underworld. With her record, she'll be stuck up on Earth forever."

The little skull sighed with relief.

Alex, however, was feeling distinctly uneasy because whilst all the monsters were fuming and unhappy, he was sure that there would be one person who'd be thrilled at any chance of going back up to Earth.

"Has anyone seen Aries this afternoon?" he asked.

The garden rasped with the scraping of finger bones against skulls as the soldiers thought. In the quiet, Alex heard a distant pounding of hooves, a pounding that grew steadily closer, until a few seconds later Aries barrelled into the garden.

"Alex! I've got something important to tell you!"

"He already knows," said the skull on hipbones.

"Excellent," gasped Aries, his face flushed pink with excitement. "That'll save time!"

"Time for what?" said Alex.

"My training!" replied Aries. "For the assault course!"

Skulls squealed round on their bone supports. Jawbones fell open. A sword flew out of the four-armed soldier's grasp and stabbed a clump of lavender.

"Well, I can see you're impressed!" Aries smiled at Alex's astonished face and slammed a hoof against the path for effect. "Let's make a start!"

Snapping off a branch of a nearby jacaranda tree, Aries began jabbing at the air. "There might be sword fighting," he muttered out of one side of his mouth. "And spear throwing. Alex, you'll need to give me some tips on improving my aim!"

"Aries," said Alex, gently taking the branch from the ram's mouth. "I don't think this is such a good idea. I mean, the soldiers tell me the course is the trickiest set of obstacles since Herakles did his **twelve labours**? It's designed for the Argonauts."

"I know that!" Aries rolled his eyes impatiently. "That's why I need your help! I have to be the one to win. No one wants to go back to Earth on a quest more than I do! Now, listen. You were always doing assault courses with your dad. What do you suggest?"

Alex winced at the memory of wading through rivers and swinging on ropes in a tunic sopping with muddy water. It had been gruelling enough as a boy with arms and legs. For a ram, with four hooves and a belly like a barrel, it would be impossible. Worse still, Alex knew it would be laughable. Just imagining tonight's spectators, cruel and gleeful, shrieking with laughter as they watched Aries struggle and fail, made his heart lurch.

"I suggest we go and watch the others make fools of themselves instead," replied Alex brightly. "Have a laugh when Herakles pitches head first into the mud."

Aries pursed his lips and stared at Alex.

"What he's trying to say," said the skull with three legs, "is that the assault course isn't meant for sheep."

"Sheep?" Aries swung his head round and glared darkly at the skull. "Me? Aries Khrysamallos? You're calling me a *sheep*?" He lifted his muzzle into the air and regarded the other bone soldiers haughtily. "Do I eat grass all day? Or stare gormlessly into space for hours? Drop steaming pats in fields?"

"I don't know," said the skull on hipbones. "Do you?"

"No, bonehead!" boomed Aries. "I do not! You're confusing me with those woolly brained four-legged carpets that loiter behind gates going 'baaa'!"

"What about parping?" asked the three-legged skull.

Aries fixed him with a steely glare.

"Pardon me, I'm sure," muttered the skull.

Aries threw back his head defiantly. "Sheep may share a few minor bodily similarities with me. However, you wouldn't see one of them in tonight's contest. And you wouldn't see them returning to Earth on a quest either!"

"Oh, Aries," sighed Alex. He reached out and stroked Aries' hot forehead. "I can understand how exciting this seems to you. But—"

"But nothing!" protested Aries. "I'm entering. It's

the only way I can get back to Earth and find my fleece. I've made up my mind!"

Unfortunately, rams have never been known for thinking things through logically. I mean, you never see them doing sudoku, do you? And they're stubborn, too. As Alex knew only too well, once Aries made up his mind up about something, his determination was like a boulder rolling down a mountainside. It flattened everything in its path.

"Excuse me," said a small voice. Alex looked down to see the skull on one foot prodding his sandal with a big toe bone. "But wouldn't it be dangerous for Aries to go to Earth?"

"Well, of course it'd be dangerous, you numbskull!" said Aries before Alex could reply. He drummed the stone path with his hooves. "That's the whole point of a quest, isn't it? It's not like popping down to the agora for a pot of olives!"

The other skulls laughed, filling the garden with the dry rattle of loose teeth and chuckling.

"Ancient Greece was dangerous enough," said the four-armed skull, jabbing his swords into the air, "but I've heard there are hundreds of countries up there now!"

"And chariots without horses that belch out smoke!" added the skull on shoulder bones.

"Says who?" snipped Aries.

"The **oracles**," replied the skull. "They've seen other things, too. Buildings as tall as the sky, metal ships that fly through the clouds, and—"

"Oracles poracles!" boomed Aries. "I'm the one who's going, so you lot can just hold onto your clackers." He rolled his head round, looking at each one of them in turn. "Unless anyone would like to come along too? You know, to sort out my bedding, do a bit of washing-up, find the juiciest thistles, that sort of thing?"

The skeletons that still owned kneecaps examined them. Others drummed their finger bones against their skulls and looked up at the cloudless sky.

"I would," said one, pointing to his sockets, "but my eyesight's not what it used to be."

"And my arthritis," added the skull on three legs, "would play merry havoc on a march!"

"Not to worry," announced Aries brightly. "Because Alex will come with me!"

Alex stared, speechless, as Aries continued talking to the skulls.

Return to Earth?

He couldn't think of anything more ridiculous than leaving the safety of the Underworld to return to an Earth they'd no longer recognise.

"He's my best friend," Aries continued, "and, as you know, we've always been a team." Looking back at Alex, the ram's treacly brown eyes glittered with excitement. He poked Alex playfully with the tip of a horn. "Do you remember the time I fell into Hydra's tank and you distracted her by tipping in a month's supply of sardines so I could scramble out? Or when the Minotaur had you by the ankle and I distracted him by butting him up the—"

"Aries, stop it!" implored Alex.

Aries fell silent, his jaw slack, waiting for Alex to go on.

"Don't enter," said Alex more calmly. "Please?" He reached out and rested a hand on Aries' shoulder. "Aren't you happy enough down here? With us?" Neck bones creaked as the skulls listened, nodding sympathetically. "Helping me at the zoo?"

"But look at me!" snapped Aries hotly. "I'm bald! Bald and ridiculous. Don't you understand? Every day people make fun of me!"

Alex hesitated, trying to choose his next words carefully. "But can't you see that entering tonight's race will only give them something else to laugh about?"

"They won't laugh when I win!" said Aries. "A quest on Earth is my only chance to find my fleece. I can't let it pass me by. Now, where were we? Ah, yes, you were about to give me some tips on assault courses."

"No, I wasn't," said Alex. "Because I'm not going to help you make a fool of yourself."

"But, Alex!" Aries snorted. "Nothing is more important to me than going back for my fleece!"

"Nothing?" said Alex, aware of a sudden tightness behind his ribs.

Aries thought hard for a moment. "No," he said, shaking his head. "Nothing at all! That's why I need your help!" Alex watched the ram's eyes grow wider, sparkling with excitement. "Oh, come on, Alex! Don't you remember what your grandfather used to say? That thing about pots and people?"

"That pots were like people," Alex replied flatly, thinking back to his grandfather carrying a tray of wet freshly thrown clay pots across the studio in ancient Athens. "He said that you couldn't tell how well they'd turn out until they'd been fired in the kiln."

"Well then?"

"Well then, what?" muttered Alex. "Some pots shatter in the heat, Aries. I should know. I was the one who had to sweep them up every evening. Sometimes it's better not to go near the fire."

"Well, that's the spirit I must say!" huffed Aries.

"Thank you very much!"

Around the garden, the skulls looked round at each other, their sockets gaping in shock.

"Come on," said Alex, much more cheerfully than he felt. He stood up and reached out for Aries but the ram twisted his head away. "Look," he persisted, "why don't we go and do something fun instead! You know, cheer ourselves up a bit? We've still got the hippocampi to feed and you love doing that."

The hippocampi were sea creatures with the heads and front legs of horses and the tails of fishes who'd once drawn Poseidon, the king of the sea's, chariot. Now they dipped and dived like dolphins each day for the visitors who took the ferry around the lake and it was one of Aries' favourite jobs to carry the bucket of sugar cubes and carrots down to the water, waiting for the creatures to rise up close to the banks, foaming and prancing.

"And I'll pick you some olives as a treat when we're finished," added Alex, walking across the garden to the long white villa where the monster feed was stored. He slid the key in the lock. "We can go back home, set a little fire in the courtyard and toast some rose hips to go with them. Forget about the party tonight. What do you say?"

There was no reply.

"Aries?" Alex looked back over his shoulder to see the ram standing on the same spot, staring gloomily at the ground.

"I'm afraid you'll have to manage by yourself today," said Aries.

He turned and began clopping back along the path, his hoof-falls slow and heavy. Pausing at the corner of the Tropical House, he looked back, his eyes dull with disappointment. "At least the Argonauts stood by Jason," he said, sniffing loudly. "I'm sorry it's come to this."

Half an hour later, Alex was sorry too.

Sorry that he'd been unable to change Aries' mind, that was.

Why, the voice in Alex's mind demanded, couldn't the ram see how foolish it was to enter tonight's competition? Why did he insist on humiliating himself? And, worse, what would happen after he failed tonight? (And let me tell you, this was no small worry when you've seen what a sulking ram can do with a pile of dung.)

Having been born and brought up in Athens, a city famed for its philosophers and thinkers, Alex had always been taught to figure things out with his brain. And up until now, it had worked well. But, as Alex began to realise, the clever old Greeks who'd worked out the distance to the moon had never had to do anything as tricky as try to stop a ram that would do anything, however stupid, to find his fleece and feel special and fabulous again.

Leaning against the moonlit bars of Chimera's cage, Alex sighed, trying to ignore the distant sound of laughter ringing out through the trees from the pavilion, hoping it wasn't directed at Aries.

"You should have gone with him," muttered a voice.

Alex held his lantern to the bars, letting the candlelight spill onto Chimera, the monster with a lion's head and body, the head of a goat halfway down its back and a viper for a tail. Slumped on the floor, it lay snoozing. Mostly. Because while its lion's and snake's eyes were shut, the goat was wide awake and staring disdainfully at him, waiting for a reply.

"To watch him make a fool of himself?" said Alex.

The lion threw back its head and yawned.

"Bleurgh!" spluttered the goat, spitting out a mouthful of mane. "Do you mind? I was having a private conversation with Alex."

"Isss it breakfasssst time?" muttered the snake-tail, sleepily rising from the floor.

"No, it's not!" snapped the goat. She pushed her

head through the bars and brought her mouth so close to Alex's face that he could smell the chewed grass on her breath. "I'd have gone with him!"

"No you wouldn't," growled the lion, "because I wouldn't have moved my paws! Like Alex, I have common sense."

"Common sense, is it?" sniffed the goat. "What about courage? Look at us monsters, moping around all day, miserable as a wet Tuesday in **Tartarus** because those glorified bullies are being celebrated tonight. Isn't it about time us fabulous animals stopped sulking and *did* something fabulous for a change?"

"Fabulous?" The lion slapped down a giant paw. "What's fabulous about Aries landing belly down, bottom up, at the first hurdle?"

Alex winced at the thought.

The goat bleated furiously. "You and Alex are so sure that Aries will lose, aren't you?"

"Of course he will," said Alex calmly. "He's a ram up against the Greek heroes."

"But sometimes things don't go the way you expect," replied the goat, tilting her head provocatively. "Don't forget what happened to the hero who killed us."

Alex thought back to Bellerophon, the man

who'd killed Chimera whilst riding **Pegasus**, the winged horse. As they'd galloped away through the skies, a gadfly had stung Pegasus's haunch, causing the horse to buck, throwing Bellerophon into the thorn bush that blinded him.

"Or Heraklesss," added the snake sadly. "He wasss only a baby when the goddessss Hera dropped my two great python unclesss into his cot. He ssstrangled them both with his tiny fisssts!"

Flies and heroes, thought Alex. Babies and snakes? Despite telling himself that they were freaky one-off events, he still couldn't ignore the tiny spark of anxiety kindling in his mind.

Rams and Argonauts?

It was ridiculous, no, it was impossible to imagine that Aries could win.

Wasn't it?

For an animal used to scrabbling up mountainsides to beat the fittest Greeks who'd ever lived? For the first time since Aries had raced back into the zoo that afternoon Alex considered what, if by some mad whim of **the Fates**, Aries actually came first. It would be amazing, he knew, unable to stop the warm feeling of pride coursing through him. Then he remembered what it would lead to and felt his skin freeze.

"He'd be stumbling around some modern city,

surrounded by strangers," he said, speaking his thoughts out loud. "But he didn't even survive ancient Greece," Alex continued, feeling his voice waver with panic. "He wouldn't last five minutes!"

"Not on his own," said the goat.

"Not even with Athena'sss help," added the snake, reminding Alex of the tradition where Athena always gave a Greek on a quest something to help them. "I mean, what's the use of magical capesssss or winged sssssandals to Aries, when he can't tie them on?"

"Maybe she could lend him the **Spartan army** instead," sneered the lion.

Alex fixed him with a cold stare.

"Well," muttered the lion, pausing to lick a giant paw, "I mean, all this fuss just for Aries to end up as some Earth person's dinner."

"But that'd be terrible," said Alex, his voice thin with panic.

"Not necessarily," said the lion. "I expect his mutton's a bit on the tough side by now, but he'd still make lovely moussaka."

"When you've quite finished," snapped the goat. She turned back to Alex and narrowed her eyes. "What I'm saying is that whatever happens tonight he'll need you. If he loses, he'll need you to cheer him up, but if he wins—"

"Wins?" spluttered Alex. "If he wins, he'll never come back!"

"Then you'd better ssstop him, hadn't you?" hissed the snake. "I reckon if you sssprint, you might jussst get there in time."

* IV *
THE FEST AND THE FURIOUS

Meanwhile, on the other side of the forest, Aries was feeling much less bold than he had done earlier that afternoon. Standing in the Grand Hall of the Heroes' Pavilion, he peered at his reflection in one of the shields tossed down by the Argonauts on their way to the Banqueting Hall, trying to screw up enough courage to pull open the door and march in.

But it wasn't easy.

Partly because, unlike typical Greek heroes, rams can't dress like champions: those horsehair-plumed helmets slip down their muzzles whilst **greaves** stop them bending their legs.

But mostly it was because of Alex.

Blinking back a tear, Aries remembered the day they'd met. Having been chased through the forest by five whooping Spartan boys, he'd become tangled in the rose bushes outside the zoo. The boys gathered around him, aiming their catapults at his bottom.

Not that that was unusual. Being teased and ridiculed was something that happened every day to Aries; no, what was unusual that day was that someone had stood up for him. Hearing the boys' jeers, Alex strode out of the zoo, seized the leader of the gang by his red cloak and dangled him upside down to demonstrate exactly what it felt like to be bullied.

The boys fled into the trees while Alex prised Aries from the branches. He'd spent hours gently pulling the thorns from his skin and cheering him up. And he'd been his best friend ever since.

Until today.

Aries flinched as another wave of coarse laughter spilled from the Banqueting Hall, chilling him like a cold tide. Shuddering, he drew himself up to his full height, braced his shoulders and took a deep breath, staring harder into the shield to try and prepare his warrior mind.

In.

If he squinted until he was almost cross-eyed and stuck out his lower lip, he could still make out the gold speckles on his muzzle and a shimmer across his brow.

Out.

Except that squinting his eyes and sticking out his lower lip made him look completely ridiculous…

He heard a snort and turned to see the bowsprit giggling.

"You'll splinter my grain if you carry on!" she wheezed.

Aries eyed her coldly. "If you don't mind," he said, sounding much more confident than he felt, "I am preparing myself."

The bowsprit burst into laughter, making the sound of a chainsaw gnawing through damp wood.

"What for?" she said. "A gurning[7] competition?"

Aries slumped.

He'd never felt more alone.

Why couldn't Alex see how important it was for him to compete? Why wouldn't he help him this afternoon? And what if he actually won? How would he cope up on Earth? A giant ram without a friend? A friend with hands who could open doors and write things down, a friend with hands to stroke your ears when you felt alone and frightened.

Like now.

He forced himself to walk towards the doors of the Banquet Hall. Grasping hold of the iron ring

---

7. *Gurning is an old English tradition in which people scrunch up their faces, pull their lower lip over their top one, puff out their cheeks and cross their eyes. Then they look a bit like your teacher.*

in his mouth, he tugged the door open, flinching against the surge of noise of singing and shouting and clapping and cheering. Swallowing hard, he stepped inside.

The Banqueting Hall was magnificent.

Crafted from marble, two long lines of majestic pillars ran down either side of the hall to support its ceiling. This was painted with scenes from the Argonauts' voyage: the ship slicing between the Clashing Rocks, **Atalanta** shooting a flock of harpies with her arrows and, coiling all around the base of the roof, a life-size portrait of Drako. However, being evening, the ceiling paintings were blotted by darkness, which hardly mattered since the Argonauts and their guests didn't give a fig for art – particularly in the middle of a party.

Slamming beer tankards together, slapping each other on the back, singing, shouting and slumping face down in their food? Yes.

Art? No.

Freshly disgusted by them, Aries peeled a hoof from the beer-sticky floor and began picking his way around the edge of the room, careful to stay hidden in the shadows between the pillars and the rows of tables. Firelight from the braziers[8] flickered over the Argonauts' ruddy faces, their shiny noses and greedy smiles.

Around him Aries could smell the mingled aromas of roast meat, woodsmoke and something so sour that he decided it could only be the Argonauts' feet and armpits. He sniffed again. Yes, he decided, it was just as stinky, mean and grubby as they were.

In front of him, Mopsus, the Argonaut who could speak to animals, slouched against a bedraggled wolfhound. Beside him, Tiphys lay face down in his stuffed pheasant and clearly, Aries decided, helmsman or not, hardly likely to be steering anything anytime soon. Taking a few steps forwards, Aries concentrated his disgust on a row of singing men lurching from side to side on a nearby bench, and as they roared into their chorus he glimpsed Athena sitting at the high table, which was set on a low platform in the centre of the room.

The goddess sat back, resplendent in her white floor-length chiton, her waist criss-crossed with silver cords, her helmet, spear and shield lying

---

8. *Braziers are metal baskets that hold fire. They are not to be confused with brassieres, which are items of ladies' underwear and, although they sound similar, do not keep straw burning nearly as well.*

at her sandaled feet. She looked fresh-faced and thoughtful, nodding in time to the lyre music, her dark hair plaited over her left shoulder, making a soft nest for her faithful owl[9]. Beside her, Jason sat back, smoothing his hair into place. Next was **Theseus**, dark-haired and craggily handsome, all gold and glittery wearing the bronze armour he'd worn to kill the Minotaur. (You could tell it was the same outfit because of the twin horn-shaped dinks in the breastplate and an enormous hoof-print in the helmet that no amount of buffing could ever smooth out.) Herakles, the strongest man in the world, sprawled beside him, taking up three spaces. Draped in the pelt of the **lion of Nemea** he'd killed, its open maw crowned his pumpkin-shaped head as he lurched drunkenly, reaching for goblet after goblet of wine and dribbling it into his beard. Atalanta was dressed, as always, in her archery clothes. She moved her

---

9. *Greek gods and goddesses often had birds with them, a bit like pirates with parrots, but not nearly as much fun. Each bird symbolised what the god it belonged to was famous for: Aphrodite, goddess of love, owned a fluffy-wuffy dove; Zeus, the king, an eagle; and Athena, being wise, an owl, although what is wise about twisting your head all the way round like a lighthouse beacon and staying up all night to catch and eat mice is beyond me.*

chair away from Herakles to whisper something to Orpheus, the Argonaut who'd played the lyre aboard the *Argo* to keep the Argonauts rowing in time.

Bracing his shoulders, Aries pushed his way towards them. It was unfortunate, though, that owing to the width of his horns and the narrow gap between the tables, he dragged the tablecloths either side with him, sending pots, candles and flasks of wine clattering to the floor in a cascade of shattering clay and furious shouts. Undeterred, he stomped up to the competitors' table, despite having a tablecloth hanging from each horn.

Jason regarded him in disgust, his mouth a perfect 'O'. The musicians twanged to a halt. And the crowd started to laugh.

Tossing the sheets furiously to the floor, Aries noticed Athena rise to her feet and step forwards, regarding him with cool grey eyes, and he quickly lowered his head, bowing clumsily.

"Majesty," he murmured.

"Ram?" Athena's voice was soft and interested. She looked brightly around the wide-eyed onlookers. "What is your business here tonight?"

Aries opened his mouth to speak but another gruffer voice boomed out instead.

"Hish business?" it said thickly, slurred with ale.

"I think I sh-tepped in it on the way in!"

At which the crowd dissolved into furious laughter.

"Silence!" Athena slammed her foot down impatiently. "Much as I love a good fight, I will have order! Aries, explain why you are here!"

Aries took a deep breath. "I'm putting myself forward for the challenge!"

For a few seconds there was a stunned silence as several ale-fuddled brains tried to make sense of what they'd just heard.

Then Jason leaped up onto the table, and looked around the crowd's bemused faces. "Is it just me," he said, "or did anyone else just hear Aries say that he is going to compete against the Argonauts?"

At which the room erupted into laughter again. Everywhere Aries looked the Argonauts and their friends stood, clutching their bellies and doubling over with laughter, wheezing for breath. Herakles slapped Orpheus on the back and sent him flying onto the floor, where he sat in a heap giggling. Atalanta dabbed away tears from laughing so hard.

"It's the funniest thing I've heard in years!" gasped Jason between gulps of laughter.

"I don't see why," said Athena sharply.

The laughter died away immediately.

"Athena?" Jason frowned. "You *are* joking aren't you?"

"No," said Athena coolly. "When I joke, Jason, I laugh. And look at my face. Is it laughing?"

It wasn't, thought Aries, brightening. In fact, it looked completely unamused and goddess-frosty.

Pursing his lips, Jason stepped down off the table and slumped back into his seat. He folded his arms moodily across his chest. "But he's something out of a farmyard," he muttered. "He's just a common sheep."

"I am not!" protested Aries.

"Oh, really?" said Jason, raising one perfect eyebrow. "You've got four hooves and a silly face, haven't you? Not like me."

"No," said Aries. "You don't have four hooves."

Jason lunged at Aries.

"Gentlemen!" scolded Athena. She waited as Jason sat down again and for the crowd to sink into absolute silence before continuing. "I would like to point out that the rules of my competition clearly state—"

A loud muttering, peppered with grunts and grumbling, rose from the back of the room and, frowning at being interrupted yet again, Athena peered out across the heads of the Argonauts and their guests as they appeared to part around someone smaller who was making their way towards her. A few moments later, Alex emerged, red-faced from running, elbowing his way through the swaying men. Wiping the sweat from his brow he knelt down beside Aries and patted the ram's shoulders.

"You've changed your mind!" squealed Aries, beaming.

Now, Aries reassured himself, everything would be all right because Alex always knew the best words to reason with people so he could tell Athena exactly why Aries should be allowed to enter.

Athena peered down. "It's Alex, isn't it?" she said.

Alex bowed his head before meeting Athena's level gaze. "Majesty."

"So," said Athena. She regarded him quizzically. "Tell me! What do you think of your friend's request?"

Aries stuck his muzzle in the air, feeling a surge of confidence rise from his hooves to his horns as he waited for Alex to reply.

"I've come to take him home," said Alex flatly.

Aries stared wordlessly at Alex, his surge no more than a cold dribble of dismay, as the room burst into fresh whoops of laughter and spite.

"Well," said Athena, raising her voice to be heard.

"I'm sorry to hear that because you're too late!"

"Too late, ma'am?" said Alex.

"Yes," said Athena. "Because what I had been about to say when I was so rudely interrupted was that my rules clearly state that anyone who was on Kolkis that night can enter, and since Aries was there he's as entitled as tonight's other contenders."

Aries blinked. He held his head up high and looked around at the astonished faces of the Argonauts made stupid by the surprise or, as he would have told you, practice.

"Besides," she added, "Aries will liven things up a bit, won't he? After all, the heroes," she said, waving at the competitors seated behind her, "never make mistakes, do they? They never break their legs or gouge out their eyeballs. In fact, they do nothing for us to laugh at, at all. But a ram on an assault course? That's more like it!"

Aries jerked his head back to look at her, feeling his forelegs wobble with the meanness of her words. Glancing across at Alex he could see the shock on the boy's face, too. Why did no one believe in him? He hunched down and scrunched his eyes closed for a moment. It would be so easy, he thought, to listen to Alex, to turn around and trot meekly back to his stable and sink his nose into a bucket of olives.

But how would he live with himself the next day? And the day after that? Stuffed with olives and regret?

So, instead he opened his eyes and lifted his shoulders, watching Athena as she drew her red velvet cloak around her shoulders and stepped down from the stage. She turned towards the open doors that led out to the gardens and the lake.

"Let the competition begin!"

❊ V ❊
How the Quest was Won

Alex and Aries followed Athena and the other competitors to the scarlet starting ribbon that had been strung between two olive trees. Peering down through the pavilion gardens they could see the obstacles, each hung with lanterns that cast patches of light on the grass, patches that grew steadily dimmer as the course stretched away towards the flagpole at the finishing line.

"I can't believe it!" growled Alex, squinting through the trees towards the first obstacle, a network of ropes, its top pegged with several peculiar objects, to the long narrow pipe lying flat on the grass beyond.

"Me neither," said Aries, frowning. "Athena's made it really different!"

Alex cast his eyes up at the starry sky. "I wasn't talking about the obstacles, you great steaming dollop!" he said. "I meant the fact you still want to enter. Anyway, what's different about a climbing net? Unless there's a ram tangled up in it?" He glanced at Aries' belly and raised his eyebrows in dismay. "Or squeezing through pipes?"

"Has it occurred to you," replied Aries dryly, "that despite your lack of support and help this afternoon, I might have a plan?"

Alex sighed, wondering what sort of plan could possibly help Aries now.

"Ladies and gentlemen and, er, rams!" Athena raised her voice as the Greek ghosts drifted out around her to take their places along the roped-off spectators' areas. "I present the Earthbound Assault Course! The oracles have helped me create a competition full of the challenges our winner will face up on modern-day Earth."

Curious whispers rippled through the crowd as everyone stared at the strange assortment of obstacles.

Which was hardly surprising. You see, the problem was that ever since the oracles' eyesight had become too fuzzy to gaze into pots they'd taken up psychic ear trumpets instead. And at Athena's request, they'd tuned these in through layers of rock and soil and buried dog bones to the sacred temple at Delphi. Or rather, the café built next to it where they'd used them to listen to the chatter of tourists and reported back to Athena on exactly what they'd heard.

"I know it may look a little unusual," said Athena. She snapped her fingers and a burly man in full armour stepped out of the crowd, jumped up onto the goddess' owl-carved chariot, reined to a white horse, and drove it over to her and waited as she stepped up demurely behind him. "But don't worry!" Reaching down, she unclipped a polished goat horn from the side of the chariot and held it to her lips. "Because I shall be giving you a running commentary to tell you about each obstacle as the first athlete reaches it, using this!" she said, her voice now ringing out through the trees. "Calling all competitors!"

"This is your last chance," hissed Alex urgently. "You have to come home!"

"No!" snapped Aries. "Shan't!"

At which Aries clamped his mouth tightly shut, feeling an overwhelming combination of annoyance with Alex, and puzzlement as to how indeed he might make it even over the first obstacle, let alone finish the whole course – and finish first too.

Whilst Alex felt a similarly overwhelming combination of annoyance with Aries, puzzlement as to why Aries remained so proudly stubborn mixed with the horrible certainty that it'd all end in disaster anyway. So he closed his mouth too, leaving them both in an uncomfortable silence, lost in their own gloomy thoughts and taking what is proverbially known as 'the hump' [10].

Casting one last tight-lipped glance at Alex, Aries took his place between Theseus, who was busily clanking through his leg stretches, and Jason, who stood basking in the breeze that rippled his hair (a breeze, I might add, filled with the sighs and murmurs of lovesick ladies amongst the spectators).

Alex had by now, as you might imagine, had enough and stumped back around the pavilion to sit alone on its front steps, unable either to stay and watch people make fun of Aries or to leave him on his own.

Meanwhile back at the starting line, Athena leaned down from her chariot and reached for the ribbon.

"Ready?" She bounced up and down excitedly on the chariot.

"Steady?" Her voice was little more than a giggle. "Go!"

---

10. *Why being grumpy should be likened to the physique of a camel is beyond me. However, it is what people say, and perhaps if Alex and Aries had been speaking at that point they too might have discussed it. But they weren't and so they didn't.*

There was a blare of trumpets as Athena snatched the ribbon away and the chariot thundered off down the course.

The crowd whooped.

Women flung rose petals into Jason's path as he sped past in a blur of leopard-skin, neck and neck with Atalanta, who raced forwards, her head down, sleek as an otter slicing through water.

Theseus sprinted a split second behind them, his spear tilted forwards, his armour glinting in the lantern lights, just a footstep in front of Orpheus and Herakles.

And Aries?

Well, I'm afraid he had an unrivalled view of five Argonauts' bottoms, bobbing up and down and growing smaller as they raced down the grass towards the first obstacle where Athena's chariot was now pulling up.

"Earth people," her voice drifted back, "love going on something called the Web! And so, we've spun one of our own!"

Aries thundered towards the Web, bemused at the criss-crossing ropes disappearing into the treetops overhead. Earth people, he decided, must be quite strange if they became so excited about such a thing.

"Now, according to Sybil," Athena went on,

giving him a withering stare as he wheezed to a stop in front of her, "Earth people go onto the Web to find things 'online'. So, tonight the competitors must choose one of the magical tools hanging up there on our line to take to Earth with them if they win."

Aries looked overhead to see Jason and Theseus clambering to the top, swift as spiders, deftly picking their way over the ropes. A few seconds later Jason dropped softly onto the grass on the other side and, pushing his hand back through the ropes, waggled a golden key under Aries' muzzle.

"This key will open every door on Earth to me!" he sneered before sprinting away.

Theseus landed next, but instead of racing after Jason he walked off the course and calmly sat down on a rock. Puzzled, Aries watched as the Argonaut slipped on the sandals he'd collected from the Web, stuck out his dusty feet and chuckled as wings unfurled from the sandal heels and began flapping like baby sparrows. Typical, thought Aries, realising that Theseus intended to fly over the remaining obstacles, and cheat, just like he had on the night he killed the Minotaur when the armour-plated trickster had found his way out through the labyrinth by following the trail of wool he'd laid on the way in.

Aries lurched up onto his hooves and waddled

over to Atalanta, who was aiming an arrow at a dark green bottle tied between a scroll and a spade, and bumped her with his flank.

"Do you mind!" she growled, stumbling sideways.

Drawing back her arrow a second time, she narrowed her eyes to dark slits of concentration. Close by, Aries noticed Orpheus busily wedging the broad base of his lyre against a rock before wrestling its top into the lowest ropes of the Web. Then, straightening up, the musician tapped his foot against its strings to check their bounce and jogged backwards. Meanwhile, Herakles appeared to be cuddling a tree.

Aries stuck his chin up and nudged Atalanta's elbow. "I'm going to win, you know!"

"You must be joking!" she muttered, as Orpheus sped past, bounced on his lyre and rose gracefully into the air.

"Not really," said Aries and stamped on her bare toes, making four things happen ever so quickly:

1. Atalanta shrieked and stumbled backwards, loosing her arrow blindly into the air, just as…

2. Orpheus grabbed hold of the top of the Web with one hand and a scroll from online with the other, just as…

3. Atalanta's arrow spliced through the hem of his tunic, making a loud *Pt-chow!* and pinning him to the ropes, just as…

4. Actually, I've decided not to mention number 4 because I've remembered how you insisted on talking about pants at the start of this book. Obviously Orpheus wasn't wearing any during the race and we are not going to dwell on his rude bits. Nor will there be any pictures. Black and white. Or colour.

"What the?" yelped Orpheus.

Spinning sideways and stuck like a fly in a cobweb, he was helpless to stop the scroll tumbling from his grasp, spiralling to the ground and landing at Aries' hooves. Snatching it up, he stomped on towards the next obstacle, leaving a furious Atalanta clutching her throbbing foot.

Yay!

Aries!

Give me an A…!

Give me an R…!

What's that?

Well of course I know they didn't have cheerleaders in the Underworld. I just felt that Aries deserved a bit of support after all that cleverness and so I was shaking my bootie for him. But you're probably right. I ought to get back to telling you what's happening.

Herakles roared his rumbling strongman's bellow, which sent bats wheeling into the dark sky and wrenched the tree he'd been embracing out of the ground. Then, slamming it down, he plucked at its branches furiously until only a sharp-tipped tree trunk was left. This he hurled, like a woody home-made javelin, high into the Web, sending its tip whistling through the handle of the spade and bringing it down with a crash, narrowly missing Aries' right ear as it speared a bank of blue rhododendrons.

"Spade![11]" cried Herakles, powering past Aries with it tucked beneath his biceps.

Up ahead, Athena squealed excitedly down the goat horn.

"Jason's through the Tube!" she cried, jumping up and down in her chariot.

A moment later Herakles thumped his meaty fist against the pipe, delighted by the metallic

---

11. *In case you're wondering, this was the Spade of Digging Coins.*
    Each time it was stuck into the soil a sack of Earth money would
    appear. Just my kind of magical tool.

echo that rang from the other end.

"Tube!" he said, rolling the word around his mouth like an olive stone.

"That's right," said Athena, speaking more slowly. "The oracles heard that Earth people use it to travel underneath their cities all the time."

"Tube," repeated Herakles, holding his ear to the pipe and chuckling.

Herakles, as you might have gathered from this, wasn't the brightest buckle on an Argonaut's tunic. Indeed, it's probably fair to say that the muscle man was, well, *all* muscle: they bulged in his biceps, rippled across his shoulders and filled the space between his ears.

Meanwhile, Jason flashed a smile at Athena and sauntered away, sniggering. Sauntering, rather like sniggering, are things you only do in a race when you're confident you'll win, and catching sight of Jason's smug face, Herakles threw himself into the pipe. *Clangs* and *thwacks* rang out as he thundered through, his spade hammering against the inside so that by the time he emerged from the other end, the pipe was pocked with dents and bumps, whilst his spade hung wrapped around his neck like a paperclip.

As he lumbered away, Aries wheezed to a stop

at the other end of the pipe, and gingerly poked his head inside.

"Oh, no!" squeaked an unfamiliar voice.

Startled, Aries peered deeper into the gloom. "Is somebody in there?"

"No!" snipped the voice. "And I don't intend to be, either. You surely can't be thinking of carrying *me*, the All-Knowing Scroll of Attica, down that grubby thing?"

Aries pulled out his head, crossed his eyes and peered down his muzzle at the Scroll.

"Oh, the page-crumpling shame of being carried by a piece of livestock!" squeaked the Scroll, glowing white with disgust. "To think I might have been won by Orpheus, musician to the gods, I could have—"

But Aries didn't have time to listen.

Clamping his mouth on the Scroll, he hunched down, sucked in his belly, flattened his ears and squashed inside. It was dark and smelled of boiled cabbage. Pushing forwards, his flanks dragged painfully against the sides of the pipe and his horns scraped along the metal. Steeling himself, he forced his broad shoulders against the pipe's cold metal, biting his lip anxiously.

What if it really was this hard on Earth?

How would he cope without Alex?

He swallowed hard. If only Alex were there too, crawling along behind him, giving him advice, pushing when necessary and complaining.

Some hopes.

Feeling his heart clench, he wondered if Alex had stomped back to the zoo in a huff. Aries wouldn't have blamed him. After all, he sighed, he'd hardly listened to a thing the boy had said.

"Can't you hurry up?" muttered the Scroll. "This is hardly my cup of ambrosia."

Aries snorted and might have pointed out that it was hardly his idea of a good time either, thank you very much, before asking whether the Scroll was aware that he was speaking to a ram of legend? However, since talking would have meant even more effort, he kept silent and squirmed resolutely on to emerge from the other end with an embarrassing squelch.

Finally free, Aries stood for a moment in the moonlight. Then, hearing an odd moaning sound coming from the oak tree up ahead, he pricked up his ears and clopped over. Looking up into its canopy he saw Theseus hanging, dazed, looped over a low bough.

"Having problems?" said Aries.

Theseus slid off the branch onto the ground.

"Actually," he said, shaking the leaves from his

hair, "I'm just getting the hang of it."

"Really?" sniffed Aries. "Won't you have to learn how to fly first?" He held out a hoof in the moonlight and admired its gleam. "Of course, whilst I don't like to brag, I was a master of aeronautics myself, you know, when I had my fleece. Those were the days, looping the loop over the Aegean Sea."

"So, it can't be that hard, can it?" said Theseus.

"Not if a sheep can manage it," agreed the Scroll, just before Aries flattened it with his hoof.

"It's not," said Aries. "Not when you know the secret, that is."

"What secret?" demanded Theseus. He folded his arms over his chest. "You might as well tell me. I mean, it's not like you're going to win, but at least if you tell me, you'll get a mention in my victor's speech."

"Ooh, that'd be nice," said Aries, careful to keep the sarcasm from his voice. "All right, then. The secret is to point your toes in opposite directions."

"Opposite directions?" said Theseus suspiciously.

Aries nodded. "Works like a charm."

There was a muffled mutter from the Scroll, but scrolls pinned beneath hooves don't make a lot of noise.

Or indeed sense.

"All right, then," said Theseus and, clicking his heels, rose into the air again, wobbling like a trainee tightrope walker.

Taking a deep breath, he splayed his feet into a letter V, whereupon each foot shot out in opposite directions and forced him into the splits before flipping him over backwards.

"Aries!" he squealed as rolled back and back towards the start, turning like a baby's push-along toy. "You'll pay for…" but the rest of his words were lost on the night air as he whirled away through the trees.

There was a distant and painful-sounding crash. Probably lots of rude words too, but luckily Aries couldn't hear them.

"That was a dirty trick," said the Scroll snootily.

"Hardly," replied Aries. "That was tactics!"

As the Scroll scrumpled in disagreement, Aries turned to look down the course towards the next obstacle. It appeared to consist of a series of banners tied between trees, stretched one in front of the other across the grass.

Close by them, Athena was leaning out of her parked chariot explaining what they were to the crowd, but she was too far away for Aries to hear.

"What are they?" he asked, starting to gallop again.

"Pictures," replied the Scroll bumpily, as Aries thumped into his stride. "Apparently Earth people like taking them. You're supposed to take one and swim across the lake with it. Though I'd be obliged if you didn't take me in to the waaaaa—"

The Scroll flew into the air as Aries shrieked and skidded to a stop. His haunches froze and he was only vaguely aware of the Scroll muttering furiously from the grass nearby.

But he couldn't listen.

Or answer.

Because Medea, the sorceress, was stdnin rit ni fornt fo him.

Oh, I'm sorry...

The very idea of her looming out of the twilight like that has made my typing go to pot.

Just give me a moment to compose myself, would you?

✣VI✣
CROWN OF RAM

Ah, that's better.

Thank you.

What had actually startled Aries was in fact simply a painting of Medea. Life-sized and horribly accurate, it's true, but still only a likeness of her copied onto Athena's banners by the Underworld artists. Now, as his breathing finally slowed down, Aries took a closer look.

The scene was of the night his fleece had been stolen and showed the *Argo* sailing out of Kolkis Harbour. Surf lapped at her bow as Jason manned the helm whilst Medea stared out of the picture, her smile more like a snarl, her hand wrapped around the fleece. She looked so real that Aries half-expected to hear her glassy laugh or see her push back that tangle of long black hair, smoothing its single lock of violet, twisting it round and round her pale fingers the way she used to when she thought hard.

He recognised it as a copy of one of Jason and Medea's wedding presents, when they'd tied the knot – bless! – although, as with many celebrity couples, the wedding presents had lasted much longer than the marriage.

Dragging his eyes from the sorceress's silvery gaze, Aries looked at the fleece and felt his heart lift like a harpy in a high wind. Even though it was just so much gold paint on canvas, it still dazzled the rest of the picture into shadow.

Now, if this were a film rather than a most excellent book, the music would swell in a cacophony of violins and romantic pianos. There'd be a glorious sunset on the screen to silhouette Aries, whilst the audience, goggle-eyed and slack-jawed, tossed popcorn frantically into their mouths and down their jumpers because that's what always happens with popcorn in the dark.

Why?

Because then, right then, at that very moment, Aries knew that no matter what anyone else had to say – not Alex, Athena, the Skeleton Soldiers, the Argonauts – he *had* to win.

Snorting, he lowered his head and thundered at the banner, jabbing it with his horns until the ropes either side snapped and the picture wrapped itself around his head like a badly wrapped mummy. Then he snatched up the Scroll and for a moment stood and looked out over the black giggling water of the lake.

That's right, *giggling*, not gurgling.

Because when the oracles had overheard the tourists complaining about sirens waking them in the night, they hadn't realised that Earth people meant the *whoo-whoo* sort of sirens that you find on fire engines. No, they had filled the lake with Greek Sirens, the supernatural water-women of old Greece, who'd once enchanted sailors with their songs, luring them to smash their boats on the rocks and drown[12]. Tonight those mermaids rose up through the glittering lake to sabotage competitors instead.

"Brilliant!" murmured Aries, picking his way through the spectators, who stood, frozen as statues, glaze-eyed and silent, hypnotised by the singing.

"You reckon?" said the Scroll.

Aries nodded.

Not because he could swim as well or as fast as the others. He couldn't. But because of the

---

12. *It's a lesser-known fact that their singing can really upset octopuses too, and has led to a number of unpleasant incidents involving tentacle fights and ink-blotting vandalism on the sea bed.*

little-known fact that Siren songs don't have the teeniest effect on rams.

But Aries could tell that Herakles was already transfixed. Standing on the lakeside with his hands on his enormous hips he swayed in time to the Sirens' song, chuckling as they brushed their long hair and flicked their fish tails in the air. But Jason didn't look transfixed at all. Looking across the water, his picture of Medea rolled up tightly and tucked into his belt, he grinned and pushed something into his ears, something soft that rolled like dough and glowed buttery-yellow in the lantern light.

"What's he doing, Scroll?" said Aries, craning his neck to try and see more.

"Bees' wax," replied the Scroll knowingly (which is, after all, what you'd expect from an All-Knowing Scroll). "One of his fans passed it to him at the start of the race. He's going to use the same trick as Odysseus."

Panicked, Aries remembered how Odysseus had blocked his ears with bees' wax on the return voyage from the Battle of Troy, making himself deaf in order to captain his ship safely past the Sirens. He watched wordlessly as Jason dived in, swam past the bobbing sirens, rendered harmless as water lilies, and hauled himself out.

"That's it then!" cooed the Scroll. "He's won!"

Aries felt the Scroll flutter in delight as the Argonaut smoothed his wet hair, adjusted his chiton and began strolling towards the artists who were already gathering around the Finishing Knoll armed with clay tablets and paintbrushes, set to capture his face as he collected the flag and won.

"Not yet he hasn't!" muttered Aries.

He began backing away from the lake, watching Herakles, who lay on its bank, wallowing like a besotted walrus, his hand tucked inside the head of his lion-skin pelt, making its jaw open and close, to make the Sirens laugh.

Then, ignoring the Scroll's papery shrieks, Aries charged. Leaping off the bank he sailed high into the air before bellyflopping into the water.

Now, as any teacher will tell you, when you drop something big into water, the same bigness (or 'volume' as they like to say in science) of water splashes out. Consequently when a gigantic ram leaps into water, a gigantic ram-sized volume of water *whooshes* out. Or in this case *up* – up and along in a moving wall of water that bowled over the lake and smashed down on the Sirens' heads, snuffing out their singing.

Herakles immediately started to come round. Sitting up, he prodded his ears with his fingers, blinking in confusion as the Sirens vanished in a *flip-flap* of fish tails and curses, beneath the surface of the lake.

"Ladies?" murmured Herakles, looking at the flat, unmoving water.

"Over here!" called Aries, from the middle of the lake.

Herakles frowned. "You're not a lady."

"No," said Aries. "Well spotted. I am in fact a ram. But I do have a message for you."

Herakles brightened. "Is it from the ladies?"

"No," said Aries. "It's from Jason. Remember him? And that little race you were in?"

"Jason?" growled Herakles, rising to his feet.

"Yes," said Aries, starting to swim gently towards the far bank. "He's too busy winning to talk to you in person, but he asked me to say, 'Better luck next time!'"

"Better luck?" Herakles roared and launched himself into the water.

A couple of seconds later he plunged past Aries in a fury of foam and froth, and clambered out on the other side.

Aries swam on, watching as the big man sprinted over the grass and pounded up the knoll behind Jason, leaving an open-mouthed Athena in his wake, before hurling himself at Jason's legs and slamming the young man to the ground. Aries scrambled out of the water and ran past the furious blur of leopard and lion skin as the two Argonauts punched and pounded each other.

Galloping on, he craned his head towards the flagpole at the top of the knoll. A fabulous trick had he been a giraffe, but being a ram, with only a short, thick neck, it didn't make the slightest bit of difference and just as he reached the flagpole Jason finally leaped free of Herakles, shot past him and began climbing for the flag. A second later Herakles threw himself onto the pole, reaching up and clawing at Jason's ankles.

Jason kicked as Herakles punched, swinging his fists like demolition balls. Jason leaned out. Herakles leaned in. Swinging around the pole, they looked like a thin man and his fat reflection in a fun-house mirror as the flagpole lurched and creaked, bending left and right, as the crowd roared, cheering and shouting for their favourites.

Not that anyone cheered for Aries, of course. Nor did they notice when he snatched one of the flagpole's straining guy ropes and began furiously chewing through it.

Except Alex.

That's right.

Because, wondering why he'd not been summoned to untangle Aries from the Web or prise him out of the Tube, he'd come to see what was happening for himself. And now, despite his annoyance at Aries' stubbornness, he couldn't help feeling a spark of delight at seeing his friend at the finish, one rope now broken and the second clamped in the ram's mouth. Only Alex watched as Aries stalked backwards with sweat dribbling off his muzzle and tendons rising in his neck, pulling the pole downwards. It arched down, lower and lower, until its tip touched the grass, but it was only when Jason felt the prickle of thistles against his neck that he glanced sideways and found himself eyeball to eyeball with Aries.

"Greetings!" said Aries, out of one side of his mouth, before snatching the flag with his front hoof and releasing the rope.

The flagpole whipped upright, firing Herakles and Jason into the sky, up, up and well, even *more* up, sailing across the starry sky like two squealing starfish and disappearing into the darkness.

The crowd stared after them, stunned. Until they noticed the drumming of horns against the flagpole. Only then did they look back down to see Aries beaming from horn to horn, the winner's flag hanging out of his mouth.

"You did it!" shouted Alex, running up the grass of the Finishing Knoll. He knelt down and threw his arms around Aries' neck, burying his face in his side. "You idiot!"

Athena's chariot creaked to a halt beside them. Stepping down, she picked the Scroll up from where it lay at Aries' hooves, her face a muddle of surprise and bright amusement.

"Come with me, ram!"

On either side of them, the dumbstruck crowd parted, staring wide-eyed at Aries as he followed the goddess to a stage lit by flaming torches and set with a golden pedestal on which a circlet of fresh laurels rested.

"Ladies and gentlemen," said Athena, looking out over the bemused faces of the spectators as Aries scrambled up beside her. "I present the champion of our competition!"

The crowd began to clap uncertainly as she set the laurels on Aries' head.

"So then, ram," she said, straightening up, "tell us the nature of your quest!"

Aries looked out over the waiting crowd and cleared his throat. "I'm going to find and bring back my fleece!"

"Your fleece?" said Athena a few moments later, her voice breaking the astonished silence that now engulfed the crowd. "That's quite a mission, particularly for a ruminant. However, since you've shown such cunning and guile in our competition, perhaps the Fates might smile on you."

"I doubt it," muttered the Scroll, drawing its papery curls in so tightly that it looked more like a reed.

Ignoring its remark, Athena lifted the Scroll with her left hand. "Aries, as our champion, you may take this scroll with you." She raised her right hand and fluttered her fingers. "I, Athena, daughter of Zeus, command you, Scroll, obey your new master."

There was a brilliant flash, a puff of ruby-coloured smoke and a shower of silver stars as Athena unfurled the Scroll to reveal an ancient hand-drawn map. Blinking against the smoke, she gave a little cough before carrying on.

"Firstly, the Scroll's map will guide you through the Underworld to the portal to Earth, which lies hidden behind a statue in my great temple in Athens[13].

---

13. *Being a rather nosy goddess, Athena had hidden the portal at the Parthenon, so that she might watch the spirits of the dead pass into the Underworld and know who was going and well, going.*

Then, once up on Earth, just as a compass reveals four directions, so the Scroll will reveal answers to four questions. But only four." She paused and looked down at Aries. "You can count to four, can't you?"

Aries glared at her from beneath his leafy crown.

"What about the gift of tongues?" he said. "Greeks on a quest are always given it to overcome language problems."

"I'm just coming to that," said Athena. She rolled the Scroll up and wound a yellow ribbon around it. "Although, given the circumstances, there's a bit of a problem."

"Problem?" Aries waited, watching as the goddess pursed her lips into a dark heart-shaped frown.

"The thing is," Athena went on, "that although you'll be able to understand every language on Earth when you hear it or see it written down, you won't be able to speak."

Aries stared blankly at her.

"Because in case you've forgotten," Athena explained, "everyday Earth rams don't talk. So, you simply can't draw attention to yourself – or us down here – by chatting."

She bent forwards and tied the Scroll around Aries' neck so that it hung down like a cowbell.

"So how am I going to find out about anything?"

said Aries miserably.

A low murmur spread through the crowd as the spectators considered this. Which was when Alex stepped up onto the stage.

"I'll do the talking for him," he said.

Aries' eyes grew wide in surprise.

Perhaps yours have, too?

Or maybe you're thinking, *Oh, how ridiculous! Alex is supposed to be the sensible one!* And indeed on a normal day Alex would have been the first to agree with you. Except that today had been anything but normal and right now Alex's emotions felt more tangled than **Medusa**'s snaky tresses on a bad hair day. Guilt at not helping Aries to prepare writhed with a grudging sense of triumph at his friend's victory and wrestled with a python-sized fear at what might lie ahead. Of course he knew that going back to Earth to try and find Aries' fleece was an outrageously stupid thing to do. Not only were their chances of success smaller than an ant's kneecaps but it was possible they might never come back. Momentarily he wondered if it hurt when a Greek ghost was extinguished. And yet, as he stood beside Aries on the stage, he understood that it would be even more stupid to let Aries go back on his own. Besides, he reflected, if a ram could beat five Greek heroes through sheer determination, wasn't there a tiny chance they might succeed?

"Ladies and gentlemen!" said Athena, lifting her shield high into the night air. "I give you our Earth-questing heroes!

✳VII✳
STYX AND STONES

Up on Earth, Rose Pottersby-Weir was bored, bored, bored.

Twelve years old with freckles and a mass of tangled red ringlets, she slumped onto a bench in the **Parthenon** room of the British Museum, listening to her iPod. Hazel Praline, the fourteen-year-old pop sensation, was singing about how nobody understood her. Rose scowled in agreement, although, as she reminded herself, it was way easier being misunderstood when you were a famous Texan star who spent your days jetting around the world sipping fruit coolers rather than being stuck in a mouldering old museum.

Staring dismally at the slabs of cream-coloured marble that hung around the walls, Rose remembered how her mother had told her that each piece of the frieze was part of a long carving showing a procession of men on horses that had once decorated the sides of the Parthenon, Athena's temple, in Athens. They'd been there for hundreds of years, until a wealthy Victorian called **Elgin** had arrived and shipped them back to decorate his Scottish estate. Soon after, he'd sold them to the museum, where they'd hung ever since. Back in Greece, Athena's temple was crumbling, eaten away by car fumes and rain and the endless scuffle of tourists' feet. Rose sighed. She was pretty sure that Athena wouldn't have been happy about that. Not that Rose actually believed in any of the Greeks' made-up gods and goddesses, of course, but she now reflected sourly, if Athena were real, Rose would certainly have something in common with her: neither of them would want to be stuck in a museum.

Rose flicked absently onto the next track, entitled 'What am I doing here?' and stretched out her long legs. Her trainers squealed against the polished floor, rupturing the quiet and dismaying an elderly lady in a tweed suit who glanced up from the glass box in which stood a model of how the Parthenon used to look and frowned.

Rose felt like sticking out her tongue.

What did that old bat know about ruined holidays?

About sitting around, day after day after day, feeling as dusty as the relics on display?

It was all very well, thought Rose, having a mother who was an archaeologist, but did she really have to spend every single second of Rose's summer holiday cataloguing South American archives at the British Museum?

And worse, expecting Rose to help her?

Each day was spent the same way: down in the basement, hunched over velvet-lined trays, scrabbling through bits of pots and plates left behind by some old Amazon tribe. Even now, Rose was supposed to be quickly collecting two cups of tea from the museum café and hurrying back downstairs with them, but she knew her mother wouldn't notice how long she was gone. Not if there was a three-hundred-year-old shard of pot with a painting of a toucan feather on it to study. Besides, Rose decided, pulling off her special anti-acid, anti-fingerprint, anti-friction and anti-having-any-fun-document-handling white gloves, she needed a break.

Shoving the gloves into her jeans' pockets, she watched as yet another tour party meandered into the room. Dressed in shorts and T-shirts, carrying the tour company's green rucksacks, they looked more like a school of terrapins learning to swim. They flapped around the statues until the tour guide, a tanned man with a long grey beard and yellow umbrella, called them over to look at the marble caryatid that had once adorned Athena's temple.

Caryatid.

Sulkily, Rose pulled her earphones out and reminded herself of her mother's lesson on the subject. "A caryatid, Rose, is a column carved to look like a woman." Rose knew so many fancy archaeological words now. Even 'museum' had been explained to her: 'muse' from the Greek word meaning to think, and 'um', Rose added darkly in her mind, as in, "Um, can't we go somewhere else, Mum?"

Somewhere else, like the premiere of Hazel Praline's new film, *Rodeo Love*, at Leicester Square in two days' time, for instance? Where the star was going to appear and sing a few songs before her new film was shown?

Some hopes.

Thinking back to her mother's drawn face, how she'd sighed and told Rose that she wished she could afford to buy her a ticket, Rose folded her arms and stuck her tongue out at the caryatid. The statue gazed loftily back from her special stage, still haughty despite her rain-pitted cheeks, her chipped nose and the way the black velvet curtain that hung across the wall behind her made her marble shoulders look grubby and grey. That was the trouble with archaeology,

Rose decided, it was just so totally dead and over.

"Are we there yet?" wailed Aries.

Two long days had passed since Aries' victory on the assault course. Two long days spent scaling the Mountains of Misery and crossing the Desert of Disappointment towards the portal to Earth. Two long days of Alex worrying about how they would find the fleece whilst Aries asked him what was for dinner.

Now, having finally arrived at the Cave of Celestial Gloom, they stood, washed in its dim light, halfway up a bank of shale. Behind them the cold black water of the **River Styx** roared, echoing in their ears and bouncing around the damp walls of rock[14].

"We need to find the Thorn Roses of Oblivion,"

---

14. *Some of you might be surprised to find the route back to Earth*
    so grim. This was because Hades, king of the Underworld, had
    always loved a bit of drama. Before he married Persephone, the
    whole Underworld was filled with shadowy grey light and bare
    trees that dripped water down the back of people's necks, but when
    she arrived, his new queen insisted on a makeover that cheered
    everything up. Now, only the old pathway, unused for several years,
    remained the stuff of spook and gloom.

said Alex, gingerly edging his way up the slope towards the dark glistening walls of rock. Beneath his feet the shale crunched, rattling down to splash in the water.

Aries shrugged, vaguely remembering the blackened shrubs draped with the precious possessions the dead brought with them from Earth, stuff that **Charon**, the boatman who ferried the dead across the Styx, insisted they leave behind in order to forget their mortal lives more easily.

Then he sniffed and stared gloomily down at his wet hoof.

Unfortunately the tattered old barque they'd used to cross the river had been cracked and leaky and Aries was now sopping to the knees.

"Who knows what creatures might be swimming in this," he muttered irritably. "Aquatic ticks of despair, I shouldn't wonder. Of course, if I had my fleece I'd be waterproof."

Alex scoured the walls of the cavern. "Would you be moan-proof, too? Besides," he went on, "if you'd kept your fleece, then we wouldn't here at the Styx at all, would we?"

"I wish," groaned Aries, imagining himself golden, beautiful and magnificent strolling around the Underworld.

"But then," Alex went on, looking at the patches of withered plants around him, "we wouldn't have met either. You'd have been the magnificent golden ram feted by the gods and I'd have been a lowly zoo hand. You'd never even have spoken to me."

Aries considered this for a moment. It was an odd and uncomfortable thought and gave him a funny lump in his throat like the time he'd eaten an overlarge stink beetle, and so he stopped thinking it and scrabbled after Alex, up the shale.

"Why don't we just ask Charon to show us where the portal is?" He looked around the deserted riverbank. "Where is he, anyway?"

"He retired years ago," replied Alex, "just after the last Greek came down to the Underworld. Give me the Scroll, Aries, I'll have a look at the map."

Aries waited for Alex to untie the Scroll from around his neck and delicately unfurl the ancient paper.

"Aries!" Alex's shout bounced off the rocks as he peered through a hole in the middle of the parchment, a hole the shape of a ram's mouth.

Aries shrugged. "I was a bit peckish, you know, after all this climbing and—"

"I don't believe it!" cried Alex. "You're supposed to be on a heroic quest, Aries! Not an all-you-can-eat picnic! What are we going to do now? You do realise that this was supposed to be our divine help?"

"Didn't taste very divine to me," muttered Aries sulkily. "I've had better tasting bog daisies."

"How-wow-wow d-d-dare you!" spluttered the tattered Scroll, crackling like a badly tuned radio.

"Just look what you've done!" fumed Alex, looking anxiously at the trembling Scroll. He waited until it stopped gasping and tried to study the map properly. "According to what's left of this, the Thorn Roses of Oblivion stand in front of the silvered rock."

"Silvered rock," muttered Aries, rolling his eyes. He hadn't had a decent meal in days and now they were playing Hunt the Tree.

"We have to snap off a branch to open the portal," said Alex, as Aries wandered off. "Give me a shout the minute you see them."

Aries stumbled irritably up the slope and glanced around him. Scowling, he took a bite from a clump of black leaves and stared sulkily at the rock face. Clearly the starvation and damp was affecting his eyes too because the patch of rock in front of him seemed to be dancing with frosted sparkles. They twinkled, flittering like fireflies, and Aries wondered whether to call Alex.

Whilst he was wondering, he bit off the rest of

the branch. This time, he felt something crunch in his mouth, hard as olive stones, and looking back at the snapped branch he saw a broken necklace dripping pearls onto the ground.

Suddenly a ripple danced across the rock face, the sort of ripple that a raindrop makes in a puddle, except that there were no raindrops and there wasn't a puddle, only granite rising in a sheer wall. And granite, as we all know, doesn't ripple. Or yowl, come to that, which it now began to do, a yowl that grew louder and echoed around the cavern in a series of wails. Dimly aware of Alex racing over, Aries spat out his mouthful of pearls and watched a second ripple pass across the rock.

"You've found it!" yelled Alex triumphantly.

A dark crack snaked up the wall, splitting the rock face like a lightning bolt as on either side the rock face began to quiver and twitch, jerking apart like stone gates. A sudden gust of wind whipped through the gap, hurling dust, grit and the unexpected smell of wax polish into their faces before dying away in the cavern behind them. The rocks jolted still, revealing a dim archway to Earth.

In the sudden eerie stillness Alex turned to Aries and looked into his eyes.

"Just remember, we mustn't draw attention to

ourselves. Our lives could depend on it, so do exactly as I say. All right?"

Half-kneeling, Alex leaned forwards into the gap and stretched out his hand. His fingers touched something that felt like material, soft and velvety. Disconcerted, he looked back at Aries. "Stone portals should be hard, not soft," he whispered. He peered into the grey Earthlight. "And where's the Greek sunshine?"

Aries stuck his nose into the gap to find out for himself. Alex was right. He sniffed at the fabric and took a small nibble, giving it a thorough chew. Finding that it tasted rather good if a little dusty, he tugged a bit harder and dragged another mouthful back through the crevice.

"Aries, no!" hissed Alex and tried to wrestle the cloth from Aries' mouth.

But it was too late.

It's funny, thought Rose, the way your eyesight blurs and makes things seem to quiver when you look at them for a long time. She concentrated harder on the curtain hanging behind the caryatid. It definitely seemed to be twitching. She stared harder.

It *was* moving!

Rippling, it seemed to be disappearing backwards,

like water drawn down a plughole. Which was completely ridiculous, she told herself, since there was only a brick wall behind that curtain. But, ridiculous or not, the curtain rings were now flying off and clattering like coins onto the floor around her feet. Squealing, the tour party ran across the room and, stopping mid-sentence, the guide looked back just as the curtain was yanked completely off its pole. It thumped down onto the caryatid, covering her for a brief moment before flicking out like a matador's cape and sliding backwards, snagging around her base.

"Someone!" he shouted, jabbing his umbrella in the air. "Call the guards!"

Suddenly the curtain was wrenched away and the statue started to rock. For a long breathless second everyone froze, held rapt as she tilted forwards, the startled hush broken only by the *click-click-click* of the statue tipping further and further off its base.

The tour guide jumped out of the way. "We need—"

But his words were lost in a smash of marble as the statue tumbled forwards onto the floor and shattered into several chunks, as priceless pieces of ancient history are prone to do when they crash onto a hard floor.

Rose watched, round-eyed, as the caryatid's head

rumbled across the floor towards her and bumped against her feet. Either side of her astonished tourists shouted, clicked cameras and squawked into mobiles as beyond the room an alarm bell began clanging. Covering her ears, Rose looked back up at the stand.

Filling the space where the caryatid had stood was a sheep – the biggest, baldest sheep she'd ever seen – and a dazed-looking boy of about her own age. Rose could hardly believe her eyes and couldn't imagine how they'd managed to clamber up there.

Kicking up its back hooves, the sheep freed itself of the curtain whilst the boy stood absolutely still, pink-faced with horror, staring at the shattered statue on the floor. Hardly surprising, thought Rose, not only had he helped demolish a precious artefact, but he also appeared to be dressed in what looked like a pillowcase, drawn in round the middle by a wide leather belt.

Just then a guard in a grey shirt and trousers raced into the room, shouting at the tourists. Tall and thin with a fierce black moustache and hair that stuck out beneath his cap like a scrubbing brush, Rose recognised Eric, because, as she would have pointed out, you didn't spend your entire life in a museum without getting to know everyone who worked there. He sprinted across the floor, scrabbled up onto the empty stand and threw his arms around the boy's chest.

"Gotcha!" he shouted, pinning the struggling boy to the spot. "Damaging the property of this 'ere museum is a chargeable offence!"

The boy twisted and squirmed, his bare feet slipping over the smooth plinth as Eric pulled him onto the floor. Bleating wildly, the sheep leaped down, just as Ron, a second guard, chubby and breathless, lumbered into the room and rolled back his shirtsleeves. Fingers twitching, he pursued the sheep through a party of Japanese schoolgirls before chasing it into a cluster of old ladies. There was a *whumping* sound as copious handbags thumped the sheep, before it reappeared wearing a straw hat, trimmed with yellow roses, over its horns. Now blinded by the hat, it skidded into a pushchair, sending a teddy bear into the air. Two tiny pink fists waved furiously from under the canopy.

Looking desperate, the sheep tossed the hat away and galloped past Rose. For a second she caught the look in its eyes: wild, angry... and something else.

Intelligent?

Rose blinked the weird thought away. And yet, she felt certain there was something different about the animal, quite apart from its size and baldness and that sparkle of gold across its brow.

Finally, the sheep gasped to a standstill and Ron, sensing his chance, seized a wooden chair that stood against the wall and walked towards it, brandishing the chair in front of him like a lion tamer. In response, the ram lifted its shoulders and lowered its head, snorting through flapping black nostrils.

"Aries! No!" The tourists' heads swung round like spectators at a tennis match as the boy shouted, straining against Eric's hold. "Don't do it!"

Rose stared at the boy and then at the sheep.

Aries?

To her amazement, the sheep relaxed, lowered its shoulders and looked towards the boy.

It's behaving more like a dog than a sheep, thought Rose. *Stranger still, as if it understands what the boy says.* And that, she reminded herself, was completely crazy.

Ron set down the chair. "That's better."

He walked through the sea of startled tourists to the spoilt plinth, unhooked the velvet crowd-rope and fashioned it into a makeshift lead.

"Easy now," he murmured, walking back towards the sheep with the rope held out boldly in front of him.

Rose blinked, certain that the sheep rolled its

eyes at the ceiling as Ron draped the rope around its neck. Holding the lead tight, Ron returned his attention to the boy.

"You one of them protestors?" he barked. "Them that wants the British Museum's marbles back in Greece again?"

The boy looked confused.

"Protestors?" gasped a nearby American lady and lifted her gigantic sunglasses off her nose for a better look. "I get it! That's why they're dressed up in such a kooky way, isn't it? Like the old Greeks?" She stepped closer and poked the boy's shoulder. "He's real convincing, but the sheep's a bit moth-eaten, ain't he?"

The sheep flared its nostrils. Quickly the boy stamped his foot and after a quick exchange of looks the sheep slumped back down on its haunches, frowning.

"Guys," said Rose hesitantly, as Ron tightened his grip on the lead. "Shouldn't we clear the room?"

Twenty-three pairs of American eyes, five pairs of Japanese eyes, two pairs of guards' eyes, the sheep's golden eyes and the boy's brown ones all turned to stare at Rose. She felt her cheeks warm with embarrassment and, if you'd asked her later why she chose to speak up at that particular moment, she couldn't have told you. Perhaps it was because a boy and a sheep turning up to demolish relics in the British Museum was *the* single most awesome thing that had ever happened to her. After all, not even Hazel Praline had her glamorous days interrupted by livestock. Or perhaps it was just because they really looked like they needed some help.

"I mean," she went on, "it'd be safer, wouldn't it?"

Eric took one hand from the boy and mopped his brow with a handkerchief.

"She's right, Ron!" He cleared his throat and turned to the crowd. "Ladies and gentlemen, if we might 'ave your cooperation, please?"

A moment later, Rose stood holding the sheep's rope as Ron and Eric ushered the tourists out through the double doors. Aware that the sheep was staring at her and tilting his muzzle from side to side to get a proper look, she turned to face him whereupon he slapped his lips together and concentrated on the ceiling instead.

A couple of minutes later the guards had bolted the doors and walked back across the empty hall.

"Forty years," muttered Eric. "Forty years I've looked after that statue lady. Never allowed so much as a lollipop to touch her and now look!"

"It's not that bad," said the boy. "After all,

she'd already lost both her arms."

Eric and Ron stared open-mouthed.

"And," the boy continued, "her stone's grey. She used to be pure white."

"Comedian as well as vandal, are we?" said Ron, his face darkening to a shade of plum. "We'll see how funny you find it when the police arrive."

"Police?" said Rose.

"Of course," said Ron. "This here is criminal damage."

Rose thought quickly. "But the police won't arrest a sheep, will they?"

"No," Ron muttered coldly. "They'll bring along," and here he made a cutting gesture across his neck with his finger, "special services."

Aries, who wasn't much into sign language at the best of times and particularly those from a modern Englishman, had no trouble deciphering this one. Rose heard a noisy gulp from the other end of the lead.

"That'd be awful!" said Rose.

"Hardly," said Eric, reaching for his mobile phone and looking around him. "*This* is what's awful. One of the museum's most important finds ruined and me with only three weeks to go till retirement. Where will me invite to the queen's garden party be now?"

"Hold on," said Rose. "I've got a better idea. Why don't I have a word with my mum? Really, she's bound to know someone who could fix the statue." She looked at the shattered mess on the floor. "You know, someone who's good with glue."

The guards looked at her, their interest piqued. Everyone knew how dedicated Rose's mother was and the hours she spent working on the museum's artefacts, and slowly their faces brightened. She was as organised as a phone directory. Of course, she'd simply make a list of who to ask and text and phone until everything was perfect again.

"And," Rose added, "I bet she could fix things before the museum director comes back from holiday at the end of the week."

Ron's face began to relax. Rubbing his chin thoughtfully he looked at the broken statue.

"Well, all right," he said finally. "But what about these two?"

Rose felt the boy's gaze. "I certainly don't think we should involve the police," she said. "The publicity would reflect badly on security."

"Quite," said Eric, looking down at his shoes.

"Anyway, Mum could sort them out, too, phone the right people, make sure the insurance was sorted without any fuss."

"Well…" said Ron.

"*Really* quickly," added Rose. She took a step towards the door marked PRIVATE at the back of the room. "Shall I take them to her now?"

"What do you think, Eric?"

Unsurprisingly Eric didn't take any persuading. "Get the kettle on!"

A few moments later when the guards had left, locking the doors behind them and pausing to take one last glance through the glass before heading to their staffroom, Rose tightened her grip on the rope and looked at the boy.

"Right!" she said, sounding much braver than she felt. "My name's Rose. Who on earth are you?"

VIII
Rose to the Rescue

More like where *on Earth?* thought Alex.

He scanned the room, searching for a window to look through, desperate for a reassuring glimpse of the clustered terracotta rooftops of Athens. But there were no windows, just four blank walls hung with stone friezes of horsemen, friezes he'd now realised he'd last seen fixed beneath the roof of Athena's temple.

His mind tumbled with questions: Why had the caryatid been indoors when she should have been out on the Acropolis? Where was the rest of the temple? The sunshine? He took a deep breath that was filled with the cloying smell of wax polish instead of the scent of cypress trees and stared down at the caryatid's face. Seeing the stark sugar-white break in her neck against those familiar carved ringlets, he felt his stomach knot tighter than a Greek fisherman's net. How would they ever return home?

"Well?" said Rose, her arms folded, waiting for an answer.

Alex turned and looked at Rose properly for the first time. Of course, it was no surprise that she was unlike any girl he'd seen before, but her appearance was still a shock. Whilst his sisters wore their hair glossed and coiled, pinned into intricate styles with pearl pins, hers was wild and loose and tangled over her shoulders. Unlike the women of old Greece, always so elegantly draped in dresses, Rose's clothes were baggy and casual. But it was the way she looked at him, her eyes bright with impatience, demanding an answer, which was the most surprising thing of all.

"I'm Alex," he said at last. He laid a hand on Aries' head. "And this is Aries." Aries harrumphed pointedly. "Aries Khryos Khrysamallos," added Alex, glaring down at the ram.

"That's some name," said Rose.

"It's Greek," explained Alex.

"Of course." Rose rolled her eyes and put her hands on her hips. "And I suppose he's a Greek sheep?"

Aries stamped his hoof furiously.

"Ram," corrected Alex.

Aries clopped forwards and snuffled against the cheek of the broken caryatid. Kneeling down, Alex put his arm around the ram's neck and looked at the statue's face, remembering the countless times he'd walked past her when she'd gleamed in the Greek sunshine.

"Can your mother really fix this?" he asked.

Rose nodded. "Of course she can. Believe me, she loves anything old and made of stone."

Alex looked across the room at the three statues of reclining goddesses and frowned, recognising them by only their poses, since each goddess was now headless.

"What happened to the Parthenon?" said Alex.

"Nothing's happened to it," said Rose flatly. "It's still in Greece."

Aries looked up at Alex with wide, worried eyes.

"And we're not?" said Alex.

Rose shook her head. "Okay. It's not funny any more."

Alex stared at her.

"This is the British Museum," she added. "In London."

"Britannia?" gasped Alex.

At which Aries bleated furiously and was about to shout something extremely rude, had Alex not clamped his hand around the ram's muzzle.

"It can't be!" said Alex, struggling to keep Aries' mouth closed. "That's the caryatid Athena chose for her portal! So, how did she move?"

"Right! That's enough!" Rose held her hands up in front of her. "Either stop acting weird and come with me, or take your chances with them out there!" She nodded towards the doors at the back of the room and Alex followed her gaze to see several tourists still clamouring against the glass, pushing for a better view, staring and pointing. "Your choice."

Five minutes later Rose had led them out of the Parthenon room and down into the basement of the British Museum. Now they followed her along underground corridors that criss-crossed like a maze and led to storerooms filled with exhibits for repair or storage. Alex looked up, fascinated by the dots of twinkling light set into the ceiling. He wanted to reach up and touch them, to see if they burned like fire or were full of lightning sparks, but knowing that it would make Rose even more annoyed he hurried on, Aries' hoof-falls ringing in his ears.

"In here," said Rose finally, opening a door at the end of the corridor and stepping inside.

Cramped and stuffy, the room was lit by dingy yellow light and filled with rows of wooden shelves that stretched almost from one wall to the other with only a narrow aisle to walk around them. Every shelf was crammed with boxes and packing cases spilling straw. Vase-shaped bundles in bubble wrap and glass trays of pinned oily black beetles were wedged between rows of leather suitcases bearing handwritten brown labels. A mummified lizard stared balefully down at Alex from the far corner, its glass eyes dull. On the shelf below, stuffed tarantulas the size of rubber gloves arched beneath glass domes. Of course, on any other day, the sort of other day when he hadn't been plunged into modern London, Alex would have loved this room. He'd have spent hours studying the beetles and lifting the spiders from their boxes to stroke the fur on their legs. Even the Underworld Zoo, with all its monsters, had nothing quite so hairy and marvellous [15]. But as Aries squeezed between the first two shelves and began to snuffle around in the hope of finding something to eat, Alex turned away from the spiders and looked at Rose who was pulling out a blanket from beneath a jar of desiccated bat wings.

Now he thought about it, she had been pretty brave in standing up to the guards. And she hadn't batted an eyelid at the rows of gigantic spiders in here. Impressive. For a girl, he quickly reminded himself,

---

15. *Marvellous, however, would not have been the first word I would have chosen. "Aaaargh!" and "Get it away from me," would have been much higher up my list.*

confident that she'd probably still just burst into tears and run away if he told her the real truth about who they were[16].

"Perhaps," said Alex, "your husband might be able to help us?"

"Husband?" snapped Rose and thumped the blanket onto the floor.

Thanks to Rose's mother's daily lectures on antiquity she knew that ancient Greek girls were married by the age of fourteen, usually to a man in his thirties, chosen by her father. She wasn't amused. "For the last time, snap out of this freaky Greek routine or I'm going for the guards!"

She sat down on the blanket and drew her knees up under her chin, scowling. At which, Aries, who hadn't eaten for at least three hours – which, as he'd have told you, in ram-terms is forever, but had now discovered a crate of tasty naval flags – looked up, the red flag of the Imperial Japanese Navy trailing from the corner of his mouth.

---

16. Of course, it wasn't really Alex's fault that he was so absolutely wrong about girls. Since ancient Athenian men didn't allow women to vote or have jobs or even step out of the house on their own, many of them simply never discovered just how capable, smart and, frankly, all-round brilliant, women are.

"Touchy, isn't she?" he muttered between chews. "No wonder her family can't find a man for her."

Rose's jaw fell open. She gasped, staring wide-eyed at Aries, and turned to Alex.

"Do that again!" she insisted.

"Do what?" said Alex, clamping Aries' mouth shut.

"Throw your voice! Make him look like he can talk!" said Rose. "It's awesome!"

Aries pulled his nose out of Alex's fingers. "How nice of you to say so!"

"No way!" spluttered Rose, scrambling to her feet. "That time was seriously spooky!"

"Spooky, my cud!" spat Aries, flinging Alex's hand away. "Do you know to whom you are speaking?" Rose stared bewildered as Aries went on, stamping his hoof in time with his words. "The ram of the Golden Fleece!"

By now Rose was at the door, her palm around its handle, but Aries was faster, in the way that furious rams always are, and he swung his weight against the door with a thump. "And there's no need to look like that about it, either!" he went on, staring up crossly at her. "I know it must be rather disappointing to see me bald, but—"

"Aries! That's enough!" insisted Alex. "Let her go if she wants to!"

Aries turned and regarded the boy loftily. "I hope all modern Earth people aren't like her!"

"Like what?" demanded Rose, her annoyance overtaking her shock.

"Fickle," said Aries simply. "Helping one minute and going as goggly as **Narcissus** the next."

Rose looked astonished.

"I can explain," said Alex, pushing his hair back off his face. "If you really want to know, that is?"

He waited, watching the flush disappear from her face as the panic seemed to fade, replaced by something else.

Curiosity.

Perhaps, Alex thought, he'd been wrong about her after all. Even though she was a girl, she hadn't dived out of the door and fled back upstairs to find the guards. He frowned. His own sisters would have run squealing from a room at the most ordinary of things or thing – a beetle scuttling over the floor would have had them lifting their skirts and sprinting away. And this could hardly be an ordinary day for Rose.

"It is a long story," he said tentatively. "And you'll find it strange and perhaps frightening…"

Rose let go of the door handle and waited for Alex to go on.

"Are you going to stay and listen?" asked Aries, bustling past to sit next to Alex. "Good. Alex is excellent at stories. In fact, the Minotaur always asks for two at bedtime and as for Chimera—"

"Aries!" said Alex.

Aries snapped his mouth shut.

"Go on," Rose encouraged him. "I'm listening."

Alex took a deep breath. "Aries is telling the truth when he says he's the ram of the Golden Fleece—"

"As in the myth?" Rose interrupted. "I thought that was just a made-up story—"

Aries tapped his horn against the shelf. "Do I sound made-up to you?"

"No, but," Rose paused, thinking. "You're in the book of Greek stories my mum gave me last Christmas. Except in your picture you're covered in golden wool. Let me think… The Golden Fleece? That's the one with Jason, isn't it?"

Aries and Alex nodded.

"So, did he really exist, too?" Rose's cheeks grew pink. Her eyes glittered. "Was he a total hunk like the story says?"

"No," said Aries. "That bit *was* made-up."

Rose turned to Alex. "So, who are you, then? You're not in the myth, are you?"

Alex shook his head. "No. I was an ordinary

potter in Attica when the Argonauts sailed."

Rose edged back against the wall, her face growing pale beneath her freckles. "But that was, like, ages ago, wasn't it? How old are you?"

Alex shrugged. "Technically, I was thirteen when I died—"

"Died," Rose repeated emptily.

"Of the plague," explained Alex.

"He's not infectious any more," said Aries, seeing the look of fear on her face.

"But you *are* a ghost?" Rose's eyebrows, which had been rising at each new thing she'd been told, now completely vanished under her fringe.

Alex nodded. "We prefer to call ourselves **shades**." He stretched out his legs in front of him.

"But you look as solid as anyone else," she said, frowning and touching him gingerly with a finger. "You know, normal," she added before glancing down at his tunic and filthy bare feet. "Sort of." She stretched out her legs too. "So, why've you come back?"

For the next twenty minutes Rose listened, her eyes growing wider and wider, as Alex explained what had really happened that night in Kolkis, of how Medea had used her spiteful magic to trick Drako and how Aries had finally won the chance to come back to Earth to find his fleece. Luckily for Alex and Aries, Rose's mother had always taught her daughter to be polite and to listen to what others had to say, even if they were Greek and dead and one of them happened to be a magical ram. And even though what they said was the most remarkable, fantastical and crazy story Rose had ever heard in her life, it was also, she knew, the only story that could explain how a boy and a talking ram had simply appeared through a brick wall of the museum.

"What I don't get," she said eventually, "is why Jason didn't look after the fleece and take it with him to the Underworld when he died."

Alex shrugged. "All we know is that he wore it on the day he married Medea. It was in all the news scrolls. But after that, well…" He shrugged.

"Lots of things vanished in the fall of Greece," Aries said. He rolled his eyes. "Those Romans. Such a shocking lack of manners. For months after their invasion, **Queen Persephone** kept going back to collect the things that her people had left behind. In the end there were so many that she asked the palace servants to open a lost property office. I went there every day. They had **Perseus**'s flying sandals, the gold statue of **Midas**'s daughter, even three of the four legs of the Trojan Horse…"

"But no fleece?" finished Rose. "So, how will you track it down?"

Alex sighed. "I'm not sure. I mean, we were supposed to start at the Parthenon." He scowled at the boxes of rolled up maps on the top of the nearest shelf. "I still don't understand how we ended up in London."

"Lots of pieces of the Parthenon were moved," said Rose simply. She tucked her hair behind her ear, thinking. "Important things usually end up in museums, which is why this is so strange."

"What is?" said Alex, relieved that she was taking them so seriously.

"Well, shouldn't the fleece be in a museum, too? I mean, if it was left up on Earth like you say it was, then surely..." she looked up at them, her brow furrowed, "surely it'd be the star exhibit somewhere?"

Aries beamed and rubbed his ears against her elbow.

Rose smiled down at him. "But if it were in a museum, like, any museum, anywhere, then I'd know about it. Believe me, Mum would have dragged me to see it from my pushchair years ago."

"So it's not?" said Alex.

Rose shook her head. "Someone somewhere must still have it." She leaned back against the shelf.

"Maybe some old duke and duchess have it hanging on the walls of their dining room," she went on, thinking out loud. "Or a Chinese emperor's using it as a bedroom rug in his golden pagoda."

Aries wrinkled up his nose at the suggestion of toes scrunching into his golden wool.

Rose shrugged. "Haven't you got any clues or help at all?"

"Only this," said Alex, rummaging in his bag for the Scroll.

It gave a grumpy rustle as it unfurled and looked at Rose through one of its ragged holes.

Rose stared blankly. "What is it?"

"An All-Knowing, talking Scroll," said Alex. "Or at least it was before someone decided to eat half of it for his lunch. I don't think there's enough of it to work properly now. It's probably useless."

"It was useless before," muttered Aries.

The Scroll harrumphed.

"Hmm," said Rose, tracing one of the holes in the parchment with her fingertip. "I'm not so sure."

She examined the Scroll, turning it this way and that, studying the edges of the holes, stroking the damage. Soon it began to purr like a cat and Alex felt himself brighten. Perhaps Rose might be able to do something? Rose would, of course, because just like her mother – although she would hate my pointing this out – she was one of nature's fixers and never able to see a problem without her mind worrying and fiddling and wondering how to solve it.

"I'm sure I could patch this up," she said, handing it back to Alex with a smile. "But right now I have to go back upstairs."

Alex felt a ripple of panic in his chest. "Why?"

"To tell Mum about the caryatid, of course," said Rose, rising to her feet. "Otherwise Ron and Eric will freak out and then who knows what'll happen."

"But you will—"

"Come back?" finished Rose. "Of course I will! Don't worry!"

Aries planted his head on her waist. "Promise?"

Rose stroked his muzzle. "Promise!"

"But what about the guards?" said Alex.

"Simple," smiled Rose. "I tell Mum that the guards dealt with you and the guards that Mum dealt with you. As long as she fixes the caryatid and they don't get into trouble, there won't be a problem."

(See, like I said, one of nature's fixers.)

She turned towards the door.

"But what shall we do while you're gone?" asked Alex.

Rose looked back over her shoulder. "Stay out of

sight and think about how I can help you. Okay?"

"Olives," said Aries.

Rose exchanged glances with Alex.

"That's how you can help me," added Aries, seeing their puzzled faces. "Do you know, I haven't eaten properly for days? Not unless you count a mouthful of withered oblivion bushes and a few furry biscuits from the bottom of Alex's bag, which frankly I do not. Green olives would be nicest, if you can find them in this London place."

Shaking her head, Rose turned away and began walking up the corridor.

There was a *clopping* noise behind her as Aries stuck his head out around the door. "And a few salty crackers to go with them."

❄IX❄

CUPS AND SORCERESS

Unfortunately, as with many of life's problems, green olives and salty crackers aren't the answer. They're not the answer to six times seven[17], or what's the capital of Venezuela[18]. They don't help ghost rams and boys who are hiding in the basement of the British Museum and they're completely useless for problems that sit at café tables in Rome, twisting a streak of violet hair around their white fingers.

Remember that violet streak?

I thought you might.

And believe me, I am sorry for having to bring Medea into this story at all. However, you might recall that I have tried to be kind to you up until now, by dropping little hintlets about her unpleasantness to prepare you. Nevertheless, I shall try to make this as quick as possible.

---

17. *Forty-two.*   18. *Caracas.*

Whilst Alex was busy scolding Aries for thinking about olives when he ought to be thinking about the mess they were in, Medea was sitting miles away sipping a latte in the Piazza Navona.

Bathed in the sunlight streaming through the café's windows, she looked magnificent. Flawless, in fact. With skin as smooth as a shark's tooth she appeared barely twenty-two of her three-thousand-eight-hundred-and-seventy-six years, which is what being an immortal sorceress will do for you, Greek-witch magic being a whole lot more effective than those anti-wrinkle creams they flog on the telly.

Of course, she'd have been even prettier if she smiled occasionally but Medea hadn't smiled for months now. Instead, she'd sulked and raged, smashing china and summoning up thunderbolts that split walls and wilted dahlias, not to mention using the sort of language that would curl your eyelashes. All of which Hex, her accomplice – or 'familiar' as they say in witchy circles – could have told you about (and shown you the bruises) except that he was at that moment hidden inside the carpet bag at her feet, a carpet bag that writhed and hissed. As you might now have guessed, Hex was a snake. However, what you probably haven't guessed is that he was a black mamba – and a black mamba, for those non-snake experts amongst you, is one of the deadliest snakes on Earth. Able to kill a man in minutes – *hiss, nip, thud!* – it's also the fastest snake in the world and can zip through a classroom in under two seconds. However, unless you live in Africa, where mambas usually live, don't worry about any black snakes you might see hanging around school, because despite their name, black mambas are grey. It's the inky-black insides of their mouths that give them their name.

Now, back to Medea.

Since she left ancient Greece all those years ago she'd turned her hand to designing clothes. Not just any old clothes, but fabulous dresses and jackets, exquisite ball gowns that shimmered like tropical fish, wedding dresses as soft as snowdrifts and suits that made the dowdiest of men look debonair. For centuries, kings and queens, emperors and politicians, artists, musicians and several Hollywood stars had clamoured for her designs. Yet no one had ever connected her in any of her incarnations – as the seamstress at King Henry VIII's court, the maker of Georgian silk pantaloons and white wigs in the eighteenth century or the modern-day business woman with a studio in Rome – to the sorceress in an ancient Greek myth with the same name. I mean that would've been silly, wouldn't it, for who in their right mind could imagine that such a fresh and glamorous young woman was really a witch? Or that she was thousands of years old? I mean, I bet you know some boys called Isaac, but did they discover gravity standing under an apple tree? How about women called Cleo? Did the one you know rule Egypt four thousand years ago? Well, quite. And just in case any smart old person with an even smarter memory might grow suspicious, Medea vanished for decades every so often, to return refreshed and ready to tempt a whole new audience with her catwalk collections of clothes. But for a very special few, shall we say her most *privileged* customers, Medea offered a special service where she herself took the customer's measurements, cut and sewed the cloth, snipping and tucking and stitching until the clothes were, well, breathtaking.

It was for just such a lucky customer that Medea was at that moment sketching, adding layer upon layer of pink taffeta to the skirts of the prom dress outlined on the page in front of her. She shrugged off her nightshade-purple jacket to reveal a short-sleeved black dress that fitted her as snugly as the skin on a spider's tummy, and took a sip of latte, glancing up at the café television, which was showing footage of

Hazel Praline arriving in London. Amused, Medea set down her sketch pad to watch as the screen filled with images of the young pop star stepping out of her pink-winged jet, adjusting her pink headband and throwing kisses to her screaming fans, her manager-father standing behind her, waving his white cowboy hat.

"Ooh," hissed Hex, peeping out from inside the carpetbag. "That's her, isn't it, Mistressss?"

Medea sighed, scanning the other customers to make sure that no one else had heard before holding her pencil up towards the screen to check the proportions of the gown she was drawing against the girl on screen.

"Daddy'd make a good meal," added Hex, slapping his lips with his black tongue. "Texasss hasssh!"

Medea shoved Hex back into the damp flannel-lined bag and jabbed him with the heel of her spiked boot, ignoring the muffled squeal of pain. Unfortunately, as Medea had recently discovered, black mambas, unlike black cats, don't make good familiars. Despite their mean looks and reputation, they're born daydreamers who'd rather snooze than squirm around a cauldron and spend most of their time lingering like a lost sock under the bed, which is hardly sorceress-chic.

"Breaking news," barked the newscaster as the screen flipped to a picture of the British Museum, "from our London correspondent, where reports are coming through that a sheep – yes, you heard me correctly, a *sheep* – has run amok through the British Museum. Witnesses say that the sheep seemed to appear out of nowhere in Room 18, home to the Parthenon exhibits."

Medea glanced up as the screen changed to a jittery video, clearly from a tourist's camera, to see Aries looking back at her.

"According to those present," the reporter went on, "the sheep was simply not there one moment but there the next, crashing into a caryatid from the Parthenon. A second vandal, this time a boy dressed as an ancient Greek, was accompanying the sheep, although museum guards now tell us that both boy and sheep have been removed from the premises and are being dealt with by the relevant authorities."

Medea stared.

It couldn't be, she told herself, the image of Aries emblazoned on her mind. It simply could not be him. Except, as her icy brain pointed out, how many other enormous bald rams with horns like bedsprings were there on the planet? Or, in fact, usually in its Greek Underworld.

None.

Flipping shut her sketchbook, she knocked her coffee cup to the floor.

"Mistressss?" Hex edged his snout up and stopped, startled by her expression.

She was smiling, actually smiling. Hex blinked to make sure. But seeing the corners of her mouth lift upwards turned his tepid reptile heart to ice cubes. Medea smiling, you see, was always more dangerous than Medea sulking.

"Mistressss?" he murmured, sinking back into the bag.

"Mind your own business," snapped Medea, dropping her sketchbook on top of him.

Snatching up her coat and bag, she hurried out of the café, as erratic as a startled scorpion. She didn't care about the muffled *ouches* as her bag knocked into one chair after another. Nor did she notice the customers nudge each other and whisper as she strode past them, out into the square where now, wholly oblivious to its baroque architecture and magnificent fountains, she hailed a taxi to Leonardo da Vinci airport and her private jet.

✣ X ✣

SNACKS AND BUGS AND
BROKEN SCROLLS

Well, that's enough of her.

Let's talk about someone nicer instead: Rose.

Now, as you might have guessed, Rose's mother didn't have much time for television news. No, I'm afraid Dr Pottersby-Weir didn't have much time for holidays, cinemas, sunbathing in the park, trips to the London Dungeon, cream cakes, bicycle rides or, if you'd asked Rose, daughters, either. And so when Rose found her mother that afternoon she wasn't remotely surprised to discover her engrossed by something small and twinkling at the end of a microscope, her elbows red from leaning on the desk.

Rose pulled up the stool beside her mother and sat down.

"Two ancient Greeks turned up in the Parthenon room this afternoon," she began.

Her mother continued to peer down the lens. "Really?"

"Yes. Both been dead for years."

"Uh-huh," muttered Dr Pottersby-Weir, straightening up.

She slid her black-framed glasses onto the top of her head, pushing back her hair, which was the same mass of red curls as Rose's, but cut to a sensible shoulder length. Then she picked up a pair of tweezers and plucked the artefact from under the microscope, a small disc of gold that gleamed in the light of the desk lamp. Laying it gently on her gloved palm she held it out to Rose.

"Take a look at this."

Sighing, Rose stepped closer. It looked like a gold charm, the sort you might find on a bracelet, but this one was crumpled with age and carved with a picture of a giant beetle, its huge mandibles holding something round.

"It was found in the black soil of the Amazon basin," said her mother, stroking it with her gloved fingers. "I've dated it to around 1650. Rose, that suggests there were tribes on the Amazon much longer ago than people think. I'm going to publish!"

"That's great," sighed Rose.

Unfortunately, life with her mother had been like

this ever since Rose's eleventh birthday, which was when her father, who'd been an archaeologist too, had left on an expedition to the Amazon jungle.

And never returned.

People deal with grief in lots of different ways and Rose's mother's way had been to devote her time single-mindedly to finding one special artefact from the Amazon rainforest, one unique and amazing thing, to research and name after her lost husband. Ever since he'd vanished she'd taken jobs at museum after museum, in city after city, towing Rose through school after school whilst she hunted for what could be the Theodore Pottersby-Weir's Arrowhead, the Theodore Pottersby-Weir's Chieftan's Crown or the Theodore Pottersby-Weir's Jaguar Mask. Rose glanced at the beetle on the crumpled gold disc and hoped that wasn't it.

Perhaps some of you might be a bit shocked by Rose's attitude? Don't be. Rose wasn't a harsh or mean-spirited person and she loved her mother dearly. And of course she understood that her mother's obsession with work distracted her from an overwhelming grief. She just wished it didn't distract her quite so much from noticing her daughter.

Rose missed her father desperately too. She still thought about him every day, missing his warm chestnut-brown eyes, his smile, his raucous laugh that filled a room, his bear hug that swept her off her feet. And, as she reminded herself now, she missed the way he'd have listened properly if she'd told him about Alex and Aries.

"One was a talking sheep," said Rose who now found herself speaking to her mother's back.

Slowly Dr Pottersby-Weir laid the charm on a velvet-lined tray and turned to face her daughter. "That's an amusing story, Rosie. But you'll never make an archaeologist if you don't stick to the facts."

Rose rolled her eyes. "Look, what I actually came to tell you was that they damaged a statue when they arrived."

"A statue?" Her mother leaned forwards, suddenly interested. "Well, why didn't you say so in the first place? Which one?"

"The caryatid," said Rose. "I told Ron and Eric that you'd know what to do because they were totally freaking out. I said you'd help them. They've dealt with the, er, vandals."

But her mother was barely listening. She stood up from the stool, the charm temporarily forgotten, and began pacing between the table and the wall.

"Now, let me see… Athenian marble… dating from 490 BC… weathered for three thousand years.

Hmm, she'll have a porosity of three-point-four to three-point-five, just like an old tooth. Structure and density will need confirming." She counted off her fingers as she spoke. "I'll need to consult Professor Spyros Papadakis in Delphi to formulate the exact marble compound resin to rebuild her, contact the museum's insurance holders to cover the costs of my flight and materials, issue a notice that all is in hand to the press, inform the Greek government." She reached for her BlackBerry. "Rose, sweetie, I'm going to be busy. Can you amuse yourself for half an hour?"

Rose nodded. Her mother's 'half-hours' were always at least three hours long. And, whilst Rose usually resented this, today she was grateful. Grateful because Alex and Aries needed her mother's exceptional talents to restore the caryatid to perfection so that they would be able to return home. After all, if anyone understood what it meant when people were lost far from home, it was Rose. Collecting her rucksack she slipped out of the room and down the museum's back stairs, out onto the street and heading towards the nearest supermarket.

Three jars of olives, two packets of salty biscuits, four rounds of cheese sandwiches, six bags of salt and vinegar crisps, an entire box of iced cakes, two bottles of pop and a bar of fruit and nut chocolate later, Alex and Aries felt much brighter. Whilst they had been eating, Rose had been busily rootling around the shelves, trying to find some suitably old paper to try and patch up the Scroll. She'd felt certain there'd be some old scrap of papyrus or calfskin lying around down here, but ten minutes later all she'd turned up was a faded teen magazine, jammed between two suitcases that had probably been left behind by a bored archivist years ago. Had her mother have been there, she would have instructed Rose to be put the magazine back, be patient, find the appropriate materials, match the gaps exactly and use a special acid-free glue. But she wasn't. Consequently, Rose, never the most patient girl in the world and hugely excited to be holding a real actual All-Knowing Scroll, had mended it her own way. I use the term 'mended' loosely, because as Rose now held it up to admire her handiwork, the Scroll hung in crumples, one corner higher than the other, a patchwork of parchment, sticky tape and glossy paper.

"And this can really tell you the answer to any question?" Rose said, hardly believing the words herself.

Alex looked up and frowned. "Well, it used to," he said uncertainly.

"Brilliant!" said Rose, her heart beginning to drum behind her ribs. Drawing the Scroll up to her mouth she took a deep breath and closed her eyes. "Scroll," she whispered, "please tell me what happened to my fath—"

"No!" Aries knocked the Scroll out of her hand with his horns. It gave a little yelp, tumbled to the floor, snapped shut and rolled under the nearest shelf.

Rose snapped open her eyes, shocked. "What did you do that for?"

"*Four* questions!" muttered Aries, hunching down to peer for the Scroll in the dusty shadows. "That's all it's got. We can't afford to waste them."

"It wouldn't have been a waste," said Rose.

"Not to you," said Alex gently, noticing her glistening eyes. "It must have been something important?"

Rose stared at the floor in silence.

There was a clattering as Aries pulled the Scroll out from under a shelf and rolled it back towards Alex. Seeing Rose's face he sank his head onto her shoulder.

"I'm sorry," he said, pressing his muzzle against

her ear. "But if I'm going to find my fleece we need all the help we can get."

Despite her disappointment, Rose smiled. After all, it's not every day you have a talking ram apologise damply in your ear and, quite apart from the novelty, it tickles deliciously.

"Look," said Alex. "Tell you what. If we can find the fleece in three questions…"

A smile lit Rose's face. "You'll give me the last one?"

Alex nodded.

"Then I'll help you," said Rose. "I know far more about Earth than the Scroll can tell you in so few questions."

"Let's make a start then," said Alex, gently unfurling the Scroll. Holding his face in a suitably solemn expression, he began.

"*Scrollius lapidus, exalto Greco…*"

"Ancient Greek," whispered Aries to Rose. "I don't know why he's using that since the Scroll speaks all languages. Probably showing off."

"Do you mind?" snapped Alex. "I am speaking to the Scroll in Ancient Greek to comfort it after its traumas."

"Don't bother," moaned the Scroll. "It's too late for that."

Aries stuck his nose underneath the bottom of the Scroll. "Where's the fleece?"

There was a rustle followed by a wisp of silver smoke.

"*My talents now are sadly skewed, from having all my best bits chewed*," said the Scroll in a wobbly voice.

"Awesome!" said Rose.

"Get on with it," muttered Aries.

The Scroll fluttered beneath Alex's fingers.

"*The tufts of gold are near you now, much closer than you think. You'll find them hid— oh, oh…*" The Scroll wheezed and stretched taut.

"Near!" boomed Aries, sticking his muzzle in Alex's ear. "Did you hear that, Alex?"

Alex tried to push Aries away, but the ram stuck his head under Alex's elbow to nuzzle the bottom of the parchment. "Tell Uncle Aries what you mean, you sweet little scrolly Scroll!"

"*It's hidden in—*" The Scroll coughed and tailed off.

"In?" snorted Aries.

"*In, in, in, n-n-n—*" The Scroll snapped shut and open. "*Don't stand sobbing by the sink, or gaze in sad dismay. For teenage spots, try new Wash Pink! And rinse your cares away!*"

"Wash Pink?" stammered Aries. "What's it on about?"

Rose bit her lip and pointed to a photograph of a bottle of face wash shown on one of the scraps she'd torn from the magazine page. "It's the advert, isn't it? See: 'Wash Pink – for teenage skin.' I think the magazine's interfering with its vibes."

"I'll interfere with its vibes," growled Aries, "if it doesn't tell me something useful soon!"

"Scroll," coaxed Alex, drawing the Scroll towards him, "we'd like you to try again."

A waft of putrid smoke curled from the Scroll's edges and hung stinking in the air.

"*Beneath… Midnight Shimmer,*" said the Scroll and burped loudly. "Oh, excuse me! *Shimmer your way into the spotlight with Glitzy Girl eyeshadow! Close to… fizz up your life with Mango Whizz — the zippiest lip gloss around!*"

The Scroll spluttered and snapped shut.

Rose bit her lip. "Maybe my repair wasn't as good as I thought."

"And now we've used up a question," sighed Alex.

But Aries wasn't listening. "Did you hear what it said? My fleece! Closer than we think! We have to start looking." He thumped his shoulder against the door and stepped back again, lowering his horns, ready to charge through it.

"No!" cried Alex and threw his arms around

Aries' horns, trying to hold him back. "The Scroll's too damaged," he gasped, jerked along the floor behind the ram's rump, "to guide us safely."

"Let me go!" Aries squirmed and twisted, his hooves squealing on the tiled floor.

Alex pulled Aries' head round to face him. "You wouldn't stand a chance up there!"

Aries frothed. The tendons in his neck strained. "The Scroll said it's near. So, it must be in the museum somewhere."

"It's not!" said Rose. She knelt down and looked into Aries' frustrated face and laid a hand on his pulsing neck. "The fleece is not an exhibit here. It never has been."

"So what did it mean?" sighed Aries, slumping onto his haunches.

He stuck his bottom lip out and stared at the floor. Behind him, Alex shook his head at Rose, giving her a look that said that there was no point reasoning with a moody ram.

Rose glanced at her watch and sighed. "The museum closes in about ten minutes," she said. "I'll have to go."

"What about us?" said Alex.

"You'll be safe as long as you stay down here, okay? No one will come in here overnight. I'll come back first thing tomorrow and then we'll get somewhere. You'll see."

And, as the author, I can tell you that Rose was absolutely right: the next day they certainly would get somewhere. However, as she hurried down the museum's front marble steps and Alex and Aries fought over the blanket before settling down to sleep, none of them could have imagined just where that was and how dangerous and unpleasant it would be.

Which was just as well, really.

❋XI❋

NIGHT AT THE MUSEUM

Groan…

      puff…

            sigh…

For those of you who've never shared your bedroom with half a ton of ram, these are the sort of sounds it makes when he's too excited to sleep.

Snort…

      scrunch (of half a biscuit discovered
            in the bedding)…

            "Hellooo…?"

Aries tried to sleep. He really did. But every time he closed his eyelids, images of lambs bounced across them, each carrying letters: an 'N', an 'E', an 'A' and an 'R' in their fleecy tails, gambolling over grass like woolly ballerinas, spelling the word out over and over again.

"Near!" announced Aries, clattering to his hooves and flinging off his share of the blanket. "Near!"

he said to the odd-shaped parcels above his head, half-lit by the dim corridor lights spilling through the glass in the door. "Near!" he told the stuffed lizard whose glass eyes glinted at him from the gloom.

Then he trotted over to Alex and leaned down close to the boy's ear. "Alex," he whispered. "Are you asleep?"

"Yes," said Alex.

That was a nuisance, thought Aries and clopped back to face the wall. Why didn't Alex understand how difficult it was to sleep, knowing that Aries' fleece was

NEAR!

And *close* added a little voice in his brain, not to mention proximate, not too far away, within a short distance, in the vicinity and quite possibly within spitting distance. His blood raced like fireflies, his heart pumped like a yearling.

"Near!" Aries announced to the darkened ceiling. He regarded the door and took a step closer to it. After all, as he would quickly have pointed out, he didn't come back to Earth to practise camping in the British Museum under a rather scratchy – and for all he knew rather flea-bitten – old blanket.

He looked back and licked Alex's ear.

"Get off!" Alex batted him away. "It's the middle of the night!"

"Near!" said Aries in a low voice.

"What?" muttered Alex, noticing the rather mad-looking glint in Aries' eyes. "Not again!"

Aries nodded wildly. "I'm going to look for it!"

"Now?" exclaimed Alex. He drew his knees up to his chin and wrapped his arms around them. "What a brilliant idea! I mean, I wonder why I didn't think of it? What with no talking Scroll, no idea where to start looking and, oh, the little matter of being in the middle of a museum in modern London full of guards who could arrest us and throw us into jail at any moment…"

"But apart from that?" Aries persisted.

Alex groaned and lay back down on the bed, pulling the blanket over his head.

Back in her tiny bedroom in Camden, Rose sat cross-legged on her bed, tapping away on her computer and humming along happily to her latest Hazel Praline CD.

And the reason she was so happy?

Because she'd discovered how to fix the Scroll.

As in *really* fix it.

Racking her brain for a way to fix the parchment, Rose had remembered the odd little map scrawled on its reverse side. She hadn't paid much attention to it at the time but this evening it reminded her of last summer's holiday hotspot: the Royal Geographic Society, where she and her mother had spent many happy hours (well, her mother, anyway, Rose having had no choice as usual) in the Cartography Laboratory. Cartography is a fancy word for maps, in case you're wondering, and the lab was rather like a hospital for crumbly old ones.

The lab's computers could scan in moth-eaten old maps, tattered with holes and rips, and work out where the missing contours, coastlines and paths would once have gone. Other machines analysed the age and density of the original scraps and, more importantly, gave directions to where, in the lab's library, the same type of paper might be found to patch the maps perfectly. Since the lab stored thousands of types of paper Rose was confident they'd have a much closer match for the Scroll. Then all they had to do was feed it into the machine to produce perfect copies of all the missing pieces. With the right sort of paper, Rose reasoned, the Scroll would practically be back to normal and much more likely to give sensible answers to Aries' questions about the fleece.

And to her own.

Meanwhile, up on the top floor of the British Museum, Aries shuffled through the deserted Egyptian Rooms, ducking the security beams and weaving between the red-eyed motion sensors. He'd already seen the cracked teapots of ancient China, the seal-fur underpants of the Viking invaders and a ghastly display of Amazonian shrunken heads with lolly-out tongues. Now he picked his way through cabinets stuffed with statues of blue hippos and green crocodiles and row upon row of mummification tools all silvery in the moonlight. He paused to peer at a line of wooden stobbers and hoikers for hooking out brains and shuddered before turning to yet another painted sarcophagus.

"Great Aken Poo Poo," he muttered, staring at the mummy case, its big potato nose glinting in the moonlight. "Know you the way to the fleece?"

The mummy case remained silent. Just as well, I suppose, since if it had sprung open and a bandaged figure had leaped out, there'd have been a brand new exhibit of Greek-Ram-Poo-Poo on the floor and the curators would not have liked that. Nor the cleaners.

Aries sighed and looked around at the mummy's rigid face. Of course it was wonderful knowing that the fleece was near, it was the best news he'd had in centuries, but really, what the Scroll had said was very puzzling. And not particularly helpful when you had three enormous floors to search, all with rooms the size of tennis courts and brimming with cabinets, cupboards and shadows.

Wearily, he meandered up to a nearby sign, which read:

TUDOR EXHIBITION
This gallery shows some of the clothes worn
by Henry VIII's six wives.

Aries walked up to the first dummy and considered it. With its bulging belly, beard and silk bloomers it was a funny looking wife, he decided, even allowing for the whims of fashion. Then he read the notice beside it, which said:

King Henry VIII – dancing costume

He might have smiled but for the frustration he felt. His hooves ached. His back ached. Worse, his heart ached because he had to admit to himself that Alex had been right: it would have been more sensible just to wait for Rose to repair the Scroll.

Shrugging, he glanced along the dresses on display. Beneath the night-lights their luxurious fabrics glowed. Extravagant damson and cream silks, swathes of emerald velvet and golden damask, braided with ribbons, their bodices picked out with tiny, glimmering seed pearls.

Except for the last one.

Intrigued, Aries clopped closer. This dress was made from heavy grey muslin, the colour of rain clouds. Pooling heavily around the dummy's feet, it was plainer by far than the others, save for a glittering row of gold stitches around its square neckline.

Sighing, Aries sank down, feeling a wave of tiredness wash over him. Laying his muzzle on the soft fabric, he muttered contentedly and read the card by the dummy's feet:

Dress worn by Anne Boleyn on first meeting Henry VIII.

Cut in the French style, its pewter colour is said to have caught the king's eye and perhaps because of this, Anne chose to wear this dress to the Tower of London in 1536 at her execution by beheading.

Execution, thought Aries sleepily, feeling his worries disappear as he sank into a doze. Taking a deep breath he snuggled deeper into the dress's skirts, paddling his hooves into its soft folds until it slid from the dummy's shoulders and covered him completely. Then, cosy and warm, he fell into a deep sleep.

✻XII✻

EARTH, WIND AND IRE

Compared to Anne Boleyn, earthworms live rather ordinary lives.

Day after day spent mooching and mulching through soil, their big moment comes when they poke their head into the sunshine and become a blackbird's breakfast. Except that tonight one London worm community was having an altogether livelier time than usual.

This community of worms lived in Regent's Park, tucked in a bed of yellow Californian roses, and up until a few minutes ago their lives had been simple and, well, wormy. But now, as Big Ben struck twelve, their soil began to quiver strangely. And thrum. With a good deal of shaking and groaning thrown in. Clay clods wobbled up, roots flapped, gravel rained down, crushing the wormholes and twirling the worms to make them look like marshmallow twists, but brown grey instead of pink and yellow.

Squirming to escape and stampeded by beetles and spiders scuttling past in a tussle of legs, the worms wriggled for the surface, trying to escape the earthquake, unaware that there was no earthquake. Simply a sorceress, chanting and stamping in the flower bed.

Draped in a moss-green velvet robe with Hex wrapped around her neck like a lively silvery scarf, Medea twirled in the rose trees, her fists above her head, flattening the earth over what she'd planted.

Dragons' teeth.

Remember how the ones planted on Kolkis had sprung up into Skeleton Soldiers? The ones she'd planted tonight were even meaner – a monster medley, if you like.

Since landing at Heathrow, Medea had worked fast, racing to her London home, a swanky three-storey mansion in Belgravia, snatching her favourite magic ingredients from the cellar and *click-click-clacking* across the park in her high heels to this particularly private spot. Sorceresses, you see, move faster at night, like spiders. This is because there are fewer people around to ask them why they are dancing in the flower beds, damaging the flowers and wearing a venomous snake around their necks, which, whatever you might have heard about

Londoners, is still considered unusual behaviour.

Breathing in the spicy scent of the roses, she tried to block out the memory of the stench in the cellar. And the squealing. We'll come to what she kept down there later on, but for now, let's just say it wasn't the usual old suitcases and a broken vacuum cleaner you'd expect.

Hex coiled round and looked into her eyes. "Can we go home now?" he hissed, thinking of how flying had rather dried his scales and he'd just love a wriggly dip in the swimming pool in Medea's garden.

"Of course not, scale-brain!"

Medea's eyes glittered like broken glass as, kneeling down, she squelched soil between her fingers, scooped up two fistfuls and held them to the sky.

Hecate! Queen of evil, Queen of night,
Helper of witches, hear me!

Fanning out her long fingers over her head, the soil drizzled down, showering over her shoulders and bouncing off Hex's head.

Be our darkest help at hand,
Raise our helpers from this land!

Three thumps rang out of the earth into the stillness and Medea stood up, her face a cold mask of pleasure. Turning, she stamped her feet into the earth, pounding a tattoo against the soil, facing the sky.

It was a good job that the park keeper wasn't around to see her, because I can tell you he wouldn't have taken kindly to that sort of behaviour in his most exotic roses. Nor would he have liked the crash of thunder and sudden wind that whipped across the park, twisting the rose bushes on their stalks and sending every rose petal into the air as she began to spin. Her skirt snagged in the thorns as she turned, muttering darkly under her breath, her face tilted to the moon, when suddenly she stopped and threw her arms up, twisting her hands, one over the other, as though winding in an invisible rope. Magic, as you might not know, needs energy and is much more like an aerobics class than any *tapsy-wapsying* of wands. Dark and primitive, it needs power and without lots of arm waving and leaping about, it's just so many dark words lost on the air.

A *whooshing* sound erupted from the soil and Medea froze, staring down, her eyes wide and gleaming like broken glass, as three holes zigzagged open around her feet. Earth poured into them like muddy waterfalls and anyone close enough would have seen the soil crumbling onto the heads and shoulders of three curiously misshapen figures below.

Kneeling at the edge of the nearest hole, Medea peered down, whispering:

Hecate! Hear your servant's plea,
Help the witch of Greece,
Lead me now with helpers three,
To Aries of the fleece.

Surprised?

I expect you were rather taken aback at how excited Medea was by the television footage at the café too?

I mean you just don't expect a sorceress to leap on a plane, dive into some London rose bushes at midnight and ask for help in tracking down a ram, do you? And much as I'd like to reassure you that it was just for old time's sake, I'm afraid you're right to be worried.

"Can I have a look?" hissed Hex, his fangs glinting silver in the moonlight.

Medea glared at him.

"I need to know what'sss going on, don't I?" the snake persisted, lowering himself towards the soil, squinting. "After all, you want a capable familiar, don't you?"

"Yes," said Medea coldly. "In fact, I'm thinking of getting one. You know, a black panther, maybe, or a Bolivian bird-eating spider."

She gripped Hex's throat and clicked her fingers above his head. A scatter of black stars rained down over his skin, dusting his scales and jerking him as rigid as a broomstick. He gulped, flicking his green eyes to look at her just as she tossed him up into the air, caught him and jammed him, snout first, down into the earth.

"Capable, indeed," she muttered, dusting the soil off her hands.

Then she paused, listening to the new sounds mingling beneath her feet: the throb of three hearts, an unfurling of knifelike feathers, a scrabbling of fingers, a throaty braying laugh.

✳XIII✳

STONE THE CROWS

Museums, like elephants, wake up slowly in the mornings.

Next morning, as the heating and plumbing wheezed into life – the museum's that is, not the elephant's, although if it's an old elephant it could be both – the night guards switched off the intruder alarms, brewed their morning mugs of tea and unlocked the doors to the cleaners waiting outside. It was behind just such a small army of men and women, struggling with bags of overalls, polish and rubber gloves, that Rose walked in. Behind her, at the foot of the steps, her mother's car zoomed off, heading in the direction of the airport and Athens to visit Professor Papadakis, the caryatid expert. She'd left Rose with a kiss, a banana and strict instructions to go straight to her friend Lucy's house that evening as she, her mother, wouldn't be back till tomorrow night. (Suiting Rose perfectly since, despite telling her mum all about it, she still hadn't remembered Lucy was on holiday with her family in Lanzarote until the following Tuesday.)

Rose hitched her rucksack onto her back and walked across the museum's Great Hall, its white floor bright with sunshine streaming through its vast glass ceiling. She knew she ought to feel relieved about Professor Papadakis fixing the caryatid, because it would mean that the portal was in place and Alex and Aries could go home again, but another part of her hoped it wouldn't be too soon. After all, it had been a long time since Rose had felt so excited or useful about anything. Or had real company.

She walked past a couple of guards scratching their heads over a collapsed dummy in the Tudor collection and turned towards the lost property office on the western side of the museum. Her footsteps echoed along the empty corridors and up the short flight of steps to the little office, stuffed full of lost things that the attendants found scattered every day round its halls and corridors. Checking first that no one was around, Rose stepped inside and worked quickly. A few minutes later she had found a navy blue jumper, a white T-shirt and a pair of boy's jeans. How someone had managed to walk out into the middle of London without their jeans on puzzled her until she noticed the price tag still hanging off them. She held them up in front of her: they looked about right for Alex and would certainly help him blend in when they left the museum. Rose stuffed them into her rucksack, hurried out of the office and made her way to the basement.

She knocked lightly on the storeroom door and stepped inside to find Alex and Aries arguing about something.

"But I liked it," Aries was saying.

"That's hardly the point!" replied Alex, his arms folded tightly over his chest.

"Hello?" said Rose. "Something wrong?"

Alex turned and smiled quickly. "Only that Aries took himself off on a midnight tour of the museum last night and went to bed in some fancy dress."

"*On* it," corrected Aries. "Not in it!"

"You were supposed to stay here," said Rose, beginning to wonder what the security cameras had picked up.

Aries sniffed and stared up at the ceiling.

"Luckily I found him before the doors opened," said Alex. "So I suppose there's no harm done."

Hardly, thought Rose, remembering the guards she'd walked past, wondering if they might at this very moment be checking the night footage and discovering where Alex and Aries were hiding. Realising that she needed to delete whatever was recorded before they checked, she hastily unbuckled her rucksack and pulled out the clothes from the lost property office.

"Put these on!" she said, handing them to Alex. "I have to nip upstairs a minute."

Alex examined the jeans and frowned. "They're like yours," he said suspiciously. "I don't want to wear girl things."

"They're jeans," she replied patiently, or as patiently as she could manage, talking to a boy in a Greek tunic that looked like a minidress. "And everyone here wears them."

"Xerxes of Persia wore trousers," muttered Aries. "And a right berk he looked in them too. Not that anyone mentioned it to his face, of course. Not with his being so handy with a sword."

"Look," said Rose, walking quickly towards the door and glancing back at Alex. "Just change into them, okay? It'll make life a lot easier."

"And what about me?" sniffed Aries sniffily. "What am I supposed to wear?"

"I'm still thinking of something for you," said Rose.

"Something in gold," said Aries as she stepped

out into the corridor. "It is my best colour, you know."

Rose hurried back the way she had come to the security office. Located at the museum's front entrance, it was a small glass-fronted room set behind a counter, which doubled as an information point during the daytime. Now, glancing through its window, she was relieved to see that no one had checked the surveillance footage because the monitors were still showing live views of the exhibition rooms. She tapped in the room's security code and stepped inside. Half a minute later she'd wiped the night's recordings and was just about to stand up and leave when a sudden rapping on the glass startled her. Twisting round, she saw a sharp-featured old woman wearing strange black-rimmed glasses with lenses shaped like lemons. Her grey hair was pulled tightly back off her face into a bun and bundled up in her thick black cape, far too warm for the summer. She reminded Rose of an old-fashioned nanny, a particularly stern and short-tempered one.

Rose stood up, wondering how the woman had even managed to get in since the museum didn't open to the public until ten, and walked over to the glass, opening the panel. "Can I help you?"

Twitching, the woman craned her neck forwards,

revealing a wattle of yellowed skin beneath her chin. "I need to see the museum director," she said, her voice low and croaking.

"She's on holiday," Rose said. "My mum said—"

"Your mother?" The woman tipped her head to one side and regarded Rose with cold glittering eyes.

"Yes," Rose went on, feeling her smile slip as a sour smell wafted through into the small office. "She works here, Dr Pottersby-Weir. She's an archaeologist. Anyway, she says that Mr Roper, the chief curator, is in charge for now."

"And when is Mr Roper in?"

"About half nine, usually. Shall I give him a message for you?"

"Tell him," the woman bustled her shoulders, "that I am calling about the sheep-related incident yesterday." She jerked her head to the other side. "I am Ms De Mentor from the Department of Art, Culture and Ruminants."

"Culture and Ruminants?" said Rose uneasily, because even though she hardly knew anything about politics, she was sure that the Department of Arts and Culture didn't have any special departments for sheep.

"This museum was a laughing stock yesterday," said Ms De Mentor, leaning towards the glass, "and it can't be allowed to happen again. Sheep's cud will stain marble permanently, you know, while stray boluses of food are worse than dried bubblegum to shift. And don't get me started on what a sheep's other end can do."

"I wasn't going to," said Rose, feeling her nose tingle. The mouldy smell was getting stronger now and for some reason reminded her of the school's budgerigar cage when it needed cleaning.

"My department requires me to track down the sheep," added Ms De Mentor.

"Ram," said Rose.

The woman drew her red lips into a tight line. "And the boy. He, in particular, needs to be dealt with."

"Look. I'm sure it won't happen again," said Rose quickly. "The ram was just frightened, you know, being a long way from home."

The woman arched an eyebrow suspiciously. "And how would you know that?"

Rose swallowed. "I'm, um, just guessing. You know, a ram turning up in the middle of London?"

Ms De Mentor smiled cheerlessly and glanced over at the wooden chairs and tables of the museum café.

"I shall wait over there," she said crisply. "And

I shall not be leaving. Make sure that you let the chief curator know."

Rose waited until the woman had stalked away. Then, horribly unsettled, she let herself out of the office and hurried back across the Great Hall and through the door to the basement stairs, unable to shake off the sensation of being watched until she stepped back into the storeroom.

Inside, Alex was stretching out his arms either side until his hands appeared at the end of the jumper sleeves.

"I've just met the strangest woman," said Rose, closing the door quickly behind her. "Says she wants to see the director. Something about improving security against ruminants."

"Charming," muttered Aries, about to add something else when the door slammed loudly against the back wall.

Rose spun round to see Ms De Mentor filling the doorway.

"You can't—" squeaked Rose, as Ms De Mentor shoved her out of the way and marched into the room.

"Khryos Khrysamallos," she rasped, her head jutting forwards on its thin stalk of neck. "So this is where you've been hiding!"

Alex stepped out in front of Aries and the woman's shadow fell across them both. Winded, Rose stared at the woman's back. Were Rose's eyes playing tricks on her or was Ms De Mentor really getting bigger? Her shoulders seemed to be straining against her cape, whilst her chest looked as though it was inflating, puffing up like a balloon. When her cape button popped off and skittered across the floor, Rose knew she was right, but still gasped as a ring of black splintery feathers sprung out from Ms De Mentor's neck.

"Harpy!" gasped Alex, his eyes growing wide.

With a quick shake the harpy flung her cloak away and stepped out of her skirt and boots to reveal the body of a monstrous bird, thick and bulbous and covered with oily black plumage. A tatter of down stuck out above spindly grey legs ending in wrinkled bird feet with sharp, yellowed talons. The smell of old birdcage that Rose had noticed upstairs was now overwhelming, filling the room with a sickening stench. The harpy rustled her feathers, drawing her jagged wings together so that they jutted out above her head, craned forwards and glowered at Alex and Aries.

"My mistress wishes to see you," she said.

Throwing back her head she cawed, piercing

the air with a metallic, unearthly screech.

"Aries," shouted Alex, his face suddenly pale behind his tanned skin. "Run!"

As Aries scrambled away, clattering down the narrow gap left at the ends of the shelves, Ms De Mentor flicked open her wings. They made a sound like an old umbrella opening and sent pots and vases crashing onto the floor. Lurching towards Alex, arching over him, her wings brushed the ceiling.

But he didn't run.

Rose gasped as he vanished behind a greasy wall of black feathers.

Then there was a thumping sound, like someone hitting an overstuffed pillow, and the harpy doubled over, spluttering. Alex, you see, knew a thing or two about harpies. You can't not when you have to step into their aviary to feed them three times a week. And what he knew was that they had a weakness. If you could get close enough to avoid their vicious beak, and not be shredded by their savage claws, or blinded by their feathers, their neck was soft, exposed and vulnerable. Just like a vulture's. Alex drew back his fist again. Sidestepping quickly, he landed a second punch at her gasping throat.

Desperate to help, Rose picked up the nearest thing to hand, which happened to be her rucksack, and began thumping Ms De Mentor across the back with it. Jerking upright, the bird-woman looked over her shoulder, cawing furiously, her thin black tongue rippling inside her beak, her eyes glittering with hatred. Her hair fell loose from its tight bun, tumbling into a greasy straggle over her shoulders. Rose trembled, drawing away as the harpy jerked forwards and sliced Rose's cheek with the tip of her wing. Rose yelped and stepped back, reaching for her face, sensing the blood trickle down between her fingers.

Turning back, the harpy cawed viciously, swinging her head from side to side like a T-rex. She didn't see Alex until it was too late. Crouched down, he seized the harpy's ankles and yanked hard, sending the harpy over backwards.

Yay! Alex!

As she slammed down onto the floor, air exploded from her lungs. Impressed, Rose jumped away from the winded pile of feathers wheezing at her feet.

"Come on!" yelled Alex. "We have to get out of here!"

Rose was just turning for the door when she heard Aries. Grunting and struggling he was wedged in the corner of the room, pinned between the end of the shelves and the wall, held tight.

Horribly aware of the black shape stirring on the floor, Rose dived towards Aries and seized hold of his horns. She pulled, digging her heels against the floor, leaning back, straining. Alex ran around from the other side and began to push.

"Aries, move!" he yelled. "We haven't got long before she attacks again!"

"I'm trying!" squealed Aries between gasps.

Rose felt as though her lungs would explode with effort. On the other side of the room, the harpy sat up unsteadily.

Furiously throwing her weight backwards, Rose pulled harder still, her arm muscles burning with effort as Aries twisted and thrashed, kicking and squirming. Behind him, Alex braced his shoulder against Aries' rump and pushed, his face wrought with strain.

Suddenly, with a loud splintering crack the stack of shelves collapsed and Aries shot forwards, knocking Rose off her feet. Parcels and crates cascaded to the floor around her.

Alex dragged Rose to her feet. "We need to find somewhere dark to hide. Harpies can't see well in poor light!"

Behind them, the harpy was blinking and rising to her feet. Rose lunged out into the corridor,

Alex and Aries at her heels, and hurtled towards the stairwell at the end. Throwing back the door, she glanced over her shoulder, glimpsing a scrawny yellow leg stepping out of the storeroom and threw herself up the metal stairs, followed by the other two.

Almost scrambling on all fours in her haste, she skidded out behind them into the empty Great Hall. A second later the stairwell door crashed open behind them. An ear-popping caw filled the room followed by a ferocious flapping of wings as the harpy lifted into the air, her silhouette black against the blue-grey of the glass roof.

"This way!" shouted Alex, noticing the dingy light bathing the Glories of Ancient Egypt exhibition room. "Hide!"

With her breath scouring her lungs, Rose sped into the room, hurtling past the mummies standing either side of the doorway and down the walkway made by two rows of tomb statues, several metres high. Giant stone cats in cobra headdresses gazed impassively down as the children and Aries raced past towards the colossal statue of Aken-Ra, Lord of the Locusts, placed at the top of the rows. Chiselled from sandstone and standing over five metres high, Aken-Ra leaned forwards, his huge hands resting on great golden knees and, desperate, Rose tucked herself behind his calves, flattening herself against the timeworn stone as Aries hunched down behind his heel. Skidding to a stop, Alex checked to see where they were hiding, before leaping behind the nearby statue of Aken-Ra's favourite pet locust, golden and leggy and over two metres high.

Rose breathed through her mouth and listened to the wet snuffling and sort of *scritchy-scratchy* sound that talons make against a marble floor. Edging her nose around the side of Aken-Ra's leg she peered out to see the harpy strutting towards them, jerking her head between the statues to check if anyone was hiding.

Drawing back, Rose lay her head against the cool stone. Which was when she spotted the display of tomb candle lighters arranged a couple of metres away on the wall. Taking a deep breath she leaped out, sprinted the short distance and snatched one up, actually a third century BC tomb candle lighter of the Amenhotep dynasty (which to those non-archaeologists amongst you is a big pole with a sharp tip at one end).

"Come on, you great overgrown crow!" squealed Rose, running towards the harpy, jabbing the pole in the air.

"Rose, no!" yelled Alex, leaping from his hiding place as Rose thrust and jabbed, striking high, low, left, right.

But wherever she aimed, the candle lighter bounced off the harpy's chest like a pin against a car tyre and now, cawing wildly, the ferocious bird-woman began lifting off the ground.

"Get away from her talons!" yelled Alex, throwing himself towards the harpy, reaching out for her slimy tail feathers and just missing as she swept up into the air, snatched the hood of Rose's top and yanked the girl off balance.

Behind him Aries thundered across the room, charging towards the harpy who was now flying a metre off the ground, dragging Rose backwards. Rose struggled and punched, her trainers squealing wildly over the floor as the harpy suddenly shot upwards, just missing Aries' horns, and carried Rose into the air, up over the tomb statues, towards the ceiling, tight in her talons.

Aries brayed furiously as Alex spun round, seized the nearest relic, a priceless tomb ornament of Neferhotep I (valued for its high craftsmanship and unusual use of two tones of marble) and clambered onto the locust statue for a better shot. Harpies, he knew, hunted by snatching turtles from the seashore, flying higher and higher up into the sky in order to drop them onto the rocks below, so that they'd, well, you get the picture. Horrified, he understood that the harpy intended to dispatch Rose in exactly the same way. He tried to straighten up, cursing as his feet slid over the statue's stonework, worn smooth by centuries in the desert, and realised he was too far away to make the shot.

"Aries!" he yelled. "Come here!"

The ram pounded across and skidded to a halt as Alex leaped from the statue onto his broad back. Spreading his feet for balance, teetering like a circus acrobat, Alex fixed his aim on the harpy as Aries clattered across the floor beneath her.

"Take that!" he shouted, hurling the urn with all his strength.

It whirled through the air and struck the side of the creature's head. Her wings jerked and collapsed, sending her toppling backwards, reeling tail over shoulder feathers as Rose vanished into a blur of black. The harpy fell, fluttering and whistling, and crashed into a heap on the floor.

Leaping down from Aries' back, Alex ran across the floor. A small hand poked out through the slimy tangle and grabbing it he pulled Rose free and dragged her to her feet.

"You all right?" he said.

"Soft landing," said Rose, wiping a smear of grease from her cheek. "That was some shot!"

Alex shrugged and looked down at the stunned creature. "Feels funny to be attacking something that I usually look after," he said. "But then, it was her or us."

Aries prodded a hoof into the harpy's side and she began to twitch and mutter.

"Come on," said Alex, "we have to get out of here."

Minutes later they hurried down the front steps of the British Museum, over its courtyard and out onto Great Russell Street. Alex gasped, covering his ears against the sudden thrum of traffic, and blinked, astonished by the cars and red buses rumbling past and hooting horns. Beside him, Aries buried his head in Alex's stomach (although when you're the size of an upright piano, any burying of heads is more hopeful than helpful, so that as well as being terrified, Alex was now buckled into a very uncomfortable right angle over Aries' back).

"It's all right," soothed Rose, knowing that traffic was every bit as alien to Alex and Aries as that creature in the museum had been to her.

Taking hold of Alex's sleeve and Aries' left horn, she wove through people – who pointed and clicked

Aries with their phone cameras – into a back street. One of a patchwork of lanes that zigzagged quietly towards Rose's home, today it felt safe, hidden from the London of postcards and plastic flags that she'd always felt at home in before, a London that had suddenly filled with wings and talons and danger.

❋XIV❋
SCROLL ON A ROLL

An hour later, Alex and Aries were sitting at the table in Dr Pottersby-Weir's cramped kitchen waiting for Rose to come back from the Royal Geographical Society. Only the day before Alex would never have let the Scroll, tattered and useless as it was, out of his sight and particularly in the care of a girl. After all, it was their only divine help up here. But sometimes in life there are situations that convince you to trust people quickly and someone helping you defeat a harpy in the British Museum is one of those situations.

Alex knew that Rose wasn't like any girl he'd met in ancient Athens but more like the Spartan girls he'd heard of, brought up to be strong and athletic, to ride horses and chariots. He'd been impressed at how she'd stood up to the harpy, even if she hadn't really known how to do it, but more than that, he'd been touched – touched that she'd helped them.

After all, Hades only knew how fantastic their story must have seemed to an Earth girl and so, when she'd suggested she take the Scroll away to fix, he'd agreed immediately, happy to follow her instructions not to leave the house or answer the telephone. Of course, since neither Alex nor Aries knew what a telephone was, that was hardly a problem.

The sound of the front door opening shook Alex from his thoughts.

"Did it!" called Rose, stepping into the hall.

She pushed back her hood and hurried into the kitchen, grinning and holding the Scroll up triumphantly in front of her.

Now, since Rose wasn't the sort to blow her own trumpet[19], allow me to tell you that she'd done a wonderful job. Really. Of course, she'd always been pretty good at fiddly things, like holding Brazilian lizard dung between tweezers for her mother to examine, but this time she'd excelled herself. Having charmed her way into the building – not hard, since most of the people who worked there

---

19. *Why being pleased with oneself should be likened to playing in a band I have no idea. It's like being compared to a camel when you're grumpy. Who makes these things up? That's what I'd like to know.*

still remembered her father – she'd nipped into the map lab during coffee break and used the machine to patch the Scroll's holes so neatly they all but vanished.

So, let me say it again:

Well done, Rose!

Which was what Alex said, too, as he set down his mug and unfurled the Scroll, only he didn't sound nearly as excited as me. In fact, he sounded subdued and rather nervous. Quite apart from all the strange people and things he'd seen since arriving, he'd been thinking about being attacked by a harpy, and he'd just reached a very unpleasant conclusion, which we'll come to in a moment.

Brace yourselves.

"It was easy really," said Rose, trying to sound cheerful despite their anxious faces. She sat down beside them at the table. "The machine calculated that the Scroll dates from around 440 BC and told me where to find the parchment to repair it with. I used some stuff unearthed at Corinth years ago, fed it into the machine and it made all the right pieces." She touched the scratch on her cheek. "So I suppose we can ask it who sent that bird thing to the museum?"

"We don't need to," said Alex, biting his lip. "Only Medea is powerful enough to create a harpy up here on Earth."

"But why?" Aries dropped the breakfast bowl he'd been tipping towards him to finish off his tea. It clattered in the stillness. "Why's she sticking her big nose in?"

"It wasn't big," said Alex, "not in the wedding portraits they sent me to paint on the commemorative pots."

"Perhaps she's still got it," muttered Rose, thinking out loud.

"Got what?" said Aries. "Her nose?"

"No," said Rose. "The fleece." She turned to face the other two. "Think about it," Rose went on slowly. "Didn't you say that neither she nor the fleece came down to the Underworld—"

"That doesn't mean she still has it, though," said Alex. "Not when it's been more than a thousand years since she helped steal it."

"But why else send a harpy after us?" said Rose. "Unless she's scared that we'll take the fleece away from her?"

"Scared?" Alex suppressed a nervous laugh. "You think Medea would be scared of a couple of kids and a ram?"

There was a mumble from the direction of top of the table.

"And a Scroll," added Rose quickly. She turned to look at the roll of paper, flipping its corner sulkily. "Perhaps we should be asking it questions instead of sitting here puzzling our heads off! We've still got three left."

At which point the Scroll unfurled with a shimmy.

> *Thank you, Rose, for down to you*
> *I'm again a Scroll ornately.*
> *My dimples now are velum smooth*
> *And flatter me most greatly.*
> *Three answers left have I to give,*
> *So, pray, ask me sedately.*

Twisting round, it shot a teaspoon onto the floor and flipped open and shut excitedly. "What's the question?"

Alex took a deep breath. "Scroll, we want to know, does Medea still have the fleece?"

The Scroll remained silent.

"Please?" added Rose.

"Thank you, Rose," muttered the Scroll. "How nice to find someone with good manners."

It huffed and rolled out taut.

The fleece has brought Medea
Dark hoards of wicked riches,
And swapping wands for needles means
Her power's in the stitches.
For, with the fleece, the sorceress
Doth conjure and bewitch us.

Aries frowned. "Alex, is it saying yes or no?"

Alex watched as the Scroll tweaked its corners up into a papery smile.

"It's a yes, I think," translated Alex.

"I knew it," said Aries, clattering the stone floor with his hooves. "That's why she's scared of us. She knows we're coming to—"

At which the Scroll snapped shut. "And a no," added Alex. "Probably."

"Make your mind up!" spluttered Aries.

Rose reached out a hand and stroked the Scroll. "I think it's telling us that it's a yes and a no."

"Yes, she's still got it," said Aries. "But I wonder what it meant by the no?"

For a few moments, everyone thought while the Scroll purred contentedly against Rose's hand.

"What about 'her power's in the stitches'?" said Rose.

But no one had any ideas about that either.

"Swapping wands for needles?" Rose persisted.

Or that.

Scrolls, decided Rose, even repaired ones, were nowhere near as useful as the internet. You couldn't just type in your search word and wait for a clear answer to flash up.

The Scroll rustled impatiently. "Do you have another question?"

"Hardly," muttered Aries sourly. "Not when you've already been so helpful!"

"I'm sorry," the Scroll replied. "But I may give you only the answers which I distil from the psychic vibrations around me."

"I'll give you psychic vibrations!" muttered Aries. He looked up at Alex. "What should we ask now?"

Alex swallowed. "The only thing we can ask. Scroll," he said. "Please will you tell us where to find Medea?"

Well, whilst they're waiting for the Scroll to tell them, I can tell you precisely where Medea was: sitting in a ruby wing-backed armchair in the living room of her London house, scowling. And as scowls go, it was an especially vile one, a real face-crumpler, compounded of annoyance at Ms De Mentor, who now trembled in front of the sorceress, and of the sickening stench that seeped up through the room's floorboards from the cellar below. Despite the bowls of fresh lilies Medea set around the room and the flickering sandalwood candles, nothing ever masked that putrid smell.

And what, you might ask, was down there making such a stink?

Well, ask away, because I'm not saying anything about *that* place until I really have to.

Medea stood up and fixed the harpy with her pale silver eyes. "I can't believe you failed to bring me the ram."

Hex, who'd been snoozing on the back of her chair, now opened one sleepy eye to see the sorceress pluck a black rose from the vase on the mantlepiece and slap it against her palm, sending showers of velvety petals to the floor.

"Well?" Medea turned back to the harpy who sank her scraggy neck low into her chest. "Do you have an explanation?"

"Mistress, I didn't expect the ram to have such help—"

"Help?" Medea's voice rose. "You're talking about children!"

"Yes," the harpy went on nervously. "But the boy was so protective of the ram and the girl, and she, well, she was so determined. And resourceful."

Medea raised an eyebrow. "Really?" She thought for a moment and regarded the harpy darkly. "How old was she?"

The harpy shrugged. "About twelve."

Hex noticed the dark smile cross Medea's face. "Ussseful, Mistressss?"

"Perhaps," said Medea in a voice that sounded like ice cracking under water.

"And I found out something else," added Ms De Mentor quickly. "She told me her mother works at the museum. A Dr Pottersby-Weir."

Medea frowned and walked across the room to check the morning's newspaper and flicked through the pages until she found what she wanted. "Dr Augusta Pottersby-Weir... Here we are," she said, reading over the article with fresh relish. "She's the woman who's going to fix the caryatid. Due to fly out to Greece this morning."

The harpy lifted her chin brightly and began preening one foot with the other, even though she was wearing boots again. "Is that useful, too, Mistress?"

Medea shrugged dismissively. "It hardly makes up for your failure," she muttered. "But you won't let me down again."

"No, Mistress," said the harpy, making a half-bow. "I promise I—"

"No," Medea cut her off. "You misunderstand me."

Raising one arm above her head, she whispered something under her breath and twisted round in three full circles, whereupon a flash of red light shot from her fingers, bounced off the ceiling and pierced the harpy's chest like a thrown spear.

"Mistr—?" The harpy gurgled and slumped to the floor, her eyes black circles of pain.

"Ooh," said Hex in the twitchy silence that now filled the living room. "Don't you think that was a bit harsssh?"

Medea glared at him. "Do you want to be next?"

Snapping his head back faster than a party blower[20], Hex ducked behind the chair and laced himself tightly against its carved fretwork as Medea swept past. She stooped to pick up the black smouldering dragon's tooth from the rug where the harpy had stood and slipped it into her pocket.

For a moment she stared into the cold embers of the fireplace. Then, closing her eyes, she whispered a name under her breath. A moment later the door

---

20. But without the feather on the end.

behind her opened and someone, or rather something, tall, broad-shouldered and immaculately dressed in one of Medea's suits for gentlemen, clopped inside. Clopped because although the creature's head and torso were those of a man, his hind quarters and legs were those of a goat: bowed, furry beneath those pressed trousers and ending in polished brown hooves.

The creature was a faun, the second of those Medea had created in Regent's Park the night before. Now, stepping into the sunlight streaming through the window, his black hair, smooth as gloss paint, twinkled almost blue. A microphone headset curled neatly around one ear. Beautifully groomed, he might have passed for one of Medea's own fashion models, save for the two horns that poked through his hair.

"Pandemic," said Medea.

"At your service, Mistress." The faun bowed and straightened up, smiling, making his face crease into lines around his deep brown eyes. "I assure you your problems are at an end."

"You'll bring the ram to me?" said Medea.

"Without fail, Mistress."

Opening one beautifully manicured hand, he revealed a set of panpipes, their long reeds glinting in the firelight. "The old ways still work," he smiled.

At which Hex slithered over the back of the chair and onto its seat for a better look.

"Don't you think he's a bit weedy?" he muttered, looking the faun up and down.

The faun raised an eyebrow. "I think you mean svelte."

"No." Hex regarded him, hissing. "Definitely weedy."

"Which is why I've created reinforcements," said Medea.

"Reinforcements?" said Pandemic, his voice rising peevishly as a second figure shuffled out from behind him.

Thickset and lumpen, he looked rather like a gorilla bundled into a dinner suit[21]. It stared back at the faun with a single watery green eye, set squarely in the centre of its lumpy forehead.

"Dear Fred!" Medea brushed a fleck of soil from the creature's jacket.

Pandemic wrinkled up his nose, disgusted, as Fred began flexing his muscles, making them squirm like octopus tentacles beneath his sleeves whilst his knuckles crunched like pistachio shells.

---

21. *A trick, I might add, which is very hard to do, since the gorilla rarely cooperates, meaning the trousers usually go on backwards.*

"Not bad," she murmured, smiling.

Now some of you might be wondering why Medea had created such odd-looking helpers.

Why not employ a vindictive vet?

Or a sheep wrestler?

Well, think for a moment about who are sheep's worst enemies. Yes, I do know I sound like a teacher, but go on, humour me.

Dogs?

Dingoes?

Coyotes and wolves?

The local butcher with his special offer on mint sauce and a glint in his eye?

Good answers, but all completely wrong, because sheep's worst enemies are, in fact:

1. Fauns
2. Cyclopes

All right, harpies too, on account of their talons, beaks and penchant for lamb chops, but we're not including them here, since the only harpy we've come across on Earth is now an ex-harpy, recently turned back into a tooth and gathering fluff in Medea's pocket.

Pandemic, being a faun, was a relative of Pan,

the shepherd-god who loved nothing better than terrifying flocks into frenzies by tooting his panpipes until, woolly doolally, they leaped off cliffs and dived into rivers. And Fred was the great-nephew of Polyphemus, the Cyclops from whom Odysseus and his sailors famously escaped by strapping themselves beneath the bellies of the Cyclops's sheep when he released the flock from his cave. This meant no sailors for tea that night and a whole race of Greek monsters that forever hated sheep.

Consequently, Pandemic and Fred represented the top of the line hoof-curling, wool-frazzling nightmare for any sheep and, more precisely, one particular ram.

"But I—" Pandemic began.

"Ram, ram!" blurted Fred.

"If you don't mind," interrupted Pandemic.

"Ram, ram! Ram, ram!" Fred continued happily.

"I have always," Pandemic tried again, raising his voice, "felt that brains are of far more use than—"

Fred poked Pandemic in the chest with a banana-sized finger. "Ram, ram!"

Pandemic bristled. "Mistress? Must I really take this oaf with me?"

Medea pursed her lips. "That 'oaf' is the brawn you'll need, if that feather-brained harpy was right.

I can't risk another mess-up. So, sort your differences quickly." Her eyes shone like wet slate. "Need I remind you that failure by either one of you will mean punishment for both." She plucked the tooth from her pocket and turned it slowly in front of them. "Understood?"

"Understood," muttered Pandemic.

"Huh?" said Fred.

Medea turned away from them and looked out of the window into the long walled garden, its coppery bricks bathed in sunlight.

"Ms De Mentor said the girl's mother worked at the museum. Find out where she lives." She looked over her shoulder, glancing at the walkie-talkie on the table beside her chair. "Then wait for my instructions."

❊XV❊
Uptown Ram

Medea's made a patch of Greece
With magical behaviour.
Now her house basks in an olive grove
In swankiest Belgravia.
But stay out, 'cause like flies in webs,
Inside, there's naught can save yer.

"Oh dear, oh dear," flustered the Scroll. "I'm sorry about that!"

"About what?" said Rose.

"The 'yer'. It's hardly proper English and I do have my standards. However, 'you' wouldn't rhyme with 'Belgravia' and 'yer' would."

"Get on with it," muttered Aries.

The Scroll sniffed and went on:

Beneath those marbled corridors,
In darkness vile and creepy,

> *The mournful cries ring out in fear,*
> *Lamenting long and weepy.*
> *Keep out! Keep out! Whate'er you do,*
> *Especially you, bald sheepy!*

"Bald sheepy?" spluttered Aries.

The Scroll blew what sounded like a papery raspberry. "Rhymed with weepy!" it said and snapped shut.

"I wasn't too keen on the bit about mournful cries," said Alex.

"Or the lamenting," added Rose. She leaned forwards, frowning at the others. "I wonder what it means by a patch of Greece. And olive groves? Here in London? As directions go, they're pretty woolly, aren't they?"

"Do you mind?" muttered Aries.

"Sorry," smiled Rose and rubbed his forehead.

Aries stretched towards the Scroll, put his mouth around its end, rather like playing a bugle, and boomed down its middle.

"That answer was fit for the rubbish pits of Attica! Please elaborate!"

The Scroll quivered angrily. "I am a Scroll of godly assistance, the gift of Athena. Consequently do not expect me to function like a common or garden London A to Z."

"But an address could really add to your last answer," coaxed Rose.

"Let me see," replied the Scroll and wobbled over to Rose. "As a matter of fact I do feel a secondary vibration coming through on this point," it murmured, unfurling.

She works in Bond Street – Seamed Desires –
Her store for wealthy girls.
To sew her skirts of harsh regret
In sequins, silk and pearls.
Seek there for next to bolts of cloth
Your answers will unfurl…

"No way!" Rose scrambled to her feet. "It can't be!"

"Can't be what?" said Alex, confused.

"I know her!"

"You know Medea?" said Alex incredulously.

"Well, sort of," Rose nodded, running her fingers through her hair. "I mean, everyone knows her. She's only the most fabulous dress designer on the planet."

"Dress designer?" said Alex.

Rose sat back, blinking. "She makes amazing clothes for people. I can't believe that she kept the same name…" Rose paced across the kitchen, counting on her fingers. "She's in the papers, she's on the covers of glossy magazines, she's all over the web."

"The Web?" said Aries. "We know about that!"

"You do?" said Rose.

"It's made of ropes," said Aries confidently.

"Actually," Rose said gently. "It's something on a computer. More like a magical library where you can find things out. Hang on, I'll show you!"

She hurried upstairs and returned with her mother's laptop, flipped it open and began searching 'Medea'.

Alex and Aries watched, wide-eyed, as Rose clicked on a picture and the sorceress began walking across a red carpet on the screen in front of them.

"She goes to celebrity parties, she meets presidents. She's, like, everywhere!" gabbled Rose. "All over the world, posing outside grand hotels and theatres, standing next to famous people who wear the clothes she creates." She turned to face them. "The Scroll must be wrong in its answer," she said finally.

"No," said Alex, his voice little more than a whisper. "That's her."

"But she seems so nice on the telly," protested Rose. "You know, all fun and giggly. And she's really pretty and everything. It's just crazy – like finding out that one of your teachers is actually a member of the royal family or something."

Aries nudged Alex. "Why's she so surprised?"

"Don't know," said Alex. "Deceiving people is what Medea does best."

"Yes," said Aries. "And she's not very honest either."

Rose thought back. "The Scroll said something about sewing skirts of harsh regret—"

"In sequins, silk and pearls," repeated Alex. "Whatever sequins are."

"They're round sparkly things," muttered Rose, distracted, "like stars, but made of plastic." She began pacing again. "Harsh regret? I wonder what the Scroll's trying to tell us."

"Who knows," grumbled Aries.

"What it told us was to seek answers in her shop," said Alex. "Which sounded much safer than going to her house in Belgravia."

"I didn't like the sound of that place," said Aries quietly.

"Nor me," said Rose, rubbing his neck gently. "Besides, the good news is that I happen to know where her shop is."

Alex brightened. "You do?"

"Sure," said Rose. "Bond Street's not far from here."

"It's in London?" said Alex.

Rose nodded.

"Ooooooh," squealed Aries. "I'll be back in my fleece in time for dinner! What are we waiting for?"

"Hold on," said Rose, looking into his eyes. "If you're going uptown, there's something we need to do first."

And now for a soupçon of geography.

Do you like that word? I do, so I shall say it again: soupçon. It's French, you know, and means 'a little bit'.

Now, the soupçon of geography that concerns us, and more importantly Alex, Aries and Rose, is the soupçon that tells us that Bond Street lies off Oxford Street, one of the busiest thoroughfares in London. Probably the world. Busy, that is, in terms of shoppers, tourists and workers. Not busy in terms of rams. In fact, you hardly ever see one there at all, which is why it left Alex and Rose with a problem.

"I look a complete idiot," muttered Aries, half an hour later, catching sight of his reflection in one of Selfridges' windows. On either side of him shoppers and tourists surged past, businessmen barked into mobile phones.

"Not at all!" said Rose, stroking his neck. "You blend in perfectly."

And she was right.

You see, Rose had strapped a couple of lightweight boards either side of Aries' body, fixing them so that they tented over his back like a rooftop, and had painted on a slogan –

> *Don't miss out like me!*
> *Choose Harrods!*
> *The best sheepskins in London!*

– so that now he looked like a walking advertisement.

Clever, eh?

Having already passed a woman dressed as a frog who was advertising beer and a couple in a purple pantomime cow costume complete with a ringing bell who were advertising Swiss chocolate, everyone simply strode past Aries and the children, believing a bald ram to be yet another wacky advertisement walking down the street.

Not that Aries saw it that way.

Well, he wouldn't, would he?

However, he wasn't the only one in disguise.

Rose, having rifled through her mother's wardrobe, was now wearing a floppy sun hat, blue floral dress and green flip-flops. Alex was wearing a pair of Dr Pottersby-Weir's sunglasses, an ancient pair with round circles of black glass with tomato red frames from her hippie days, and a baseball cap backwards. After all, it's hardly wise to walk into a sorceress' shop looking exactly the same way you did when she sent a harpy to attack you a few hours earlier, is it?

"I still don't like it," grumbled Aries. "I mean, could you imagine Achilles riding into Troy like this? Looking down from his horse, with a, 'Hello, Hector. Nice day for a fight! Thought I'd wear my best wooden tent for the occasion!'"

"Only because Achilles wasn't as bold as you," Alex told him.

Aries looked at him suspiciously.

"Well," Alex began. "Who'd believe that the world's most important ram would ever be dressed like this?"

"Most important ram?" said Aries, brightening.

"That's right," added Rose, exchanging a knowing glance with Alex. "Only someone as truly noble as you are could carry it off with such flair."

Aries drew himself up taller. "Well, I suppose when you put it like that, I am being rather clever."

And so all three walked on, content and relaxed in the knowledge that, for the first time in public in London, Aries wasn't the centre of attention. Tourists and street cleaners, buskers and backpackers all bustled past without a second glance. And I expect that you might be sitting back, too, taking a deep breath and thinking, *Thank goodness for that.*

Well, don't.

Because when I say *everyone*, I'm not being strictly truthful since I'm not including the tall figure in the unseasonable trilby hat and his squat, lumbering companion, who hadn't taken their eyes off Aries and the children from the moment they'd stepped out of Rose's house and had been following them ever since. And whilst we know who they were, Aries, Rose and Alex didn't, which meant that they weren't the least bit troubled by them.

Yet.

Medea's shop shone like a pearl.

Framed by lavishly carved pillars that were topped with gold-painted leaves, its sign, picked out in gold and turquoise mosaic, twinkled in the sunlight. On either side luxury shops stretched away: jewellery shops glittered with conker-sized sapphires, cafés served Hawaiian coffee, auction houses groaned under the weight of portraits of Georgian ladies in marshmallow-pink dresses.

But of course all this swagger together with the shop's ENORMOUS price tags meant two important things:

1. You'd never find a children's writer shopping there – unless it was that really good one who wrote about the boy wizard – and,
2. They are simply not the sort of establishments to welcome rams through their doors, no matter how famous, noble or important to ancient myths they are.

And so Rose, Alex and Aries had had no other choice than to split up.

"You will be careful?" said Alex for about the fifteenth time.

They were standing in a small public park, just around the corner from Bond Street. Black railings and froths of fiery red rhododendrons bound its clipped lawn. Two wooden benches faced each other over a green-looking pond, noisy with frogs burping in the shade.

"Of course," said Rose, pushing back the brim of her hat again. "I'm only going to walk in there—"

"Checking Medea isn't around first," interrupted Alex.

Rose nodded impatiently. "And have a mooch round to see what I can find."

"I'm not sure," said Alex. "It feels too dangerous."

Which, frankly, it was.

But Rose was adamant.

Of course, as she'd explained, she was the only one of them who could walk into Medea's boutique without raising suspicion or, in Aries' case, the police. But what she didn't explain, because she'd have felt far too silly, was how much she wanted to walk in there and help them. Not because they were the most amazing friends she'd ever made (although they were) or the only ones to rescue her from a Greek monster (ditto) or even because of that last question on the Scroll (although thinking about that felt like fireworks exploding behind her ribs). But because, whilst they couldn't have been more different from her, she hadn't felt as much in common with anyone for years. She understood how Aries felt on losing the most precious thing he'd ever known, because she had too. She understood Alex's loyalty, how he'd come to Earth with Aries even though he was clever enough to know it was probably hopeless and certainly dangerous, because she'd risk just as much to find her father again.

Consequently she wasn't about to let her new friends down. (And, let's face it, if you're not prepared to stand up to an immortal sorceress for your mates, what sort of friend are you? What's that? One who isn't snatched up by a harpy and cracked like a nut? Okay... I suppose you might have a point.)

Rose unfastened her watch and handed it to Alex. "Look, if I'm not back in ten minutes, come and find me. Okay?"

Alex turned the watch around in his palm, staring blankly.

"It's a watch," said Rose patiently. "You use it to tell the time."

Alex and Aries exchanged blank looks.

Rose smiled and took the watch back. "Just count up to five hundred," she said. "Then come looking."

Rose shivered.

She'd walked this street loads of times, and in the past it had felt magical too, but in quite a different and much nicer way. Now it felt strange and unfriendly and, standing in the shadow cast by Medea's shop, her heart thumped against her ribs. Worse, she felt that eerie sensation of being watched, you know, that prickly feeling on the back of your neck when someone is standing close behind you.

Being a sensible girl, she put it down to the trio of mannequins standing in the window. Petulant as prom queens, posed with their hands on their hips, the way they seemed to glare down their long noses was frosty enough to make anyone feel uncomfortable. Each wore a black wig and a simple black dress, brightened by belts in different colours: one red, one silver and one green. Three jackets, one red, one silver and one green were laid along the bottom of the window, together with a blue one, each threaded onto wire around the mannequins' feet, so that they rose like petals of jungle flowers. The sort of jungle flowers that poisonous toads make their homes in, thought Rose with a shudder.

Taking a deep breath she walked towards the door and took hold of the golden handle. Pushing the door open, she glanced back at the mannequins and jumped. Had their eyes moved? She stared at each hard face in turn, feeling frightened and silly, and reminded herself that they were only made of moulded plastic and as harmless as lemonade bottles.

Which I think, given who owned the shop, was just a tad optimistic.

❈ XVI ❈
JUST ONE FAUN-ETTO

"I can still smell it," said Aries, pushing his nose against Alex's sandals. "Are you sure it's not you?"

Alex pushed a rhododendron out of his face, searching the crowd, willing Rose to appear from the thronging street.

"Three hundred and eleven," he muttered, "and it's definitely not me."

"Hmm." Aries snuffled at Alex's jeans. "You're right."

In fact, thought Aries, flaring his nostrils in the breeze, this new smell was quite different from what you'd expect a zookeeper who'd not had a bath since he'd left the Underworld to smell like. It was, he decided, much hairier. What makes a smell hairy is indeed a good question. Maybe it was rank like an out-of-sorts hamster or musty like a yak in a rainstorm. I don't really know, but I do know that sheep have an awfully good sense of smell, and if

Aries thought it was hairy then it was hairy. And, what's more, he didn't like it.

"It smells grubby," sniffed Aries, "with overtones of goat." He nudged Alex with his horn. "I want to go!"

"Use the – three hundred and thirteen – bushes," hissed Alex.

"Not like that!" said Aries. "I mean go *go*. As in *go away*!"

He stomped backwards out of the bushes, the boards at his sides and his copious rear pushing the branches sideways, so that when he stepped clear they all sprang back and slapped Alex's legs.

"Ouch!" yelped Alex. "That hurt. Aries, I've told you before to be more careful. You always..."

But as usual, whenever Alex was getting grumpy, Aries wasn't listening. Now he shrugged off the advertising boards and sniffed the air. There was a second, zestier smell, more like freshly sliced lemons. It was, he decided, as though something goaty had tried to hide its mangy smell under something fruity.

And failed.

Aries trotted back and tugged on Alex's jumper.

"Get off!" said Alex, still rubbing his stung legs. "Three hundred and forty-two. You know a smell can't hurt you."

Aries sighed and slumped onto the grass. For a moment he considered sulking properly. After all, he had had the most dreadful morning, what with giant birds, ridiculous outfits and now, being stuck like a garden ornament in the middle of a frog-heavy park. However, at that moment, something somewhere started chugging nearby. Pricking up his ears, Aries turned his head and was surprised to see what appeared to be a funny-looking metal chariot, painted pink and green and blue, splutter to a halt on the path. A trumpet-shaped horn on its roof crackled into life, filling the air with a tinkle of music-box notes.

"Ice creams! Delicious ice creams!" said a voice. "Come and get yours now! Double helpings! Super creamy! Best in London!"

Aries peered harder at the vehicle, wondering if these *ice creams* were like the ones they used to sell in Athens: clay cones stuffed with crunched ice and sultanas. The painted ones on the chariot's sides looked a lot tastier and he was sure they'd make him feel better.

"Mouth-watering flavours!" continued the voice. "Rum and Grazing!"

And no, I'm afraid it wasn't interference on the loudspeaker.

"Grass-berry Ripple," the voice went on. "With silage sprinkles. Mint Dock Dip and Meadowslippi Mud Pie!"

Aries rose to his hooves and shuffled onto the path, drooling.

"What are we waiting for?" he muttered to Alex.

"Hang on," Alex called, stepping out from the bushes.

But it was too late and Alex could only watch as Aries clopped towards the van, licking his black lips, unable to resist flavours that sounded so delicious and unusual. Just like the ice-cream seller, as he was about to discover. Well, apart from the delicious bit.

Rose stepped into Seamed Desires feeling an odd mixture of fear and relief. Fear because she'd half-expected harpies to be perched on the glittering chandeliers that hung from the ceiling and relief because they weren't.

Taking off her sunglasses she looked around her. Despite the creepy trio in the window, the shop appeared perfectly Bond Street normal: oceans of golden carpet, chaises covered in ruby-coloured silk and the sort of marble counter you find in foyers of grand hotels. In fact, the only strange thing was the rather odd smell. Musty and stale, for some reason it reminded her of animal stalls. She walked across the room looking around her. Ballgowns glowed like blossom over the walls and hung in rainbow drifts behind carved alcoves; summer dresses were draped over the branches of stands carved to look like golden trees; all around the walls, shelves sparkled with gold and silver spiky-heeled shoes.

"Deception." Alex's voice floated back into her memory. "It's what she's best at."

There was a chinking sound and Rose turned to see a slender woman, wearing the same black dress as the mannequins in the window, with a blue belt, walk through a glass-beaded curtain. She had a heart-shaped face and shiny green eyes tilted like a cat's. Blinking, she smoothed her blonde hair, which was pinned up elegantly above her long neck.

"Good afternoon," she said softly. "Are you looking for something in particular?"

Rose looked round awkwardly. "An outfit," she said finally, turning to face the assistant's fixed smile.

The woman was stunning, Rose decided, feeling a strange chill, not just sophisticated or well-groomed, but actually flawless. Weirder still, her skin was so taut that it didn't even wrinkle as she smiled.

The woman blinked. "And the occasion?"

Rose's skin prickled. She looked at the woman's

wide brow, her long nose, those sooty eyelashes.

"Occasion?" repeated Rose.

The woman tilted her head prettily. "For your Seamed Desires creation, of course."

Rose bit her lip. "A, um, birthday party."

"How lovely," the woman replied. "I think we may have the very thing for you in our Junior Diva collection."

Stalking on impossibly high heels she moved to a rail of dresses the colours of tropical fishes and slid each hanger along, glancing at each one in turn before sliding the next into its place. Rose followed her across the room, glancing at the gold-legged tables set around the room. The nearest was piled high with copies of *Vogue* magazine, with Medea's picture on the top. Rose stared into the photograph's grey eyes. Despite the warmth of Medea's skin, they remained steely and cold.

"Is Medea here today?" asked Rose with a casualness she certainly didn't feel.

Behind her, she heard a giggle. She was certain of it, or rather she thought she was, because when she turned round to look, there was no one else in the shop. Apart from the mannequins, that was, and she wasn't about to count them as alive.

"Not today," replied the assistant. She smiled at

Rose, the light bouncing off her sharp cheekbones like sunshine on a glacier.

Rose tried to calm her nerves. Just because she was standing in a sorceress's shop, she reminded herself, was no reason to start imagining ridiculous things, hearing giggles and feeling scared of an assistant. Although, if you'd asked me, I'd have said it was an excellent reason. Furthermore, I'd already be sitting on the next bus rumbling away down the street.

"Medea's busy adding the finishing touches to Ms Praline's dress for the premiere tomorrow night," the assistant continued.

"Hazel Praline?" said Rose, for a moment forgetting her nervousness.

"Oh, yes," the woman nodded brightly. She pointed to a framed photograph hanging nearby. "Ms Praline is one of Medea's *special* clients."

Rose stared round-eyed at the picture: Hazel Praline, *the* Hazel Praline, beamed back. Giggling, her hands hidden in her curtain of long blonde hair, she looked out at the camera whilst Medea knelt at her feet, her face obscured by folds of the dress's skirt, the layers of taffeta so sugary pink and gauzy that it looked as though it had been spun from a giant's candyfloss machine.

The sudden clang of hanger against rail snapped her out of her reverie.

"How about this?" said the assistant, holding up a trouser suit.

And even though Rose was hardly in the mood to comment on fashion, she felt her jaw drop. The suit was beautiful. Cut from sapphire-blue cloth, its fabric fell like waves, rippling into wide-legged trousers, whilst its jacket was long and loose, edged with silver piping and fastened by silvery-pink buttons shaped like seashells.

"It's gorgeous," said Rose truthfully.

"Perhaps Miss would care to try it on?" The assistant pointed to the glass-beaded doorway leading to the back of the shop.

Sensing her chance to explore, Rose nodded.

"I knew you would," smiled the assistant and led Rose through the beaded-curtain into a long corridor, spotlit on either side like a catwalk. Curtains to changing rooms lined one side of the corridor, whilst the other was a blank wall, hung with framed fashion awards. A door marked 'STAFF ONLY' stood at the far end.

Rose followed as the woman ushered her into a cubicle with a full-length mirror ringed with lights.

"I'll leave you to it."

The assistant smiled quickly, hung up the trouser suit and snapped the curtain closed behind her. Rose waited, staring back at her anxious reflection, until the woman's footsteps faded away.

Then she stepped out again and hurried towards the door at the end of the corridor.

Alex had lost count.

If he had still been counting he'd have been up to eight hundred and seventeen.

Except he wasn't.

Because he was now lying on the floor of the ice-cream van, trying to stop sliding into Aries' bottom as the van sped out onto the street. It's never great being kidnapped, but being kidnapped with a rolling ram is something else again.

"You and your ice creams!" muttered Alex as the van veered left, sending Aries steamrollering on top of him.

"Don't go blaming me," gasped Aries, paddling his legs in the air. "You always worry too much. How was I supposed to know that this time you'd be right? I was just a bit peckish."

The van shuddered beneath them and Aries rolled the other way, crashing into a crate of cones that that showered down on him.

"My head hurts," he muttered, taking a nibble from a nearby cone. "Thanks for asking. And I can still hear that terrible noise."

Now I expect you're probably wondering how Alex and Aries ended up in such a mess?

Well, when Alex caught up with Aries and asked the ice-cream seller for a Walnut and Horsefly Whip on his behalf he discovered three things:

1. That the ice-cream seller's hands were hairy enough to belong to a Cyclops;
2. And that the smell reminded him of a Cyclops, too;
2. Because – yes – he was indeed a Cyclops. A fact that Alex could easily confirm when the aforesaid hairy hands dragged him in through the ice-cream van's window and brought him up to its solitary eye for a better look before pinning his arms behind him.

However, it was only as he was struggling against Fred's crablike grip that he heard a tooth-achingly-awful warble of pipes and realised that the Cyclops was not alone. As the shrill squeal reverberated around him, he was horrified to see Aries freeze rigid and topple over sideways to land with a soft thump on the grass. Panpipes, you see, immobilise sheep by turning them into sheepy statues with just a few terrible toots, making the animals so much easier to handle.

Alex squirmed, trying to free himself from the Cyclops, but such creatures are like walking padlocks and Alex had been snapped firmly around the arms. Resistance was hopeless and all he could do was watch from the ice-cream van as a faun – beautifully dressed, but a faun nevertheless – leaped out from behind a nearby clump of bushes.

"Good afternoon," he said and bowed to Aries, lifting his hat to reveal two small horns. "I am Pandemic. How do you do?"

Of course Aries couldn't reply. All he could do was lie there with his legs stuck out rigidly like an oversized ram-shaped piano stool.

With a malicious smile, Pandemic seized one of Aries' horns and dragged him over the grass and, still playing a tune that would curdle milk, jammed him into the van on top of Alex.

Which is where they were now.

No Walnut and Horsefly Whip.

No flake.

And no hope of escape.

✻XVII✻
A Private Viewing

Rose took hold of the brass knob of the door marked 'STAFF ONLY', hearing the blood thump in her ears. Pushing, she was surprised at how easily the door gave, opening into a dimly lit space from which a flight of steps led up to another floor. Peeling off her flip-flops – hardly the footwear for spying and swiftness – she stepped inside and raced barefoot up the stairs. At the top stood a small landing and another door and for a moment she strained, listening hard, for any sound from inside. Nothing. Her nerves fizzling like sparklers, she opened the door.

The room was a sewing workshop. Dominated by a scarred wooden table, strewn with swatches of blue satin and scattered with dress patterns that fluttered like giant butterfly wings in the draught from the open door, the room was edged by bolts of cloth. Tall columns of fabric stood around the walls, unfurling pillars of satin and silk, voile and velvet,

streaking the white-painted brickwork with colour.
The Scroll's words floated back to her:

> *Seek there for next to bolts of cloth*
> *Your answers will unfurl…*

Rose felt her breath catch and looked around her.
At the far end of the room stood a wardrobe and
a low bank of cupboards, tucked behind a row of
six tailors' dummies draped with swatches of silver
sequins and layers of dove-grey satin. For those non-
tailors amongst you, tailors' dummies aren't like shop
dummies. They're headless, padded torsos fixed onto
poles and bases, made for a tailor to fit the cut fabric
around and tack quickly before sewing the seams up
properly. Rose tiptoed past them and pulled open
the doors of the wardrobe. It was empty, save for
the musty smell of dust mixed with dry wood. Rose
tapped against the wardrobe's base to check for a
false floor – she'd seen the odd spy film or two with
her mother – and discovered it was disappointingly
solid. Next she turned her attention to the cupboards,
opening each in turn, crouching on her hands and
knees to squint past pincushions and tangled tape
measures to reach into the gloom for, well, for what
she wasn't sure. The Scroll had talked about answers.

But there was no glint of fleece in here.

Sweat prickled her forehead as her fingers stretched to touch the cupboard's back walls. Chunks of white tailors' chalk and scattered sequins scratched her skin. A reel of ribbon clattered onto the floor.

"Hopeless," she muttered.

She sat back, feeling hot and disappointed, and leaned against the nearest dummy.

It moved.

She jumped as it tilted backwards, but intrigued, turned and leaned back a second time, pushing her weight against it, feeling the dummy lean back with her, creaking on its slender wooden pole. A thin scraping sound filled the room and Rose blinked as the panel of floor beside her slid backwards to leave a square gap. Beneath it, metal rails clanked either side of the new hole, sliding down as a staircase into the darkness pooled inside, clicking into place. Then the room fell silent again.

Scrabbling on all fours Rose peered down into the gloom, jumping as a row of wall lights flicked on, *click-click-click*, one after the other, illuminating the stairs and the room below.

Excitement overcoming her fear, Rose stood up and clattered down the steps to find herself in a large room whose brightly lit walls were covered with framed photographs and pictures. In the centre of the room stood a carved stone table, surrounded by matching stone chairs scattered with gold velvet cushions. An orange-coloured Greek pot, painted with a gigantic black snake, stood on the table. It held a bottle of champagne beside a lone goblet.

Rose shuddered.

The place seemed ancient and more like an exhibition from a museum than something in modern London. Just right for an ancient sorceress, her mind prompted. The thought made her shiver. Turning, she saw a sprawling vine, dried and woody, stretching up from a bank of gravel set into the floor. Gnarled and craggy, the vine's branches were brown with age and it looked, Rose decided, more like the sort of thing you'd see in a reptile house at the zoo, something for a lizard to hang off or snake to coil around.

Still, she realised, there was nowhere down here to hide a fleece. She turned back to the stairs and was about to climb back up to the sewing room when one of the photographs, of the many that lined the walls, caught her eye.

It showed a long, black open-topped limousine, with mini American flags flapping either side of its bonnet, rolling down a wide sunny street. Men on motorcycles were pictured, riding either side of the car in which four people sat. The camera was focused on the back seat at the man and woman sitting there, laughing and smiling, waving to the crowds. He was fair-haired, rugged and handsome, wearing a grey suit, whilst she smiled prettily in a pink suit and a matching pillbox hat over her dark bob. Beside the picture was a hand-drawn sketch of the man's suit, pencilled jottings about its fabric and lining and numbers that must have been the man's measurements. The customer's name was scrawled at the bottom: John F Kennedy.

Rose had no idea who John F Kennedy was but with the happy crowds on either side of the motorcade she knew it must have been a special occasion.

Intrigued now, she looked at the next photograph. It, too, had a framed sketch of a dress beside it. The photograph was of glamorous woman, with a shock of blonde hair, standing in a white dress, the same one in the sketch, her long legs exposed and teetering in high white shoes over a grate in the street. The grate must have been blowing air because the woman's skirt was fanned out around her, frothing up like a wave, billowing up at the back as the woman tried hopelessly to hold it down in the front. Her eyes were closed, her head thrown back, her short blonde curls framing her face, her red mouth laughing. The name jotted at the bottom of the sketched dress was Marilyn Monroe.

Rose recognised the person in the next photograph, an old rock star. Dark-eyed with a mass of curly hair, Marc Bolan wore a silver shirt and a feather boa draped around his neck. She only knew who he was because her mum had liked his music. Even though he'd died years before Rose was born, when his car crashed into a tree, Rose had seen his picture enough times, staring out from her mother's old record covers, to recognise him now.

As Rose walked past the pictures, the dresses became longer, the faces grainier, fainter in old photographs. But beside each one hung a sketch of the outfit the person in the picture was wearing.

Rose felt a chill ripple up her spine. These pictures were proof that Medea couldn't possibly be twenty-six. Forensic proof, her mother would call it, although she'd usually be talking about dinosaurs and waving a prehistoric bone around her head at the time. Soon grainy newspaper cuttings gave way to pen and ink sketches on mottled paper and oil paintings, but still, each dress was drawn in the same confident style and the handwriting was identical.

Of course, had Rose been a little older and known a little more about the people in the pictures, and perhaps listened a bit harder to her history teacher,

Mr Cartwright, instead of giggling about his trousers being too short, then she might have realised that these pictures were evidence of something else. Something far more sinister. However, Rose was only twelve years old and I suppose Mr Cartwright really did have the brightest socks in the school, and since you can't know everything at that age, no matter how clever you are, she was none the wiser.

But she was going to find out, and unfortunately through a much more devious teacher.

However for now she simply wandered along the third wall, drifting back through the years: here was Nelson, she recognised him from his statue in Trafalgar Square. White-haired and unsmiling, he was painted dressed in a dark navy coat, with one gold-ringed sleeve pinned to his jacket; in the next picture Marie Antoinette giggled, decked out in a dress as frothy as a cream gateau; here was Anne Boleyn, wife of Henry VIII, painted on the morning of her execution. Rose peered harder into the picture, feeling a twinge of something half-remembered. But, like an itch you can't scratch, she couldn't quite reach the thought. And besides, as her mind pointed out, neither looking at pictures nor racking her memory was helping her find the fleece.

Still, as she stepped back onto the bottom rung

of the stairs, she couldn't help feeling rather pleased with herself at just how much she had discovered. Aries and Alex would be so impressed. After all, while those two had been lolling around enjoying the sunshine, she'd searched the workroom, found a disguised lever and opened up an amazing secret room. And, hadn't it all been easy? In fact she was just on the brink of wondering if it'd perhaps been just a teensy bit too easy when the panel above the stairwell slid shut and all the lights snapped off.

A few minutes after darkness engulfed Rose, Amelia Smythe, the manager of Seamed Desires, turned the corner into Bond Street. She heard an ice-cream van tinkling behind her but thought nothing of it. After all, as an ex-model, she was rarely tempted by an ice cream since a vanilla cone might put a millimetre on her flat tummy. Now as she clicked along the pavement she was more concerned about opening the shop because, having been called away on an urgent errand by Medea that morning, the shop had been closed all day.

That's right.

Closed.

Are you thinking what I'm thinking?

Oh, dear.

Eager to open the shop, Ms Smythe hardly noticed the man in the dark suit and hat approach her as she opened up the door, mostly because she was too busy looking at the fourth mannequin in the window, which was looking decidedly rumpled. Some of you might remember there being only three mannequins when Rose walked in and if so, I'm impressed. And grateful, since it makes it a little easier for me to break the news that this fourth mannequin was wearing a black dress with a blue belt and a blonde wig. She had a heart-shaped face and green eyes, tilted like a cat's.

"Good afternoon!" the – ahem – man in the suit said to Ms Smythe whilst flashing a business card that she didn't bother to read. "I'm here to collect the faulty roll of crêpe de Chine."

"Crêpe de Chine?"

Ms Smythe frowned. She couldn't remember any faulty material, crêpe de Chine or otherwise, but waved him into the shop. She didn't have time to supervise him as he walked through the bead curtain into the back of the shop and down the stairs. Nor, since she was still fussing with the fourth mannequin, did she notice how bulky or indeed wriggly the roll he carried was as he left the shop.

A pity, really.

✴XVIII✴
A Patch of Greece

Six-and-a-half elbow-jarring, rib-bruising, teeth-rattling minutes later, during which every rude word Aries and the children knew had been hurled into the air at least once in both Ancient Greek and English, the van screeched to a halt.

"Where are we?" muttered Aries, who now lay wedged under a collapsed shelf of Tootilicious Fruit Ices – Buy One Get One Free!

Alex sat up gingerly and rubbed his head. He had a bad feeling that'd begun when he'd been hoicked through the van's window and had grown steadily worse. "I think I can guess."

Rose, lying on the floor and still rolled in the crêpe de Chine, was furiously kicking her feet in the air making her look like a giant silkworm spinning its cocoon. "Will someone please get me out!" she demanded. "I totally have to tell you about what I saw in the shop!"

Of course, what with the faun's terrible driving, the droning of the van's engine and the avalanches of cones and flakes and bottles of raspberry sauce as they sped round corners, Rose hadn't been able to tell the others a single thing. If she had, things might have been different. I mean, she *might* have mentioned seeing Anne Boleyn's portrait, and wondered why it seemed so familiar. And, that *might* have prompted Aries' memory about the queen's dress in the British Museum. And maybe between their three clever brains (all right, two clever brains and one ram's brain) they might have worked out what Medea was up to. But since they didn't it's all academic[22] and no one was any the wiser.

Alex stepped over Rose to peer out of the window and gasped.

"What is it?" demanded Aries, drumming his hooves on the floor.

For a moment, Alex was too surprised to speak.

---

22. *Academic here doesn't mean a subject you study at school. It means something that's just a what-if – that will never happen. For example, it's academic how you would feel as an elephant, since you are never going to be an elephant. (However, if there are any elephants reading this, then how you feel is not academic at all, and indeed, I hope you're enjoying the book.)*

He squinted sideways across a lawn dotted with orange trees to where an enormous whitewashed villa loomed three storeys high beneath a roof of terracotta tiles. The roof overhung a top floor balcony with an iron fretwork as intricate as a spider's web, splashed with swags of purple bougainvillaea. Beneath it a row of tall windows stared out blindly across the garden, above a row of stone arches that encircled the villa's ground floor as a veranda, made shadowy by jacaranda trees.

"A patch of Greece," said Alex, recalling the Scroll's words and feeling it shiver in the rucksack at his feet.

"Greece!" Aries squirmed free in a clatter of ice lollies. "Let me see!"

Together, Alex and Aries looked out across gardens dotted with creamy marble statues to a swimming pool, twinkling blue and silver in the sunshine. Beyond it olive trees nodded in front of high garden walls. Extravagant and luxurious, it was just the sort of Mediterranean villa that you and I would imagine a movie magnate might own[23].

---

23. *A magnate is a very wealthy person, not someone who attracts metals. That is a* magnet *and would hardly make you rich, although constantly attracting metal objects could make you more interesting, if a little clanky.*

"Olives!" Aries licked his lips. "Hey, didn't the Scroll say something about olives?"

But before he could ask anything else, the back door of the van swung open and the Cyclops leaned in. Seizing Aries' back legs he whipped them away like a magician pulling a cloth from a dinner table and flung Aries belly first onto the van's floor before pitching him on to the pathway like a sack of common turnips.

Alex was horrified. "You don't have to be so—"

At which the Cyclops finished his sentence for him, by reaching in again, this time grabbing Alex's shoulders and throwing him out beside Aries. Too winded to speak, Alex lay beside Aries on the grass and stared up into the grey-green leaves above him. Each bough was laden with olives the size of plums, and Alex stared, dimly aware that such fruit needed a lot more sun that the cold grey skies of Britannia his uncle had told him about[24].

---

24. *And indeed, Alex was right. As any gardener will tell you, olives need heaps of sunshine to grow. However, since no gardener had ever seen over the villa's wall, no one apart from Alex had ever thought Medea's garden strange before; and anyway, gardeners being highly normal people would have found another explanation for it, since they don't understand about ancient Greek sorceresses. Unlike people reading this book who do know about them, and consequently, aren't normal at all.*

Pushing himself up onto his elbows, Alex noticed another vehicle, long, gleaming and pink, parked alongside the villa. We'd have recognised it as a stretch limousine. With windows made of rose-pink glass and headlights the colour of strawberry icing, it actually belonged to Hazel Praline, who at that very moment was standing inside the villa, twirling round and round in her sparkly rose-coloured dress for the premiere.

At the sudden slam of the ice-cream van door Alex jerked his head round to see the faun stepping neatly along the pathway towards him, stopping only when his highly polished shoes almost touched the tip of Alex's nose.

"We haven't been introduced," he crooned, leaning over to take hold of Alex's ear by which he pulled the boy up. "I'm Pandemic, or Sir to you."

"Who's that?" squealed Rose from inside the van.

"A faun," replied Aries.

"A prawn?" said Rose.

"No," muttered Aries. "He's not that clever. A faun: half-man, half-furry bottom."

Alex noticed the Cyclops start to chuckle before seeing Pandemic's face and stopping abruptly. He turned away and looked down at the wriggling material, poking it with his finger.

"Get off!" squealed Rose.

The Cyclops began rolling the cloth to and fro. "Fred, play play!"

"No," said Pandemic crisply, laying a hand on Fred's shoulder. "Fred not play play. Fred work work. Remember?"

Fred growled low. "Fred like talkie-talkie cloth!"

"It's the girl, you potato-brain!" muttered Pandemic. "Now be quick and take her to the mistress whilst I—"

Alex reached out for Pandemic's arm. "No!"

"No?" said Pandemic, plucking Alex's hand from his jacket sleeve and smoothing the crumpled material.

"Don't take her to Medea," said Alex, feeling fear rising behind his ribs. "She's just some girl we met. We hardly even know her. She hasn't done anything wrong!"

"No," said Aries. "And neither have we. So, can we go now, too?"

Pandemic bent down to Aries and gave a polished smile. "Do you really want to leave us, Aries?"

"Yes, please," said Aries, offering his best smile.

"Well, forget it!" snapped Pandemic and straightened up. "With what the mistress has planned for you, you'll never see the Underworld again!"

"But—" protested Aries before Pandemic snapped his hand around Aries' muzzle and spun round to listen to a noise from the house.

Above the sound of Aries' furious snorting, there came the sound of footsteps on gravel. Alex followed the faun's stare to see a girl with long blonde hair, wearing huge pink sunglasses and dressed in a pink jacket, pink jeans and pink sheepskin boots, jump down from the villa's doorway and half-walk half-dance towards the limousine. She nodded her head in time to whatever was playing through her earphones.

"Hey!" Alex shouted desperately, waving at the girl. "Can you help—"

Fred threw a greasy hand over Alex's mouth and dragged him behind the van, although he needn't have bothered. The girl was too busy lunging across the path, kicking and sliding, practising what looked like a dance routine to notice them.

Aries twisted and squirmed before Pandemic silenced him with a peep of panpipes and slammed the ice-cream van doors shut on Rose with his foot.

Two men now stepped out of the house. They were dressed in black suits and scrunched along the gravel behind Hazel. One carried a huge Seamed Desires box, tied with gold cord and decorated with a corsage of fresh pink roses; the other talked into a tiny phone. Whilst the first man stashed the box in the boot, the second opened the back door of the limousine and ushered the girl inside, walked to the driver's side and got in.

A moment later the car glided past. Neither Hazel nor her bodyguards even glanced out from behind their rose-tinted windows. The men were too busy chatting to one another whilst Hazel was too busy being famous and glamorous, which as anyone knows, involves listening to songs on one's iPod and examining one's fingernails for chipped varnish. The car rolled towards the gates, which began creaking open.

Pandemic chuckled, a sound like a goat with hiccups, sort of *maah-hup maah-hup*, although I am a writer, not a professional faun impersonator, and so you will have to imagine it for yourself. Then he opened the van doors and slid the cloth out.

Alex squirmed against Fred's vicelike grip. "Let her go!" he pleaded.

"Sorry," smiled Pandemic, reaching in for Rose's rucksack. "Apart from anything else this cloth's enchanted. No one except the mistress can undo it."

"No!" Alex jabbed his elbow back as hard as he could and caught Fred in the ribs. Wheezing for breath, Fred loosened his grip for a split second and, seizing his chance, Alex broke free. Dimly remembering how his father always taught him to aim for his opponent's weak spot, he smashed his shoulder into the faun's stomach, sending him sprawling against the side of the van.

"Aries, run!" yelled Alex, straightening up to aim a kick at Pandemic's ankles, knocking him off his feet.

The cloth bounced onto the ground with a yelp.

Aries charged after the car, which was now turning out onto the road.

Squealing, bleating, leaping, desperately trying to attract its attention, he slipped and skidded over the path. Now if you or I'd been in the limousine we'd have noticed him and probably recorded him on our mobile phones for YouTube and uploaded a film that'd score thousands of hits. And stepped out and helped, of course. But nobody noticed a thing and the car swept out onto the road.

"No!" squealed Aries as the gates clanged shut in front of him.

Bolts the size of sledgehammers flew across the gate's wrought ironwork and clanged viciously. Padlocks snapped shut like crocodile jaws. Dumbstruck, Aries stepped back straight into Fred's bulging knees.

"Can't go that way way!" said Fred, chuckling, and taking hold of Aries' tail he began dragging him, like a child's pull-along toy.

I can't begin to tell you how much Aries hated this and so I won't.

Meanwhile, back on the lawn, Alex was clamped onto the faun's back, flinging furious punches. Roaring, Pandemic charged across the lawn and ducked his head like a horse refusing a jump, sending Alex spiralling onto the grass. The boy landed, winded, his head spinning.

"Boys! Boys!" Icy as a steel knife kept in a freezer, a woman's voice seemed to slice through the warm air and stop time.

Feeling his breath scouring his lungs, Alex blinked and tilted his head to see a pair of small feet wearing gold pumps standing in front of him. He lifted his eyes slowly.

Medea was standing in front of him, looking exactly like her Underworld painting: the angular face, the full lips, the seawater-grey eyes, all framed by long black hair and that single lock of violet, twisted into a rope over her shoulder. Wearing a long white dress with golden ribbons criss-crossing its bodice, she stood with her hands on her hips, her long sleeves trailing at her sides.

"We've been waiting for you," she said. Turning, she walked over to Aries, who braced his shoulders and stuck his chin in the air. "And especially you, Aries Khrysamallos."

Aries' ears twitched despite the bravery in his stance. It was the way she said *especially* that did it.

"What's the matter?" said Medea. "Cat got your tongue?"

"Not cat," said Alex. "Witch."

"Witch?" squealed Rose from the cloth.

"Oh, Alex!" Medea scolded playfully.

Without looking, she snapped the fingers of her left hand. The cloth jerked taut, jackknifed in two and twisted into a tight knot, a knot that squealed.

"You'll put my special guest off," said Medea.

Special guest?

No, I didn't like the sound of that either.

"Pandemic!" Medea turned to the faun, who stood brushing out the crease marks Alex had left in his jacket, leaning with Fred against a statue of a girl holding a basket of roses. "Take the girl inside! Then return the van to the park. We don't want the police sniffing anywhere around here. Got it?"

Pandemic nodded, threw the cloth over his shoulder and strode towards the house. Alex stared after him, feeling hopeless, as Rose squirmed and shouted, trying to wriggle free. Even if he could overpower Fred, he reasoned, even if he could weave through Medea's magical gates, even if he could somehow get Aries over those two-metre-high walls, there was no way they could leave Rose behind in the sorceress's house.

"Fred?" The Cyclops lumbered forwards, dribbling. "Rope the ram!"

They made a grim procession. Led by the sorceress turning circles on the sun-dappled path, Fred towed Aries, his hoofs squealing over the stones, whilst Pandemic strong-armed a silent, stony-faced Alex. This was because fear had tightened the boy's throat like a scarf tied too tight, leaving him no voice to say things like, "It's all right, Aries," which it wasn't, or, "I'll get us out of here," of which there seemed no chance. Making the whole scene far too horribly depressing for someone like me to dwell on. So, turn the page, would you?

❊XIX❊
THE FLOCKY HORROR SHOW

Around about now, were I an estate agent, I'd be telling you how Medea's house was 'one of a kind' and 'full of her own personal style'. I'd point out the long row of Greek-looking pillars that stretched the width of the building, and its spacious entrance hall, turned into a garden room, with its black-and-white chessboard floor and huge glass doors that folded back to open up one wall of the room to the outside. I'd probably rave on about the mansion's high ceilings, black glass chandeliers and marble staircases, and mention its twelve bedrooms and vine-entwined greenhouse, too.

But I wouldn't say anything about its secret passages.

And definitely not the vile-smelling one Medea was now ushering her unwilling guests down, the one that led deep underground to the cellar. No, I'd hurry straight past that, holding a tissue delicately to my nose, and mention that some parts of the house had potential. However, even though I'm not an estate agent, I can tell you that the only potential that cellar had was for misery and suffering.

With his stomach heaving against the stench, Alex followed Medea, Aries and Fred down the gloomy corridor. With each step he took the dreadful stink seemed to grow stronger, until it became so thick he thought he might reach out and touch it. Sweet and rancid, it made him think of the Hydra's tank when the water needed changing. (Personally, I couldn't comment, never having met a Hydra, but in my writerly wisdom I imagine that they whiff of bad eggs and kippers mixed in a bin and left to rot for about four weeks. Possibly five.)

Up ahead, in the firelight cast by iron **sconces**, Alex glimpsed the ripple of Medea's dress, luminous against the dark stone of the wall as she vanished around yet another corner, sprightly beyond Aries' struggling bulk. Her footsteps echoed back over the cool stone as his mind raced. Where was she taking them? Why had she kidnapped them? Where was Rose? How would he get them all out of there? Questions jangled in his head like the squall of Pandemic's pipes until, turning another corner, he almost crashed into Aries who was hunched on the floor, blocking the way. Alex felt his throat tighten, although whether it was from the rancid air or the unearthly squeals he could now hear from beyond a huge wooden door set into the wall ahead of them, he wasn't sure.

"Let's get this over with!" muttered Medea.

Holding her sleeve against her nose, she drew back the giant bolts on the door and dragged it open.

Terrified shrieking flooded out on a tidal wave of foetid air.

"You're not taking me down there!" shouted Aries over the din, desperately trying to clop backwards from the doorway.

Tightening the rope around his meaty fist, Fred's eye blinked furiously.

Behind them, Alex stepped forwards and looked through the doorway, down the wooden staircase that lay beyond it and gasped.

The cellar was full of sheep.

Sheep with black faces, white faces, buck teeth and no teeth. Sheep with curly horns, straight horns and horns like bedsprings. Sheep with grey coats, white coats, tight coats, stringy coats and spirals of trail-in-the-mud coats. All jammed together, miserably packed into lots of small pens set side by side in long, bleak rows criss-crossed by walkways covered with greasy straw. Their bleats and wails filled the air, suddenly louder, as Medea appeared in the doorway.

Feeling sicker than ever, Alex realised that the stench in the air was a disgusting brew of dung, sweat and lanolin [25] all mixed together with pure shivering fear.

Dragging his eyes away from the sheep he looked around the rest of the cellar.

A bench ran the length of its opposite wall. Lit by spluttering candles in black candelabra, it was littered with stone bowls, pots of smoking liquids, branches of ivy and yew and scattered crystals. Two electrodes lay in a bowl of ruby-red solution surrounded by clumps of glassy green rocks. A long syringe lay dribbling gold-coloured liquid from its needle into a gleaming puddle. Nearby, a sheep's skull lay overturned and half-covered in tangled hanks of wool.

Aware now of a slow, grinding creak above his head, Alex looked up to the ceiling where a wide wheel turned slowly. Others wheezed and spluttered in the shadows. Further away banks of rollers, spikes,

---

25. *Lanolin is a wax that sheep produce in their skins, which makes their wool waterproof. People use it to make shoe polish and lotions that stop babies getting rashes on their bottoms. (Obviously these are two different products, otherwise your baby brother or sister would have a polished black waterproof bottom.)*

long poles and prodders hung from glimmering tracks criss-crossing the ceiling high above the animals. In the middle of the room, two multi-legged contraptions scuttled along the ceiling like giant spiders, their slender metallic arms pummelling the backs of a pen of sheep underneath. Beyond them a line of cranes bobbed fiercely, fitted with long handled rakes that tugged at the fleeces of some shaggy brown sheep; in the far corner, something resembling a rubber seal hung motionless above three grey sheep, ready to slap its flippers against their flanks.

Alex turned back to Medea. "What is this place?"

"My workshop," she smiled.

"It looks more like a torture chamber!"

"Why, thank you," said Medea sweetly.

Lifting the hem of her dress, she stepped through the door and down the steps into the first walkway. Bleating, the sheep drew back from her, receding like a woolly tide against the far walls of their pens as she passed.

All except one.

A ram with wool as shaggy as ostrich feathers and light brown horns that curled back over its head stood in the space left by the retreating others. Standing firm, he met her glare with caramel-coloured eyes. Was it his imagination, Alex wondered, or was the ram looking at her in disgust?

"You?" sniggered Medea.

She pulled a lever and released a jet of water onto the animal's back. Shivering, the ram gasped and closed its eyes as the water drenched his straggly wool.

"Now, come along," she called back up the steps. "Nice as it is to entertain guests, I haven't got all day."

As you might imagine the next part of the story was even more stinky and unpleasant and so I'll make it brief.

There was squealing and scuffling as Fred dragged Aries down the steps and pummelled him into a solitary pen set apart from the others. Made with thick metal bars and roofed in, it was quite different from the rather ordinary stalls that held the sheep and more like a cage.

Followed by a hammering off hooves as Aries tried to break free.

Then there was a lot of yelling as Alex tried to stop Fred slamming the door shut on Aries by wrapping himself around the Cyclops's stubby legs.

And a horrible new odour as Fred broke out in a sweat making him smell even more like a mouldy onion left in the bottom of a bucket.

Finally, there was muttering.

Now I'm only mentioning the muttering because

with that racket going on, no one else would've heard it. Except possibly a bat, picking it up on its satellite dishes of ears, save that no self-respecting bat would've flown within a mile of the cellar. So, you'll just have to take my word for it.

The mutterer was Hex.

Having been banished earlier that morning to another part of the cellar, with Medea's list of unpleasant preparations for Aries' arrival, he'd been distracted by the rumpus next door and, tasting strangers on the air, had slithered in to investigate. Now, looped over an upturned crate like a discarded pair of tights, he dangled with his job list hanging from his right fang, watching.

Aries, as he'd expected, was hunched miserably in his solitary pen, sulking.

But the boy's behaviour intrigued him.

Sitting there, skinny as an antelope, he hardly looked like the Greek hero Hex'd expected after the harpy had failed so miserably that morning. Even more puzzling, despite the boy's own precarious situation, he was reaching through the bars to Aries, trying to console him with strokes and whispers.

"Having a lie down are we, earthworm?" Hex jumped at Medea's voice and looked up to see her pointing her finger casually at Alex. "Kill him!"

Hex spat out his job list and shot over the floor. Then, swaying from side to side like a snake charmer's cobra, he rose until his snout was level with Alex's eyes. Doing his best to ignore Aries' thunderous bellows, he froze as rigid as a walking stick and adopted his death-strike position. Humans, as he'd discovered back in the African savannah, always collapsed into trembling wrecks at this and gibbered for mercy through blood-drained lips.

Except that Alex hadn't flinched.

Instead, he looked back at the snake with an oddly suspicious expression.

Puzzled, Hex drew back his lips and made his terrifying mouth-of-doom face, intent on reducing the boy to a wobbling bundle of fear that would tenderise him for biting.

Yet the boy simply continued to stare into Hex's eyes, his face quite tranquil.

Feeling slightly embarrassed now, Hex resorted to the mini death-jabs his father had taught him and began jerking his head violently, left, right, up, down, in, out.

They never failed to horrify.

Except today.

"Hex!" The sorceress's voice chilled the scales on his back. "Will you please do your job?"

Stretching his mouth wide, Hex revealed his sparkling fangs and lurched forwards. As Aries roared in horror, Hex felt cold venom shoot into his teeth, took one final look in Alex's eyes…

… and recognised his expression.

Unimpressed.

It was written all over the boy's face.

Hex's mamba mind reeled as the word buzzed through it like a mosquito, distracting him completely since he'd not encountered it on a victim's face before.

Terror, desperation, paralysing panic?

Yes, often.

But unimpressed?

No.

He'd only ever seen that on the mistress's face (usually when she was talking to him) her 'whatever' face, as he called it.

"That does it!" shrieked Medea, incensed at Hex's hesitation. Grabbing him by the throat, she lifted him up and fixed him with a furious stare. "How dare you show me up like this? I've seen scarier looking cucumbers!"

It was unfortunate (for Hex's neck) that he hadn't known how well Alex knew snakes. Having cared for Drako, the biggest and most ferocious snake who'd ever glided over the earth, Alex had long ago learned that snakes only attacked when they felt truly threatened by an enemy. The rest of the time they preferred mooching about and snoozing to striking someone dead for no good reason. And so, wholly convinced that Hex was only driven by the sorceress's spiteful demand, he knew he could be put off.

"Fred!" snapped Medea, turning to the Cyclops, who'd been busy smelling his armpits.

"I need a new familiar!" she spat. "Old jelly-fangs can't even scare a boy! I want you to ring London Zoo and organise the generous donation of a mamba. I'll get rid of Alex myself!"

"Dodo?" said the Cyclops.

"Do-na-tion," said Medea impatiently, flinging Hex in a heap on the floor. "It means gift, goggle-brain! Pack him in one of my old sewing baskets and get rid of him immediately!"

Hex's tongue quivered in fright as the sorceress swept past him, up the steps and out of the cellar. Life with her, as you can imagine, was ghastly but the sudden prospect of being sent to snake prison, held captive in a cramped vivarium with a bunch of bolshy boas whilst children poked their fingers against the glass all day was utterly unthinkable.

The sudden slam of ram against metal snapped

Hex out of his panicked thoughts.

"Alex!" bellowed Aries, hurling himself against his stall bars as Fred began bumping the boy up the stairs behind him, dragging him over the steps like a bad-tempered child with a teddy bear.

"Let him go!" bellowed Aries, throwing himself at the bars again and again.

Hex's ears rang. Around him the other sheep bleated wildly, their shrieks almost drowning out the cacophony of ringing metal.

"I'll – come – back!" gasped Alex from the top of the stairs, a squirm of flailing arms and legs. "I prom—"

The door clanged shut.

In the shrill din of the cellar, Aries slumped against the bars, snorting rapidly and sinking to his haunches.

For a moment, Hex paused, pondering why Alex would even think of trying to rescue such a ridiculous bald ram. Then he remembered that he had far more important things to worry about thanks to this same boy who'd caused him to fail so spectacularly in front of Medea. Feeling his fear crystallise into anger, and wondering what sort of revenge might save him from the zoo, he slithered down a gap in the stonework floor.

XX

A TOMB WITH NO VIEW

Things weren't going well, were they?

But then, I suppose two children and a ram were never going to be much of a match for a sneaky, all-powerful sorceress, were they? After all, how many ancient Greek superheroes with farmyard sidekicks have you heard of?

Well, quite.

Ten minutes later Alex was having a lie down. That was the good news. The bad news was that it was because the sorceress had strapped him to a marble plinth, hidden inside a building in her garden that was fashioned to look like a miniature Greek temple. Indeed, from the outside the building's carved pediments and columns made it appear a charming spot for a summer glass of lemonade. However, such architectural merit was of little comfort to Alex since he:

a. Was imprisoned on the inside, and
b. Couldn't see anything but coffins.

That's right.

Coffins.

Dark wood, golden wood, crumbling wood and mouldering wood coffins that lay stacked on the stone shelves rising either side of him like some ghastly filing cabinet of the dead. Unfortunately this was because Alex was now inside Medea's private crypt. And, although he (luckily) didn't realise it, each coffin actually held the remains of some curious person or other, some courtier, maid, model or journalist, who'd over the centuries come a tad too close to discovering who Medea really was and precisely what she was doing. Caught snooping, each nosy parker had consequently been strapped to the very same plinth as Alex and forgotten about. Whenever this happened one of Medea's servants had been dispatched months later to 'tidy up', sweeping the scatter of bones into a fresh coffin and stacking it on a shelf.

Straining against the leather straps that bound his chest, arms and legs, Alex's mind returned to the sheep in the cellar. He knew it wasn't logical for a sorceress, and a glamorous one at that, to keep such animals.

Cheetahs or leopards?

Yes, maybe.

Even a hulking vulture with a razor-sharp beak.

But never sheep.

Suddenly an icy feeling seeped into his stomach and turned his insides to frozen slush. But, much as we need one of those candles-lighting-in-the-lantern moments, where Alex would realise what Medea was up to, I'm sorry, this wasn't it. No, Alex's sudden dread was because the crypt door had groaned open and now he was aware that someone else was in the room too, and that their breathing was growing steadily closer…

Meanwhile at that precise moment, the only breathing Aries could hear was his own.

Slumped on the floor, he gulped and wheezed, sucking in great mouthfuls of air and gusting them out again, utterly exhausted. This was because he'd spent the last twenty minutes hurling his considerable bulk against the gate of his stall in a frenzied attempt to escape. But unfortunately, not only was he just as trapped as he'd been when he started, but his ears were now ringing painfully from the jangle of his horns against metal (which in case you're wondering is a sound much like that produced by a troop of monkeys armed with wooden spoons let loose in a saucepan factory) and his head throbbed violently.

But still, he absolutely couldn't give up.

Not when he was sure that the fleece was here with Medea. Not when being stuck down here was the closest he'd been to his magnificent coat for over three thousand years. And not when every time he closed his eyes, he saw the terrified look on Alex's face as they'd dragged him out of the cellar.

He had to get out.

Hauling himself to his hooves, he lowered his head and fixed his stare on the gate again. And jumped when a small voice piped up from the gloom. "That metal's magic!"

Aries swung his head round and stared in astonishment at a lamb with a face as bumpy as a potato grinning at him from beneath a helmet tangled with red and blue wires that spiralled in all directions.

Aries blinked. "You can talk?"

The lamb nodded.

"We all can," said an ewe, stepping out from the woolly wall of sheep behind the youngster. Sturdy, with the same tightly coiled wool as the lamb and honey-gold horns that curled back over her head, she looked sadly at Aries. "Medea likes to hear how frightened we are, so she bewitched us into talking."

Aries looked from the ewe to her lamb and back again. "How long have you been down here?"

"Nearly a year," answered the ewe. "I'm Martha. I was captured from Somerset. But my little Toby was born here. He's never seen anything but this disgusting place."

Aries couldn't help but remember his own lambhood, spent leaping around the sun-drenched hills of old Greece, glittering like a starburst, the scent of jacaranda in the air. And despite his urgent desire to find the fleece, his gnawing worry about Alex, not to mention his throbbing headache, Aries felt an overwhelming surge of pity course through him from hooves to muzzle as he pictured Toby, growing up in this mouldering candlelit prison full of machinery.

More furious than ever, he thumped the bars again with his horns, sending a resounding clang bouncing around the walls.

"Give up," said a deep voice with a lilting sing-song accent.

Aries looked through the clustered sheep to see the shaggy-coated ram that Medea had drenched half an hour ago step away from the others. Slender, with bright, questioning eyes, the ram tilted its head, regarding him haughtily down a long creamy muzzle, still glittering with water. "No matter how hard you try, da metal of your pen never buckle will. It's enchanted to be super-strong."

"But you don't understand!" Aries shook his head impatiently. "I have to get out of here! I am Aries Khrysamallos!"

"*Já, já, já,*" muttered the ram. "And I am Olaf."

"Mr Olaf," said Aries coolly, "you do realise that I am the ram of the Golden Fleece?"

"Golden golden blah blah blah," murmured Olaf. "Yes, we know all about you, ram. Medea and da serpent talk of you much."

"They do?" said Aries, for a moment forgetting his annoyance with the sullen ram. He stuck up his ears, expectantly. "And what do they say?"

At which Olaf turned away and started to polish his horn against the bar of his pen.

"Well, come on!" prompted Aries. "This is important."

"Dey talk of using da fleece," said Olaf. "Dat's all."

"Using it?" said Aries, frowning. "How?"

Olaf shrugged. "For her magic, I suppose."

"What magic?"

Olaf looked up at him and sniggered. "You think sorceresses confide in dere livestock, *já*?"

"No, of course not!" snapped Aries. "But one of you might have overheard something helpful. About where they keep it?" He looked quickly up and down the long rows of sheep faces in case anyone had. But no one spoke. Instead, they continued chewing and staring dismally into the gloom.

"Anyway," smiled Aries, "the wonderful thing is that it's still here!" A tingle of excitement shot down his legs at speaking the words out loud. "I just have to get it!"

At which Olaf, looking rather bored, stretched out his front leg and examined his hoof.

"Mr Olaf!" Aries felt his anger rising again. "I would appreciate your help! Must I remind you, I am a ram of legend? I've never been held in a stall in my life."

Now Olaf turned to Aries, pulling his head up against the rattle of chain, a glint of rage in his caramel eyes. "Is dat so, famous ram? Well, neither had I!" He stood tall and proud. "I am from north of Iceland where snowy skies match my wool." He tossed his head to the left. "Here are bighorn sheep from Rocky Mountains, dere are Booroolas from Australian ranch." He jabbed his horns in the direction of the pens lining the shadowy wall at the back of the cellar. "Over dere are Dorsets, Cotswolds and Wensleydales from English meadows. You think we belong in stalls?"

"Well, no," said Aries, uncomfortably aware that the other sheep were now staring at him. He glanced at their faces, long or round, white or blotched with black, framed with ringlets, fuzz or tight curls, beginning to wonder why there were quite so many breeds of sheep down here. "But I can assure you that if I had not been robbed of my fleece, I certainly would not be down here."

"Had you not been robbed," replied Olaf hotly, meeting Aries' gaze, "neither would we."

Aries paused, searching the Icelandic's disgruntled face, wondering what he meant.

"What are you talking about?" he said. "It's Medea's fault you're here, not mine. But if you'd be so kind as to help me get out of here so that I might find my fleece, then I'll leave you all in peace."

"In peace?" scoffed Olaf, casting a glance at the grinding machinery overhead. "Certainly, let's all help da poor golden ram!"

Aries snorted. "Mr Olaf, I don't like your tone!"

"Oh really?" said Olaf, bristling. "Maybe dere are other things here you will not like, also!"

Aries felt his anger cool into confusion. "Like what?"

For a moment the Icelandic looked away.

"Olaf?" persisted Aries.

"Like da fact your fleece you never will find!"

Aries shook his head. "Don't be so absurd! Obviously, I'll need to be careful and I suppose it might take a few hours to search the house, but—"

"It's gone, ram!" Olaf's face grew pink with impatience. "All gone!"

"Gone?" Aries snorted, incredulous. "What are you talking about?"

"Da sorceress has used it all up! I hear her say last week to snake, 'Only one ringlet left. Den nothing!'"

Aries felt the air gush from his lungs. "Don't be so ridiculous!"

"Ridiculous, is that? You don't think sorceress with cellar full of sheep is ridiculous?" Olaf took a step forwards. "You don't wonder why we all here?"

Aries took a step back, his mind whirling, his head suddenly pounding with the slap of paddles and groan of turning wheels.

"I don't know," he said finally, aware of a very bad feeling in the pit of his stomach, a feeling that was getting stronger.

"Golden ram, she is trying to make new fleece!"

Aries lurched backwards on wobbling legs and crashed into the back of the pen.

"Look round you! She try everything," said Olaf. "Every breed! Slapping, drenching, combing with magical wood! She inject us, bathe us, shock us with sparks."

Aries slid down, floored by the horror of what he was hearing. That the fleece was gone! That Medea could be so cruel! He scrunched his eyes tight shut and wished he could shut his ears too as Olaf went on. "She feed three sheep with mixture of gold and magical roots. Now all die. None of her plans work! But now see! Finally, she has herself da highly very important ram of da Golden Fleece! Perhaps now her scheme work and she leave rest of us alone?"

And so saying he bustled round and pointed his bottom towards Aries. At which, the other sheep, being sheep, copied him immediately, so that just a few seconds later, every sheep in the cellar had turned their bottom towards Aries in a great big woolly wall.

And I'm sorry.

This whole episode has just been far too ghastly for me to talk about any more. If I had a woolly bottom I'd probably join in with the others, because words fail me. But I don't, so I'm off.

Unlike Alex and Aries, Rose wasn't having an unpleasant time at all. In fact, whilst Alex lay captive in the crypt and Aries endured his most terrible night since his fleece had been stolen in the first place, Rose was standing on the ornate balcony of a bedroom in Medea's villa sipping a cool blackcurrant cocktail. She'd found it waiting for her, fizzing in a crystal glass on the ledge and now, as it popped and bubbled on her tongue she gazed down at the swimming pool and the candles encircling it, splashing spangles of light in the water.

Perhaps you think that drinking something made by a sorceress is a bad idea? Well, of course it is. But before you lose heart with Rose for being silly, just remember the sort of day she'd had. Frankly, it had left her horribly frightened and anxious, not to mention thirsty, and seeing that dark, sparkling drink had simply been too tempting. Now, as she let its blackberry bubbles burst on her tongue, she began to feel deeply relaxed.

However, as you've probably guessed, blackberries weren't the only ingredients in Rose's drink.

There were also:

a. Poppies – the lush Bolivian sort that make you feel chilled and confident that everything is going to be lovely, not the ones you see in hedgerows;

b. Moonwort – a fern that dissolves all your

worries with a fizz and a burp;

c. Parsnips of Petrinus – the super-sneakiest
    plant in any sorceress's allotment, one
    spoonful of these and you're ready to believe
    anything. (Believe me, if plants had jobs,
    which obviously they don't since they can't
    wear trousers and catch the bus to the office,
    then these harmless-looking vegetables
    would work as stage hypnotists, the sort that
    convince people they're squawking chickens
    or sailors swabbing decks.)

Making the mixture a potent cocktail of carefree
optimism, mixed in with a measure of dreamy
gullibility, all topped off with a double dollop of
wishful thinking.

Of course, there was another ingredient that
Medea intended to add to Rose's evening. More
bewitching than her herbal mix, more ancient and
powerful, too, this one isn't found in any flowerbed,
but since she intended to serve it later, that's when
I'll tell you about it otherwise you'll only forget and
we'll have to go through it all again.

Rose stepped back in from the balcony into
her room and gazed at the gorgeous four-poster
bed that stood at the far end, made up with cream

sheets and an embroidered emerald silk cover. It was a world apart from her faded duvet cover at home. Whilst her bedroom at home was carpeted in one of her mother's bargain buys, now stained and patchy with wear, the polished wooden floor here was scattered with sumptuous rugs. An ornately carved chair stood plumped with velvet cushions in front of a huge dressing table spread with jewel-coloured bowls of powder puffs, lipsticks and pots of glittering eye shadows, and a basket brimming with bottles of nail varnishes in golds and pinks and reds. Rose had never seen such beautiful things and she longed to try them.

She walked over and sat on the dressing table's stool and gazed at her reflection in the mirror. She smiled as the mixture of poppies and moonwort washed away her worries, and, unclipping her hair, shook it free. She imagined Alex and Aries in equally exquisite rooms. Perhaps, right now, Alex was relaxing in a room full of ancient Greek boy stuff, whilst Aries was munching through a tossed salad of olives and nettle.

Giggling, she felt a fuzzy warm glow rise up from her toes, through her legs and body, muffling the tiny squeak from some remote part of her brain that tried to tell her that it wasn't likely. She glanced into her bag, noticing that the Scroll had now folded itself tightly into what appeared to be a half-hearted origami elephant.

"Everything's all right," she soothed, stroking its paper edges. "You don't need to worry."

At which the Scroll shrank into itself even more tightly.

Rose frowned, wondering fleetingly why the Scroll was behaving so oddly but the thought was instantly snuffed out like a bonfire smut in rain as she felt her legs growing heavier and her whole body filling with a warm sleepiness, like being snuggled under a duvet on a winter night.

Behind her, the wardrobe was reflected in the dressing table mirror, its doors open to reveal an interior crammed with clothes and boots and shoes. She turned and walked across the room to take a closer look. Reaching into the wardrobe, she clicked the hangers over the rail one by one to reveal glitzy silver tops, cashmere sweaters in sapphire and ruby-red, short skirts and long skirts and four pairs of jeans, some ripped denim and others sparkly with glitter swirls, and all in her size. Spotting a flash of candy-pink, Rose pulled out a pair of jeans and caught her breath, recognising them as the same design that Hazel Praline had worn for her last music video.

Rose glanced down at her old sun dress. Two minutes later she had changed into the pink jeans, teamed with a pair of over-the-knee grey suede boots and a grey T-shirt splashed with pink glitter. Smiling, she twirled a full circle before reaching for a pot of pink nail varnish and, pulling out the brush and breathing in the heady scent from the bottle, she began to paint her nails.

What's that?

You want to know about Alex, pinned to the plinth in a tomb room filled with breathing? Well, all right, but I'm not staying down there long.

Unfortunately, the breathing outside the crypt had now become the breathing *inside* the crypt. It had grown louder, closer and – worse – much shallower. Worse, that is, because Alex now recognised it as the sniffling snorts a snake makes when it's about to attack, and straining against the straps, he twisted his head to see Hex slithering towards him, the snake's tail whipping furiously over the dusty floor. Seconds later Hex sprang up beside him, the top third of his body as stiff as a broomstick, his tongue frantically quivering in the air.

"What're you doing?" spluttered Alex, feeling a sudden panic punch behind his ribcage.

Hex's eyes glittered like emeralds. "I've decided to kill you," he hissed, flinging open his jaws to display two enormous fangs hanging like glittering stalactites a centimetre from Alex's nose. Staring into the inky black coffin-shaped void of the snake's maw, he imagined the even darker void that Hex could send him to with a single bite.

"Why?" gasped Alex, trying hopelessly to shrink back further against the plinth as the snake puffed out his neck-flap to make himself even more menacing. His mind scrambled back to what had happened in the cellar, desperate to discover what had made the snake suddenly so truly ferocious. And realised.

Alex snatched a breath, hoping it wouldn't be his last. "This is about London Zoo, isn't it?" he said. "You want to prove yourself to Medea!"

The snake jerked to a standstill and blinked. "Yesss," he said, his eyes glittering with surprise. "The mistressss always loves an agonisssing death."

Alex shook his head. "You poor thing," he said, trying to keep the tremor out of his voice.

Hex snapped his mouth shut. Throughout his life he'd been called many things: Silver Bringer of Death, Murder-Fangs, He Kills in Screams, Middasypoo-poos (although that was his mother and he didn't make it public) but not once had anyone called him a poor thing.

Or ever felt the teensiest bit sorry for him.

Until now.

"Medea doesn't treat you very well, does she?" said Alex, sensing the snake's breathing start to slow. "I expect she's always been short-tempered and unduly disappointed at the things you do, hasn't she?"

Slowly, the snake nodded and opened its mouth.

"Then why don't you tell me all about it," soothed Alex, trying not to notice the venom dripping from Hex's fangs. "I'm sure it'd make you feel better to get it off your chest. And you can always kill me afterwards."

Hex considered this for a few seconds before slithering up onto the plinth and lacing himself over the boy's body like icing on a doughnut.

"You wouldn't believe what ssshe did to me with a bucket of frozen sssquid," he began softly, his face a few centimetres above Alex's neck. "It wasss ten yearsss ago now, but I can ssstill remember the headache. And asss for the black ssstains on my ssstomach ssscales…"

"That's dreadful," said Alex.

"But that wasss only the ssstart," Hex sighed. "Ssshe sssaid ssshe couldn't be ssseen with sssuch a sssplotchy familiar and decided to get the ssstains out in the fassst cycle of the wassshing machine. I wasss burping bubblesss for weeksss."

For the next ten minutes Alex listened as Hex rasped about his miserable life with Medea. Glad to have stalled the snake's attack, the boy's mind fizzed, desperate to think of something to steer Hex from his murderous plan. Yet, despite facing near-certain death at the fangs of the world's most venomous snake whilst being trapped in a sorceress's crypt full of coffins, Alex couldn't help feeling both angry and sad on Hex's behalf. Like the monsters in the Underworld Zoo, like the sheep in Medea's cellar, Hex had been cruelly mistreated. But as Alex consoled the serpent, he slowly became aware of something slightly more useful to him than sympathy: the unmistakable tingle of an idea forming in his mind.

"Ssso you sssee," concluded Hex, pausing to utter a long hissing whoosh of dismay, "I can't bear the thought of a one-way trip in a sssewing basssket to ssshare sssome glassss box with a podgy boa conssstrictor," he said. He rose up and regarded the boy with wide gentle eyes. "Thanksss for lisssstening. If you try and relax, I'll make thisss asss painlessss asss possible."

"Hold on!" said Alex, as Hex loomed above him. "You're a clever reptile. What you do think killing me will really do?"

"Endear me to Medea, of courssse," said Hex.

"Today, perhaps," said Alex thoughtfully. "But what about tomorrow? Or next week? How about the next time you annoy Medea? You know she'll go back to her old ways again. So, you'd be no better off."

"No better off," muttered Hex, his tongue drooping like a bootlace between his lips.

"Unless…" said Alex.

"Unlessss what?"

"Come closer," said Alex, trying not to imagine just how big those fangs would look close up. "I've got an idea."

Seconds later, excited hisses punctuated by the slap of snake tail against coffin sides echoed around the ancient stillness of the crypt, as Alex told Hex his, quite frankly, brilliant idea.

And no doubt you want to know what Alex was saying, too. Well, I'm sorry. I said I'd tell you whom the breathing belonged to and to be honest I've hung around in this grubby crypt far longer than I intended. I'm going back to Rose.

So there.

✵XXI✵
DADDYS' GIRLS

I do so enjoy a good meal out, with interesting company and an enormous sticky pudding and Rose was on the point of enjoying all three. Of course, it was a pity she'd be sharing it with an ice-hearted sorceress, but then you can't have everything in life, can you?

Blissfully relaxed thanks to the blackcurrant potion, Rose stretched back in her chair and gazed admiringly at the dining table laid out before her. Candles in crystal holders twinkled, making the silver cutlery sparkle. Ruby-red goblets gleamed. A bowl of fresh white roses glowed like a fresh fall of snow. She sighed, comfortably. It was all so different from the draughty old terrace she shared with her mother, with its hard wooden chairs, cramped rooms and windowpanes that rattled in the slightest wind. Smelling the scent of jasmine blossom drifting in through the open doors to the garden, Rose closed her eyes and listened to the tinkle of wind chimes hanging from the roof of the quirky little temple building that stood amongst the trees.

However, charming as it is up here, I'm afraid I have to tell you that there was nothing jasmine-scented or tinkly-winkly happening two floors below, where at that precise moment Medea was chanting over a vast iron pot.

And I am sorry to have to do this to you, just when you thought the day couldn't get any worse, but I have to tell you something dreadful: Medea had taken a shine to Rose.

That's right.

And if there's one thing worse than incurring a sorceress's wrath, it's winning her admiration. But Medea liked Rose's courage and the way she'd squared up to Ms De Mentor that morning. She liked her curiosity too, and how it had led her into the secret room at Seamed Desires. Then there was her loyalty – even if it was wasted on those two over-baked baklavas, Aries and Alex – in searching for an answer in the pictures she found down there. All wrapped up in her willingness to accept crazy things like Greek ghosts running around London in the first place. But, unfortunately for Rose, all of these traits are essential in budding sorceresses. And rather like a judge on one of those talent shows on telly, Medea had spotted a potential in Rose, a flair ripe for twisting into sorcery, a sort of Hexfactor, if you like.

But she would still have shrugged and dispatched Rose horribly if it hadn't been for one other thing and that was how Rose so strongly reminded Medea of herself at that age. Even all these hundreds of years later, the sorceress still remembered how it stung to be twelve years old and forgotten by a distracted parent; more importantly, she recalled just how delighted she'd been when her Aunt **Circe** had turned up and taken Medea to live with her to teach her the dark arts. Now, spotting that same brittle loneliness glittering in Rose, Medea was drawn like a magpie to a gold ring left by an open window.

However, before Medea could enrol Rose into her private school of sorcery, there was the small matter of winning Rose's trust. And that was why Medea was at that moment steeped in tendrils of smoke that wreathed upwards and pooled beneath the ceiling in a cloud the grubby-green hue of an alligator. Having used her blackcurrant potion to soften Rose, as a chef might tenderise meat with a hammer before tossing it into a sizzling pan, Medea was now preparing the evening's final ingredient, the one I mentioned in the last chapter.

You remember that I mentioned another ingredient? Good.

Lifting her hands over her head, the ruby-red sleeves of her cloak fell back to reveal pale arms marked with strange symbols as she hurled a handful of dried crocuses into the crucible. Picked hundreds of years ago, these were the first flowers to clamber through the war-torn rubble of Troy. Now they hissed and bubbled, their purple and green essences mingling with the silvery deposit in the bottom of the dish.

As the mixture hissed and spat, Medea tilted her face to the ceiling.

Hecate, goddess of the night,
Hear your handmaid's plea.
Release bright dreams in Rose's heart
And paint them here to see!

Suddenly the room exploded in a storm of green lightning, splintering the air with skittering veins of electricity before vanishing with a squeal. Every candle extinguished as the eerie sound of a girls' choir rose in the velvety darkness only to dissipate in a hiss of whispers, like a room full of snakes each calling Rose's name.

"Illuminati!" commanded Medea.

The candles instantly relit.

Smiling, Medea pushed back the hood of her cloak and peered down into the crucible at a puddle of smouldering mercury-bright liquid. Consisting of a mixture of those Trojan crocuses, splinters from the anchor of a Greek ship that survived ten storms, the wick of a candle that'd burned through the night and a snip of the red wool that had led Theseus out of the Minotaur's maze, all melded with Medea's dark incantations, it was the very essence of hope.

That's right: hope. The same stuff that knots your stomach on Christmas morning when you spy your wrapped presents under the tree and so want them to be what you've hinted for since September; the same stuff that fizzes in your chest when you long for something so much it hurts. One of the most powerful forces on Earth, hope has stuck to human hearts throughout history, like a blob of chewing gum on the bottom of a shoe that no amount of common sense or logic will clean off.

Medea took a small square of card from her robe pocket and dipped it into the gleaming liquid, coating the card's surface with a skin-thin layer. For a moment she waited for it to dry, watching its colour fade from silver to the creamy-yellow of a pearl before shrugging off her robe, tucking the card into the back pocket of her jeans and hurrying up to the dining room, a fresh spring in her steps.

Back in the dining room, Rose was busy gazing at her kooky grey boots when Medea appeared in the doorway.

"Hey! Look at you!" gushed Medea, admiring Rose's outfit.

"Do you like it?" said Rose, who would usually have shrivelled up at such a compliment. But not tonight, oh no, tonight she was ready to believe whatever Medea said and now she sprang out of her chair to perform a model's twirl complete with pout.

"Way cool!" enthused Medea, her grey eyes twinkling. Wearing a simple white T-shirt and jeans, Rose thought Medea looked more like a big sister than the mega-famous fashion designer she'd seen countless times on television and in the pages of magazines. She pointed at Rose's feet. "I just love the way you teamed those jeans and boots. Look, they're the same as mine!"

Rose giggled and looked down to see Medea wearing exactly the same style grey suede boots.

"Have a seat," said Medea.

Rose sat down and looked over the table at Medea.

Dappled by candlelight, the sorceress's face looked softer tonight, the sharp bones of her face mellowed in the golden glow.

"Apologies first," said Medea, watching Rose's reaction carefully. "I'm really sorry about the way you were brought here, but as you can imagine it's difficult for me to invite people to my house without the paparazzi turning up."

Rose smiled and shrugged at a foggy memory of an ice-cream van, the tender patchwork of bruises on her elbows and knees for the moment dissolved by the blackcurrant drink.

There was an uneven click of heels on the marble floor as the butler, who'd escorted Rose down from her room, wheeled in a trolley laden with food. Despite his dark green tail coat and bowtie he was still the strangest looking butler she'd ever seen (not that she'd seen many, of course, and then only in old films) but there was definitely something odd about that lolloping walk of his. Perhaps, she thought sympathetically, as he set out hamburgers and hot pizza, bowls of chips and tacos, dips of guacamole, salsa sauce and soured cream, he had a touch of gout[26].

"I wasn't sure what you'd like," shrugged Medea, "so I thought we'd have some of everything! Tuck in!"

Rose glanced at the other chairs around the table.

"Shouldn't we wait for Alex and Aries?"

Medea looked up, a flicker of annoyance passing over her face. "Oh, sweetie," she said, "don't worry about those two. To be honest with you, I expect they're absolutely exhausted."

Which was true, of course. The fact that they were exhausted because she'd imprisoned them horribly was, however, something she didn't bother to point out.

"They were a bit worried about meeting you," Rose went on, reaching for a burger.

"Me?" Medea looked puzzled. "Oh, because of our differences in the past, you mean?" She shook her head. "That was all so long ago. Time to let bygones be bygones, if you ask me."

Rose listened happily and took a giant bite of her burger, feeling the warm cheese trickle over her fingers as she munched on the beef and spicy jalapeños.

"They thought you," she began, between mouthfuls, "were the last person to see the... the..." Rose stopped, aware of her thoughts trickling away like rainwater down a drain. "The..." She stared down at her plate and shrugged.

---

26. *Actually, a touch of goat, which just shows how much damage that blackcurrant tide of moonwort, poppies and peculiar parsnips was wreaking.*

"Mmm!" said Medea, dabbing a dot of tomato puree from her lips. "This pizza is absolutely delicious! Like some?"

Rose took a slice, sinking deeper still into her carefree torpor, rather like one of those lizards basking in the sunshine, but unfortunately in her case, without hope of scooting down a sand hole when danger's looming.

"'S fun to have a girls' night in, isn't it?" said Medea. She poured some red wine into her own glass and more blackcurrant into Rose's. "Especially when you and I have such a lot in common."

Three hours before Rose would have choked on her pepperoni at this remark. But now she simply looked up expectantly. "We do?"

"Certainly!" Medea nodded. "We're both cool, we're good to our friends, we love animals, hey, we even have the same taste in boots," she said, giggling. "And," she added, fixing Rose with her silvery eyes, "we both lost our fathers when we were little girls, didn't we?"

Despite her super-chilled mood Rose felt the pizza cloy in her mouth. Her heart drummed against her ribs and she had to lay down her knife and fork in order to concentrate on swallowing.

"My mother," Medea went on, watching Rose

over her wine glass, "died when I was born. My dad and I were everything to one another." She sighed. "Until..."

Rose cupped her chin in her hands. "Until…?"

"Until my cousin, Phryxus, brought some special treasure to Kolkis." Medea paused for effect. "It was so remarkable, so sought after, that Daddy simply doted on it and forgot all about me."

"Forgot you?" said Rose, shocked.

Medea sniffed theatrically. "I never saw him from one morning to the next. I missed him so much. So, I know what it's like for you. One parent lost, the other always so horribly busy, hardly even noticing you're there and—"

"Mum just wants to—"

Medea held up her hand. "No, I understand," she said. "Your mother is grieving. But that's hardly a consolation for you, is it? Day after day, so lonely." Medea leaned forwards on her chair. "It was just the same for me as a child, until my Aunt Circe took me under her wing and taught me all about magic."

Rose felt her eyes grow wider.

"I was never lonely again, Rose. It utterly changed my life." Medea spread her arms, indicating the beautiful room. "This house, my career, my life, my friends, my success. Everything.

It's all built on what she taught me."

Delighted by Rose's transfixed expression, Medea took the magical piece of paper from her back pocket and slid it across the table. "Just imagine what it could bring you. All the things your heart ever wanted."

Rose stared at the paper.

Were you or I to look over her shoulder, it would have only appeared as a piece of shiny white paper. But for Rose's eyes its creaminess melted into a twirling spiral of colours, colours that swam and blended into a photograph of her father. He grinned up out of the picture at her, his lopsided smile framed by a neatly trimmed beard, his eyes twinkling and loving.

"Dad?" whispered Rose.

To anyone but a sorceress with a freezer box where her heart should be, the moment would have brought tears to the eyes.

But not Medea.

All she felt was the delightful fizzy *frisson* of knowing her plan was working perfectly.

"You can have it all. The things you want the most, Rose," she murmured. "And I can teach you how."

Now unless you have a relative who disappeared in the Amazon jungle, and have since spent countless nights worrying that they became an anaconda's breakfast, you can't imagine what feelings even the tiniest chance of finding them elicits: delight, trepidation, disbelief, euphoria, impatience, all of those. But for Rose they were galvanised by a bewildering red-hot explosion of hope as the blinding magic that Medea had saturated the paper with erupted, zapping through her like a shower of sparks, electrifying every cell in her body.

"I could find my father," said Rose. She looked up at Medea, her eyes blurry with tears. "But why would you help me?"

Medea's grey eyes glittered in the candlelight. For a split second the wine glass in her hand magnified her mouth, making her teeth as long and white as a jaguar's. "Because I like you, Rose, and I think we would work well together."

"But how?" said Rose. "I'm nobody. What could I give you in return?"

"Well," said Medea. "For starters, how about giving me a hand tomorrow?"

"Tomorrow?" said Rose, uncertainly.

"Oh, it's nothing too difficult for a bright girl like you," said Medea. "The trouble is that my assistant, Mr Hex, has unexpectedly resigned, leaving me in rather a mess. I simply need someone to carry the bags, make lists, run a few errands and brew tea. I'm booked to visit Hazel Praline, you see, to make the final adjustments to her dress before her premiere tomorrow afternoon."

"Hazel Praline," gasped Rose.

"Oh, you know her, then?" smiled Medea. "Well, that's lucky."

Excitement lit up Rose's bewitched imagination like the illuminations on Blackpool Pier. The chance to meet Hazel Praline. The chance to learn magic. The chance to find her father again.

"So," smiled Medea, watching Rose's face melt into an enormous grin, "shall I take that as a yes?"

✲XXII✲
Upscares Downscares

Aries wasn't grinning.

Nor was his mind electrified by hope, fake or otherwise. Because as Rose was saying goodnight to the sorceress before going upstairs to her marshmallow-soft bed, he lay sprawled on the stinking floor of the stall, tears wobbling down his muzzle into the soggy straw beneath his chin. He'd been like this for the past two hours, ever since Olaf had spoken to him. Because what the Icelandic had told him was the single most terrible thing he'd heard since Drako's rumbling snores had echoed through the trees on the night Jason crept into the Forest of Kolkis.

Overhead, the machinery droned relentlessly on, combing and spinning wool, grinding against the fitful bleats of the sheep as they slept, huddled in their stalls. Looking over the tangle of wool and limbs, through the forest of horns, he made out Olaf's thick golden-brown pair, rippled like cockleshells. Now he understood why the Icelandic had been so unfriendly. After all, had it not been for Aries and his fleece, everyone would still be blissfully grazing in the pastures and mountains that Medea had snatched them from months ago. He stared at a tin bath lying upturned in the walkway, its sides pocked with hoof marks. Beyond it, a vicious-looking machine hung like a bad-tempered bat on the wall, crackling and spitting out flashes of green light. Aries tried to imagine the sheep's miserable existence down here, day after day after day, as the sorceress tested her endless mixes of experiment and magic to make a new golden fleece. Then Aries saw Toby, nestled against his mother's side, and hated Medea with all his heart.

Just wondering about what awful thing Medea had been doing with his fleece made him feel sick. He thought back over all those minutes and days and months that he'd yearned for it, longing for its softness on his back so that he could be magnificent again, only to discover that all that time she'd been twisting it through her small white hands and using it, for what?

How did you *use* a fleece?

He sighed, thinking back to how sure he'd been

that morning in the kitchen at Rose's house that Medea had sent a harpy to stop them from taking the fleece away from her. It seemed laughable now.

Whimpering into his forelegs, Aries realised just how stupid he'd been. Blinded by his own vanity and pride, he'd walked straight into Medea's trap. Worse, much worse, he'd dragged Alex and Rose with him. If only he'd listened to Alex in the first place. His heart tightened as he thought back to the boy, dappled by sunlight in the Skeleton Garden, reasoning with Aries, asking him to reconsider, to see sense, not to try to come back to Earth. And of how Alex had still come with him, knowing it was stupid and dangerous, how he'd felled the harpy, saving Rose from her, and of how hard he'd fought Pandemic to try and save them all. Wonderful, practical Alex who could always see so much more clearly than Aries could, driven by his own stupid obsession. Alex, the best friend he'd ever had in life or death and who, he now realised for the first time, had never even seen Aries when he'd worn his fleece.

A teardrop rolled off his muzzle and pooled with the others. Alex hadn't been dazzled by a golden coat or stupefied with admiration because a ram could fly. He loved Aries, for who he was on the inside and for the bald, lumpy and ridiculous-looking ram he was on the outside, too.

Only in the crystal clarity that spending a night in a sorceress's stinking cellar with a hundred other sheep brings did Aries understand: there were some things that were more important than his fleece. (And yes, I know. I never thought I would ever see myself type those words, either.) The thought that he had been so blind to what was truly priceless right there in front of his muzzle all these years brought him out in shivery goosebumps.

If they ever returned home, he now promised himself, he'd do all of Alex's most horrible jobs for him. He'd muck out the Minotaur, he'd drain the smelly water from Hydra's tank, he'd even chip the rock-hard splatter off the floor of the Stymphalian birds' aviary. And he'd never complain about sore hooves or how the smell made his nose ache again.

If they ever returned home.

The words sounded hollow and hopeless in his mind. Lying on the filthy floor he began to feel a deep ache in his belly. Swollen and sour, it hurt like the time he'd been poisoned by eating clover, when Alex had poured warm water and castor oil down his throat to save his life. Except that tonight's pain was sharper and all the water and castor oil in the world would never cure it.

Carpet.

It's a much worthier use of a fleece than an ingredient for Medea's magic. Not that Alex and Hex had time to appreciate the sumptuous Turkish weave on the staircase as they sprinted and slithered towards Rose's room on the top floor.

That's right, Alex and Hex, because Alex's idea, the one he'd whispered to Hex in the crypt, was for the mamba to betray Medea and help them instead. In return, Alex promised to take Hex back to the Underworld (after all, King Hades had always allowed just a few of the living to stay down there – just ask Persephone) to nest amongst Greek orchids on a diet of ghost locusts and bogey-bugs. Hex hadn't taken much persuading and quickly made the same choice we all would, given the alternative of moving into the boa constrictor tank at London Zoo.

Alex dived onto the landing behind Hex, skidded around the corner and into the hallway that led to Rose's room. And froze.

Mannequins lined the walls.

Stationed like some creepy guard of honour, they stood in two rows, facing each across the hall, positioned between the doorways. Alex felt his skin prickle as he walked past them, shuddering at their hard pink-white faces, their blank glass eyes.

Each one was dressed in a unique outfit: a fluttery white dress, a cream gown with a neckline of velvet roses, a Roman soldier's uniform draped by a purple cloak, a dark blue uniform piped with gold with one sleeve tucked into its jacket.

Hex stopped at the far end of the hall and looked back at Alex.

"They're copiesss of the clothesss the mistressss herssself made for her ssspecial clientsss," he hissed. "Marilyn Monroe, Marie Antoinette, Juliusss Caesssar and Nelssson. There are ssseveral more downsssstairs, in the mistress'sss locked roomsss."

Even though the names didn't mean anything to Alex, the mannequins' eerie stares made him feel horribly uncomfortable. He took a step closer to the last one for a better look. Dressed in a long blue naval coat with a gold starburst medal on its chest, gold epaulettes and buttons, and wearing a white pigtailed wig, the figure looked faintly displeased by the boy's interest and for a fleeting moment Alex experienced the weird sensation that it was staring back. Scolding himself for being so foolish, he reached out and gingerly touched the cloth of the old coat. Dusty with age, it smelled of must and seawater.

"That'sss a copy of the Admiral'sss coat," said Hex, sliding up the glossy white door of Rose's room.

"Wore it to lead the Britisssh Navy in the Battle of Trafalgar, two hundred yearsss ago."

"And the original?" said Alex.

"On disssplay at the naval mussseum in Greenwich with a bullet hole through itsss chessst."

Shocked, Alex snatched back his hand and hurried after Hex's tail as it vanished into Rose's room.

Rose was sound asleep. In the buttery glow of night lights dotted around her room, she lay as serene as a princess in a fairy tale, her face creamy, her hair fanned out in waves across the pillow. How lovely, you might think, for our two heroes to discover her safe and enjoy a moment of calm before waking her and leading her to safety. However, don't. Remember that this is a book of gloom and ghastly happenings. It doesn't do five minutes peace and a nice sit down, muffins or cups of tea, for that matter.

Hex quickly arranged himself like a draught excluder, quivering his tongue under the door to pick up any scent of danger, while Alex tried to wake Rose. And I mean *tried*. He whispered, cajoled and pinched. He pulled the duvet up, down, off, on. He thumped the bedsprings and the headboard and pummelled the pillows. Finally, seizing a nearby bunch of roses from their vase he was just about to upend its cold water on her when Hex shot through his legs and vanished out onto the balcony. Straining to listen, Alex heard muffled footsteps approaching. He dropped down and tried to roll under the bed, but it was too low. The wardrobe was too full and the dresser was pushed flat up against the wall, which left only one choice. He threw himself over the balcony rail and hung down over the garden just as the bedroom door clicked open.

Hanging on by his fingers, Alex saw Pandemic's shiny black shoes walk around Rose's bed and stop. There was a goaty grunt and he lifted the foot of the bed off the floor and dropped it again.

Rose didn't wake up.

"Sound asleep, Mistress," said Pandemic.

Small feet in grey boots appeared around the bed and clicked over to the balcony doors at which Hex shot over the edge and dropped inside Alex's T-shirt in terror. Biting his lip, Alex willed himself not to cry out, which, as anyone who's had a ticklish snake squirm down his or her shirt will know, is really rather hard. He watched Medea's feet, willing her not to see his fingers, white in the moonlight, clutching the sill. Luckily for Hex and him she didn't. Unluckily she closed the balcony doors and bolted them.

"Now what?" whispered Hex, sticking his head out of the boy's collar.

Beneath them Fred crashed through the shrubbery, a butterfly net slung over one shoulder, a wicker basket in his other hand, muttering something that sounded suspiciously like, "Snakey snakey!"

Hex tucked his head back in.

"I won't let him get you," Alex whispered down his now trembling T-shirt.

He watched as Fred stubbed his toe on a statue of a rather mean-looking dolphin, used lots of rude Cyclops words that won't be repeated here and finally disappeared around the corner of the villa. Then, gingerly, turning his attention to the drainpipe that ran down the side of the building, Alex began stretching his arm out towards it.

And, I know. After all this horridness you probably wanted this chapter to end on a note of triumph. Well, I'm sorry about that.

❊XXIII❊
PIRANHA SOUP

A couple of hours later Rose finally woke up.

Sunshine streamed through the balcony doors, bathing her room in brightness. Blinking, she sat up in bed and groaned, feeling as though two miniature sumo wrestlers had picked a fight inside her skull and were now taking turns to furiously thump and throw each other to the floor. Since she didn't understand why her head throbbed so much it's lucky that I'm here to explain that the numbing effect of the blackcurrant fizz had worn off during the night, and now half of her brain was thinking clearly enough to squeak that she was in danger whilst the other half, enchanted by Medea's magical hope spell, attacked it.

Medea could not be trusted, the clear-thinking side piped up.

How ridiculous, trumpeted the other side, insisting it was wrong to judge someone before you knew them properly.

Rose must not help Medea today, whispered the clear-thinking side.

Of course she should, boomed the hope-addled side, otherwise how would she ever learn the magic she needed to find her father?

Rose rubbed her forehead and threw back the luxurious bed covers. Gazing around the beautiful room, she noticed a smart black trouser suit and striped red T-shirt hanging on the wardrobe door. An outfit chosen by Medea for her to wear today.

How thoughtful, trilled the hope-bewitched side of her mind.

Don't wear it! snapped the logical side.

Feeling sick with confusion, Rose stepped out of bed and pulled the picture of her father from the pink jeans she had worn last night. She propped it against the ornate dressing-table mirror and tried to think clearly. Unfortunately, this is largely impossible when a sorceress has branded your mind with molten hope, but she did her best.

Whatever Medea was really like, she tried to reason, surely she couldn't just let the chance to learn magic, magic that might help her find out where her father was, slip through her fingers?

Of course she could, needled the logical half of her mind. After all, she was talking about a sorceress, wasn't she? And besides, there was still the Scroll and its last question, wasn't there?

The Scroll!

Rose threw open her rucksack and thrust her hands inside, reaching down to the bottom of the bag to make sure that the parchment was still safe. Her fingers touched its soft paper and she pulled it out. It lay scrunched up in a tight roll, its ends over like flaps in her palm. And yet, staring at its creamy glow, she felt her heart sink like a rock in a deep lake. Even with her muddied thinking, she knew that the way things were going, they'd have to use its last question to find the fleece.

Now, don't be mistaken: Rose wanted to find her father more than anything in the world. But whilst Medea had been right in spotting a fledging apprentice and had started, ever so gently, to warp Rose's mind into believing that learning magic would make her life so much easier, a bright and good part of Rose remained untouched by the sorceress. Like a drop of oil immune to water, Rose's true nature remained kind, unspoilt and thoroughly loyal to her friends and now, feeling tears of frustration prickling her eyes, she tucked the Scroll safely back in her bag, knowing its last question must belong to Aries.

Even more reason then, the hope-spiked side of

her mind piped up, to trust the sorceress. After all, with Medea's magical teaching, Rose would have a much better chance of finding out what happened to her father herself, wouldn't she?

Dressing quickly, Rose imagined flying to the Amazon and using magic to find her father. And yet, as she dragged a brush through her tangled hair, she knew that she could only give in to such wonderful daydreams if she was sure that Alex and Aries were safe.

Safe? chirped the enchanted side of her brain. *Of course they are safe.* What did she think a fabulous sorceress needed from a boy and a ram?

So, where are they? countered the withering voice of Rose's true mind.

By now thoroughly tired of her fractious brain and knowing there was only one way to find out, Rose hitched her rucksack onto her back. She walked over to the door and placed her ear against the wood to listen. Beyond it, Medea's house lay silent, still slumbering, and, taking a deep breath, Rose stepped out to investigate.

"Ready so quickly, Miss?" said a polished voice.

Jumping, Rose looked around the door frame to see Medea's butler standing a metre away, half-bowing, a syrupy smile on his face.

"Madam will be so pleased," he added with a wide sweep of his arm. "If you would come this way? She asked for me to escort you directly to the car."

Wondering about his dad, being escorted to a limousine or having the teeniest spark of hope brighten his desolate mood would all have been improvements on Aries' morning, because at that moment Fred was dragging him by a chain through the criss-cross of corridors that tunnelled beneath the villa. Fred's meaty arms bulged with the strain as he pulled Aries around yet another corner into a long passageway that ended in a pair of shining metal swing doors marked by skull and crossbones[27].

Aries' hooves shrieked against the stone floor. Twisting and bellowing, he threw his head from side to side, desperately trying to butt Fred with his horns. In his mind he imagined himself breaking free of the Cyclops's ironlike grasp and galloping down the corridor to smash through every wall of the villa until he found Alex and Rose. He saw

---

27. *In polite circles, this sign means 'DANGER! KEEP OUT!'*
    However, this skull was laughing and winking its right eye socket,
    which just goes to show how centuries of wickedness will warp a
    sorceress's sense of humour.

himself rescuing the children and carrying them to safety. But unfortunately for Aries, Cyclopes are tough and wily creatures, canny enough to avoid jabbing horns and strong enough to deal with ram rage. Backing through the doors, Fred hauled Aries into a room flooded with light and padlocked the chain to a metal post bolted into the floor.

"Ram, ram!" muttered the Cyclops and poked Aries on the nose for good measure.

Then he lumbered off through another door into what appeared, in the glimpse that Aries caught, to be a storeroom.

Blinking, Aries caught his breath and looked around. Stark white walls rose on every side, enclosing a room with a white tiled floor and lit by star-bright dots in the ceiling, dominated by a rectangular tank. Slightly larger than bath-size, but with higher sides made of metal, it seemed to be filled with something slimy and green. Something that churned and frothed and dribbled over the tank's rim in thick sprout-coloured fingers of goo that slid down and splattered on the floor before gurgling away through a metal grille. Clusters of greasy bubbles rose on the liquid's surface, growing under their slick skins, stretching until they popped in loud explosions of green drops.

A big metal hook hung from a rope wound over

a pulley fixed in the ceiling. On the other side it ran tautly down to wrap around the spindle of a winch, bolted to the floor. Feeling a cold dread rising up his hooves and legs, Aries looked away at the steel benches that ran around the walls of the room, scattered with chunks of stripy grey and white rock that seemed to twinkle under the lights.

He was just puzzling what a sorceress would want with the strange assortment of things in the room when a wet spume of goo flew up out of the tank and landed near his hooves.

"Good morning!" said a cold, familiar voice.

Startled, Aries swung his head back towards the doors to see Medea walk in, her high-heeled red shoes *click-clacking* against the tiles. (And, since I'm mentioning the shoes, I might as well add that Medea was looking especially glamorous this morning, in a black trouser suit, red stripy T-shirt and silk scarf, with her hair fixed in a messy bun pinned up with red chopsticks. Not that Aries had any time for fashion right now.)

"Where's Alex?" snorted Aries.

"Oh, still around," said Medea, patting her hair. "He's not going anywhere."

Aries breathed a sigh of relief. "You haven't hurt him?"

Medea shook her head. "Not yet. I haven't had the time."

She gazed lovingly into the tank and pulled on a dark waterproof coat.

"*Penibilium auriculus*," she said, in the tone of voice most people would use to soothe a kitten. "Such a big old scientific name for gold bugs."

"Gold bugs?" said Aries, feeling a sour dread wash into his stomach.

"A rather gorgeous little bacteria[28]," explained Medea. "Not that I fancied myself as much of a scientist before, but it's amazing what you can turn your hand to when the need arises. Watch this!"

She snatched a rock from the nearest bench and held it up to Aries, rather like a magician showing an empty top hat to the audience before pulling a rabbit from it.

"Gold ore," she said and tossed it over her shoulder into the tank.

There was a splash, a slurp and a rude gobbling noise followed by a long disgusting belch as something shot straight back out of the mixture and clattered across the floor.

Giggling, Medea picked it up and showed Aries.

---

28. *Yes, I know. Only a sorceress could find bacteria gorgeous.*

He peered down at the dull piece of rock in her hand. "Where's the gold gone?"

She nodded at the gurgling tank. "It's still in there, ready for me to collect and use on the sheep."

Aries blinked, staring at the writhing green mixture. "The bugs suck gold out of rocks?"

"Sweetheart." Medea pushed her face towards him, a dark gleam in her eyes. "These little darlings will suck the gold out of *anything*!" She picked up a long wooden paddle that leaned against the wall and began stirring the mixture. "Mining companies have used them for centuries. Think of them as microbes with big teeth, just like piranhas. Not that you'd have heard of those either, I suppose. Well, Aries, piranhas are meat-eating fish." Her eyes grew dreamy and she rested her face against the handle of the paddle. "They'll strip a ram down to its bones in about six minutes. These little beauties are much the same."

Aries gasped, straining backwards against the chain. But before he could speak, the door to the side room crashed open and Fred bustled out carrying a cage. A ram-of-legend-sized cage. And, straining to see over the Cyclops's wide shoulders, he spotted stirrups, one bolted into each corner of the cage floor. A padded leather halter, like the ones horses wear to pull carts, hung down from its roof.

"No!" Aries jammed his hooves hard against the polished tiles, but it was no good. They slid like skates over a rink. "You're not going to—"

"Oh, but I am," said Medea coldly, snapping her fingers. "Finally, I see why my work has been failing. As if ordinary gold could ever be good enough to use on the sheep. Silly me. But the gold from your bloodstream, Aries? The gold of the fabulous ram himself?"

The Cyclops hurried over, unfastened the padlock on Aries' chain and threw his bulk against the ram's rump, pushing him, the way a motorist pushes a broken-down car, into the cage. A moment later Fred had forced the ram's neck into the halter and his hooves into the stirrups and slammed the door shut.

"At last, I'm going to have a new fleece!" said Medea. She stepped towards the cage and peered at Aries through the bars. "Because yours is all gone!" she added spitefully.

Aries glared back. "I know!"

"You do?" Disappointed by his response, Medea pursed her lips like a sulky child. She straightened up. "Those sheep tongues been wagging, have they? Who'd have thought it? Aries Khrysamallos, always too important to speak to the sheep of Greece, chatting away with that motley herd? Don't tell me that you've finally learned some manners?"

"I've learned a lot of things lately."

"Like what?" she sniggered. "Coming all this way to find out that your fleece is no more?" She shrugged. "Well almost. There is one teensy tuft left."

Between them Fred attached the hook to the top of the cage.

"One tuft left?" said Aries. "Are you saying you pulled my fleece to pieces? Why?"

"To make it easier to sew into my clothes, of course."

Aries stared at her blankly, bracing himself as the cage lifted off the ground and began to rise jerkily.

The sorceress's face looked as hard as marble. "Didn't you ever stop to think of what your fleece did to me?"

Aries, who'd not thought about Medea for a second more than he'd absolutely had to over the years, shook his head.

"My father was so besotted by it he forgot all about me. Left me to play with a giant snake in a forest. I was six years old, Aries!" Medea stalked across the room and sat on a counter, watching as the cage rose. "Then, years of loneliness later, Jason sailed into Kolkis." Aries saw her cheeks blush pink and heard her voice soften. "I really thought he loved me. I left my home for him, my people, my life as a princess. All for a so-called hero who dumped me for someone else as soon as the fleece made him king of his own island!" Her voice hardened, becoming as cold and brittle as ice. "Your fleece cursed my life, Aries! So I've used it get my own back. I've cursed the lives of hundreds of others!"

"Cursed them?" Aries stared, barely aware that the cage had reached the ceiling. "How?"

"Remember **Glauce**?" said Medea mischievously.

Aries thought back to the beautiful young woman for whom Jason had left Medea. According to gossip in the Underworld, Medea had pretended to give her blessing to their marriage and had made Glauce's wedding dress. Woven from swans' down it was the most beautiful thing the new bride had ever seen, at least until she tried it on, whereupon it burst into flames, engulfing her in an inferno.

"Then the rumours were true?" gasped Aries. "You killed her?"

Medea nodded brightly. "I suppose you could call her my inspiration! She was my first attempt. But it worked, didn't it? Your fleece, my magic, what a perfect combination! After that it was easy. Julius Caesar, the great Roman emperor, wanted a fancy purple cloak to wear to the Senate. So not the colour for hiding stab marks and bloodstains." The sorceress laughed thinly. "Cleopatra was next. She loved the softness of my linen kaftan. And so did the asp that killed her in it! Must have, because they found it hours later, still curled up in the folds of her dress. Then there was Boudicca, William the Conqueror, Sir Walter Raleigh, Marie Antoinette!"

Aries reeled back against the bars of the cage as Medea went on, adding name after name, appalled at what she was saying. His fleece had been responsible for every one of these deaths? His mind whirled, filled with a blizzard of confusion and horror. Medea, meanwhile, was clearly warming to her subject.

"American presidents, film stars, highwaymen and pirates, I've dressed them all, though to tell you the truth, men in uniform were always my favourite! Like Captain Edward Smith!" She fluttered her hands together, remembering. "What a devil he was for gold brocade! Still, at least he looked his best on his trip to the bottom of the sea after *Titanic* hit the iceberg."

Aries stared at her, trying to take in the dreadful things she was saying.

"They all died because my fleece was sewn into their clothes?"

"Doomed from the glorious moment they put them on!" trilled Medea, clasping her hands together.

"Ooh! Nearly forgot to tell you the best bit! That dress Rose said you found in the museum? The one that was so snuggly-wuggly you fell asleep on it?"

"Anne Boleyn's?" said Aries, dimly aware that the cage was now moving sideways, sliding along beneath the ceiling, to line up over the tank.

Medea threw back her head and laughed. "Remember the line of golden stitches around the neckline?"

"My fleece?" Aries voice was little more than a whisper.

Medea smiled triumphantly. "That's why you were so drawn to it."

There was a thick popping sound and Aries looked down, suddenly remembering the slurping green goo roiling beneath his cage. He glanced over at Fred, who bounced up and down on the spot, chuckling and turned the winch handle again. The cage juddered and jerked downwards.

"All dead." Aries shook his head sadly. "And the last tuft?"

"Hazel Praline," said Medea, examining her glossy red nails. "I'll be sewing it into the dress she wears to this afternoon's premiere."

Aries hadn't the faintest idea who Hazel Praline was, but he was sure that she was in terrible danger.

And all because of his fleece.

The thought made him feel dreadfully sick. And he might well have thrown up, there and then, had he not been distracted at that moment by the first slimy green tendrils wobbling through the floor bars of the cage and slithering towards his hooves.

"And to think I was resigned to the end of my curses," she sighed. "But you came back, Aries, and thanks to you, I'll soon have the gold of the gods to inject into every sheep I own!" She paused, her eyes widening in delight as the slime turned his golden-brown hooves to the colour of mouldy seaweed. "Imagine all those Golden Fleeces!"

Except Aries was no longer listening.

He was too busy looking down, thinking about teeth, thousands of them, needle-sharp and nibbling away from inside the cold slop that was now rising up his hocks. He closed his eyes to shut out the acid brightness of the room and knew that this was the end: this was the place that his blinding obsession and stupidity had led him, to this one terrible moment.

"Well," said Medea brightly. "Much as I hate leaving a party that's in full swing, I have to go. Can't be late for Hazel!"

Forcing open his eyes Aries met the sorceress's amused gaze. "Wait!"

"What for?" she said impatiently. "The traditional last request?"

There was a muffled thud as the cage settled onto the floor of the tank. Now the deadly bacteria frothed up quickly, enveloping his belly and closing over his back like a sodden blanket.

"You've won," said Aries, blinking back the tears that threatened to roll down his muzzle. He took a deep breath just as a particularly vile-looking bubble burst, squelching clammy green slop into his face. "You'll soon have all the gold you need for your wickedness. Please just let Alex and Rose go home."

Medea tilted her head. For a moment she seemed to consider his request and he felt his heart lift. Then her face grew as hard as marble again.

"Actually," she said lightly, "I'll never let either of them go!" And so saying, she walked out of the room with Fred.

The doors *swooshed* shut behind them and for a moment Aries heard the click of Medea's shoes and rumble of Fred's coarse laughter fade away down the corridor. Then the gruesome sucking noise of the mixture took over, filling his ears with the revolting slurp, burp and dribble of his own unhappy fate.

❋XXIV❋
GREEN FOR GOO

Hazel Praline, being a total star, didn't just stay in a room at The Glorchester Hotel, she and her crew occupied its entire Moonlight Penthouse. This suite of rooms was laid out over the whole top floor of the hotel and included several bedrooms with four-poster beds, a spa with a bubbling hot tub, a kitchen stocked with cookies and jellybeans and a private cinema with just a handful of squashy velvet seats.

Not that Rose was in the mood to appreciate such luxury. Not with her mind squawking like an overcrowded aviary, the shrills of one side fighting with the shrieks of the other about what might have happened to Alex and Aries.

"You're going to be fabulous," said Medea, smiling into Rose's worried face. She linked arms with Rose as Hazel Praline's PA, a flustered young woman with a glossy chestnut bob, gabbling into a silver mobile phone, led them down the penthouse's hallway.

Around them, Rose was aware of Hazel's entourage, who'd stopped chatting amongst the potted ferns and jewel-coloured velvet chairs to watch them pass. She supposed they made a striking pair, she and Medea in their matching black trouser suits and stripy T-shirts, more like a couple of carefree sisters visiting a famous friend than a fashion designer and her new assistant. *Or,* squeaked the clear-thinking part of her brain, *an ancient sorceress and her utterly confused apprentice.*

Snapping her phone shut, Hazel's PA showed them into the penthouse's main living area. This room was the size of a tennis court and dominated by a floor-to-ceiling window that stretched the whole length of the far side of the room. London's skyline twinkled in the morning light beyond the glass and from where she stood Rose could make out the London Eye, Big Ben and Westminster Abbey, standing mistily in the early morning light behind the blue-black Thames.

Around her, yellow satin sofas and curly legged tables stood on soft sapphire blue carpet. Oil paintings in gold frames hung on the walls. Pots of pink roses and lilies stood on almost every surface, their spicy scent filling the air, each bunch displaying cards with messages from fans.

"If you'd like to make yourselves at home," said the PA, plumping up one of several gold cushions on the nearest sofa, "I'll let Miss Praline know you're here. She's rehearsing in the cinema room."

Rose watched as the PA walked towards the pair of tall cream-coloured doors at the far end of the room. A snatch of music wafted out as she opened them and Rose recognised the song as one of Hazel's, with a second identical voice singing along on top. Despite her bubbling anxiety, Rose's heart flipped like a pancake.

"Gorgeous place, isn't it?" said Medea, dropping her sewing satchel on the floor to walk over to a giant aquarium in the corner where glittery silver dollar fish flashed through the water.

Rose gazed around her. Soothed by the luxury and reassured by the normality of the familiar London she could see through the window, the bewitched side of her mind began reassuring her more confidently, its voice like a tendril choking her worries.

Things would be all right, it said. She should simply enjoy the morning. After all, wasn't it already beyond her wildest dreams? Or would she rather be sifting through trays of rhino beetle with her mother? She'd find Alex and Aries again, it promised, and they'd be absolutely fine. After all, if the sorceress were with her now, what could she possibly be doing to them?[29]

"Miss Praline will see you now," said the PA, dragging Rose from her thoughts. "I've some calls to make, so if you need me, I'll be down the hall in the office."

Medea smiled and waited for the PA to leave.

"This is it then!" she said, looking into Rose's eyes. She tucked a lock of Rose's hair gently behind her ear. "Just think what we'll achieve together."

Feeling brighter, Rose picked up the sewing satchel as Medea tapped on the cinema room door.

"Come in!" called a warm Texan voice.

Hearing Hazel's famous drawl coming from the other side of the door, Rose's legs felt wobbly as she followed Medea in.

Hazel Praline, *the* Hazel Praline, stood smiling, dressed in a pink towelling robe, her long blonde hair piled in glossy curls on top of her head. Her movie *Rodeo Love* played on the screen behind her but as Medea and Rose entered she snapped a button on the remote control, freezing a picture – of herself in rhinestone cowboy chaps riding a white horse – on the wall.

---

29. *And yes, I do know that the correct answer to this question is in fact, "Plenty."*

"Haze," said Medea. "This is Rose Pottersby-Weir, my new assistant – and a huge fan of yours."

"How flatterin'!" said Hazel. Pressing more buttons on the control she brought up the overhead lights and picked her way over the empty jellybean boxes scattered in the gap between the seats where she'd been dancing to hug Rose warmly. "'S good to meet ya!"

Rose beamed, hardly able to believe her eyes.

Hazel was just as spectacular in real life as she was in her Saturday morning television series. She seemed to glow with health, her skin golden, her eyes bright, her teeth a perfect white.

"It's amazing to meet you," said Rose honestly.

Hazel smiled whilst Medea examined the beautiful pink dress hanging on a silver clothes rail, wheeled against the wall. She lifted its skirt into the air and released it so that layer upon layer of chiffon floated down, each seeming to hang in the air for a moment like pink mist. Under the overhead lights, the crystals sewn onto its top layer sparkled like raindrops.

"Did you ev' see anythin' so beautiful?" said Hazel.

"It's incredible," agreed Rose breathlessly.

And it was.

Believe me, the way it drifted was more like a wisp of cloud, tinged to a Turkish delight pink by a glorious sunset, than anything as commonplace as a dress.

Medea slipped off her jacket before gently draping the dress over her arm, letting its skirts pool gauzily around her legs.

"Give me about ten minutes to set up," she said. "Then we can make the final alterations."

"Sure thing," said Hazel. She turned to Rose, smiling. "Y'ever had a Texan hot chocolate?"

Rose shook her head.

"Then come with me!" said Hazel.

Hardly able to believe that she was actually here, Rose followed Hazel out into the penthouse's kitchen. Bright and airy, it was twice the size of her mother's kitchen at home and gleamed with marble-topped counters and shiny gadgets.

"Secret's in the cream," said Hazel, opening the giant fridge and taking out a bar of chocolate, some milk and a small china pot of double cream. "It's from my uncle's ranch! Never tour without takin' some with me." She set everything down on the island unit. "You find a bowl to mix it with the milk and I'll grate the chocolate."

Temporarily distracted from her worries, Rose

began stirring the milk into the cream, delighted to be here, to be wearing fabulous clothes, making hot chocolate with a pop star and having fun instead of grubbing around some dusty archive with her mother.

"'S nice to have some company my own age," said Hazel, tapping the grater. Curls of chocolate fell onto the plate below.

Rose smiled, thinking exactly the same thing. "I suppose it must be hard, travelling so much of the time?"

"It is," said Hazel. "I mean, it's excitin', an' I know I'm lucky. But when we're tourin', Daddy's so busy fixin' ev'thin' we hardly see each other. And even though there's loadsa people around, it can be real lonely sometimes."

Rose sighed. "I know what you mean."

"You do?"

Whilst Hazel heated up the milk, cream and chocolate on the huge stove, Rose warmed two red china mugs and told the star about her father's disastrous expedition and how her mother had buried herself in work at one big museum after another ever since he'd disappeared. It was funny, Rose thought, the problems they shared, even though their lives couldn't be more different.

Suddenly the girls heard a rapid frothing noise.

"The milk!" they shouted together.

Hazel grabbed the pan from the stove and poured the steaming chocolate into the waiting mugs before flipping the lid off the cream and adding another hefty dollop to each.

"And finally!" she smiled, plucking a silver shaker off the counter to sprinkle multicoloured sugar crystals over the top.

Rose beamed. She'd never seen hot chocolate so huge and sparkly and crazy-looking. She lifted her mug and took a sip. Or so delicious.

"Like it?" said Hazel, setting hers down and noticing a blob of sugar-speckled cream on the tip of her neat nose. She looked at it cross-eyed. "Like my new image?"

The two girls giggled together.

Hearing Medea calling her, Hazel rolled her eyes and swiped the cream from her nose. "Duty calls!"

Together they walked back into the living room. Medea stepped aside for Hazel to slip into the cinema room and looked at Rose.

"I don't want to be disturbed by anyone whilst I'm doing this," she said. "So, please stay out here and take any messages. Okay?"

Rose looked up from spooning the cream from her hot chocolate and nodded happily. Above her the chandeliers scattered rainbow light and she sat down on a squashy sofa thinking, as Medea closed the door behind her, that she might just love this job.

Could this really be her life from now on? Working with Medea in a totally amazing job? *And* learning magic. A magic that would transform her own life in just the same way? A magic that might help her find her father? A fresh surge of optimism electrified her from her toes to the top of her head.

Which was when she noticed something white and gleaming on the floor. Long and polished, it wasn't until she'd picked it up from the carpet that she noticed the eyehole at the end and realised it was a needle. It felt warm, like porcelain, and looked ancient. For a moment she wondered what to do. She turned it over in her fingers. Clearly, it must have fallen from Medea's bag when she dropped it onto the floor. She bit her lip. The needle looked special and she could imagine Medea's frustration at not finding it, caught mid-adjustment, as Hazel stood for her alterations, the dress pinned, whilst the sorceress cast hopelessly about for the missing needle. Standing up, she looked at the closed door. Medea had said she hadn't wanted any disturbances. But surely that didn't include her. Not when she had something that was probably really important to her. After all, she reminded herself, she was Medea's assistant.

Making her decision, she strode briskly over to the cinema room door and walked in.

And froze.

Hazel wasn't standing for her alterations. She wasn't standing at all. She was floating, actually floating, as though invisibly suspended in mid-air, a metre above the floor. Rose felt a small squeal die on her lips as she watched the young singer, just hanging there, her arms outstretched, the gorgeous pink dress rippling around her body. For a moment, Rose thought she looked like an angel. Or at least she would have, if she didn't have her head thrown backwards, and her eyes staring glassily at the ceiling.

Beneath her, Medea squatted menacingly on the floor, muttering in hisses, her back hunched and uneven between her knees, her right arm little more than a blur as she sewed furiously around the hem of the dress, stitching in something that glittered like gold in the light beam from the projector.

Stepping silently backwards out of the room, Rose's attention was caught by a flicker on the screen behind Hazel. A film was playing but it wasn't Hazel's. It was a clip of what appeared to be a funeral procession. Two black horses, with pink plumes in the crown pieces of their bridles, filled the screen, drawing a glass hearse behind them. A hearse that carried a small pink coffin.

Horrified, Rose crashed back against the door. Startled, Medea spun round as quick as a spider, and stared at her.

"Rose," she soothed, her voice perfectly calm. "I asked you to wait outside."

Suddenly a burst of music exploded from the speakers and when Rose looked up, the movie was playing again whilst Hazel herself was standing on the floor, smiling at her.

She held out the skirt of her dress out and twirled like a model. "What d'you think, Rose?"

Rose stared, feeling as though her insides had turned to ice and that if she moved she might crack and fall into pieces. Her feet wanted to turn and run, sprint out of the living room, down the hallway and never come near this place again. Her fingers trembled against the door frame as Hazel waited for her answer.

Meanwhile, down in the horribly white room, Aries' horns and ears had vanished beneath the sludge, leaving only his upturned face exposed and bobbing like a chunk of white bread in a bowl of revolting green soup.

"Goodbye cruel gods!" he muttered flatly.

Being an ancient Greek it was traditional to depart in a classical fashion, which meant a flowery death speech. Not having had time to compose one of his own, Aries tried to remember **Hector**'s speech at the battle of Troy. Just before Achilles stabbed him with his spear.

Except that his heart wasn't in it.

Because, quite frankly, when you're certain you've lost your best friend and are up to your chin in something green and toothy, you're just not in the mood for fancy words.

He stared down.

Even the tank of bacteria wasn't listening. Having stopped bubbling altogether, it now lay as still as a swamp.

Then he heard a voice.

"Is that the only bit of the speech you know?" it said.

Aries jerked his head up. It sounded like Alex's voice and, feeling his heart leap, he scanned the room as the voice went on.

"The next bit goes, 'For Zeus and Athena have willed it.'"

Aries twisted round to look but the room remained gloomily empty. Freshly disappointed, he decided that the bacteria must be busy after all. They'd simply taken a short cut down his ears and chosen to start their dinner party with his brain cells, which explained why he was hearing voices.

"Oh, Alex," he sighed to himself. "Even at my darkest moment, it's your voice I hear."

"That's because I'm here, you great steaming dollop," answered the voice.

Flinging his head up a second time, Aries squealed with delight as Alex appeared in the doorway of the storeroom.

"Alex!"

Aries bounced madly in the mixture – not easy in a halter and floor-stirrups combo, but spectacular in terms of the froth it generates – as Alex hurried over. Plunging his arms into the goo, he laced his arms through the cage bars and wrapped them around Aries' neck.

"I've missed you, too!" he laughed as the splatter dribbled down his face. "We tried to free you last night but she'd put some enchantment on the cellar door. We had to wait until now. Oh, I'm so glad to see you!"

A moment later he drew back, his face pale and anxious (and a little bit green). Laying a hand on the ram's mottled brow he softened his voice. "I'm sorry,

Aries," he said. "I don't know how to say this... But, your fleece, it's all gone."

"Oh, Alex!" gushed Aries. "I already know!"

"You do?" said Alex, astonished to see that Aries' excitement hadn't diminished at all.

"And I'm the one who should be sorry," said Aries. "Sorry for all those years I spent pining after it. I've been so stupid." He sighed. "Proud and foolish. It doesn't mean as much to me as..." Aries paused, feeling his face grow pink, "well, other things. I'm sorry I dragged you back to Earth, back here to this place. Can you forgive me?"

"But it means so much to you," said Alex.

Aries shook his head. "Meant," he corrected. "Once—"

Aries stopped. Because what appeared to be a weed-covered loofah was now rising from the green liquid around him.

"Have you two quite finissshed?" hissed the loofah, spitting out a straw.

Aries looked questioningly at Alex.

"It's Hex," said Alex. "Remember him?"

Aries brought his lips up to the cage bars, closer to Alex's ear. "But he's one of hers," he whispered.

"Not any more," snapped Hex. The snake's eyes glittered indignantly behind the mask of dripping goo. "No, now I've been promoted to hiding in cake mixture—"

Aries' ears flew up. "Cake mixture?" he said and licked some off his muzzle. He took a second mouthful. "It's delicious!"

Alex rolled his eyes. "Last night, whilst Fred wandered around the garden looking for Hex and Pandemic guarded Rose upstairs—"

"Rose?" demanded Aries, between mouthfuls. "Is she all right?"

"For the moment," hissed Hex.

"Go on," urged Aries.

"Hex told me what Medea had planned for you," said Alex. "We tipped the real gold bugs down the drain and refilled the tank with what we could find in the kitchen. Flour, water, eggs and butter, anything that made it lumpy and thick and then loads of mashed cabbage and sprouts to make it green."

"But the bubbling?" said Aries.

"Hex," said Alex. "He hid at the bottom of the tank and spun round to make it churn."

Aries looked at the mamba. "What about the gold ore turning to stones?"

"Easssy," replied Hex. "The mistresss lovesss the way the bacteria do that. I knew ssshe'd have to ssshow off, ssso I took a tail full of plain rocksss with me."

"Oooh!" squealed Aries. "I could kiss you!"

"I'd rather you didn't," said Hex coolly and slithered hastily out of the tank. He lowered himself onto the white floor and slid towards the winch, leaving a green smear in his wake. "In fact, if you two are quite finissshed with the big sssoppy reunion, maybe we could think about getting out of here?"

Even though boys aren't as strong as Cyclopes and mambas have a tendency to accidentally wind themselves around rope winches only to spool out giddily, ten grunting, groaning and griping minutes later, Aries was free. And, having told Alex all about what Medea had used the fleece for, the boy was now thinking hard.

"I should have worked out what she was up to," said Alex, as Hex shot out into the corridor, tasting the air for the scent of Cyclops and worse, his basket. "I mean, it's what the Scroll was trying to tell us all along, wasn't it? 'Her power's in the stitches.' Remember?"

"Power's in the stitches, my hoof," muttered Aries, shaking his head and sending a spray of green into the air. "The Scroll's answers were fuzzier than a statue in Athenian fog. You should have let me eat it."

"All clear!" muttered Hex, bolting down the corridor like a grey-green lightning streak.

Alex and Aries hurried after him out of the room.

"Imagine all the hurt she's caused," said Alex crossly, now breaking into a jog to keep up with Hex who whipped over the stony floor ahead. "All those people she killed."

"And Hazel's next," wheezed Aries. "Whoever she is."

"Hex!" shouted Alex. "Who's Hazel?"

"Ssssh! Keep your voice down!" hissed Hex, coiling back at them. "Ssshe's a sssinger and her film premiere'sss thisss afternoon. Ssshe's going to sssing a few sssongs before they ssshow it. Medea will have taken Rossse there."

He flicked his tail and slithered on.

"So, how does Medea intend to kill her?" cried Alex in a loud whisper.

"No idea," replied Hex, vanishing around the next corner. "And neither hasss ssshe. Ssshe never knowssssss how the curssse will work. Ssshot, ssstabbed, hanged, beheaded, asssssssassssssinated," he shuddered, "finding out isss all part of the fun for her."

Alex ran after him and turning the corner recognised the same dreary passageway that Medea had led them down the day before. The one that led to the villa's entrance hall.

And out!

His heart soared. They were almost free!

Which was when he realised that Aries wasn't behind him any more.

❊XXV❊
WHAM! BAM! THANK YOU, RAM!

Well, whilst they're retracing their steps and slithers, I can tell you that Aries had turned and doubled-back to the sheep prison. Now, lowering his head, he aimed his horns at the middle of the locked door and leaped, hurling his huge bulk against it. There was a crunch as the wood cobwebbed into splits beneath his bony brow. Snorting furiously, he stepped back and threw himself at the door a second time. Now it gave way, exploding in shards of flying wood that disappeared into the gloom beyond as he skidded through the hole to a halt at the top of the stairs.

Startled, the sheep stared up at him, like a display of woolly statues[30]. Only Olaf moved, bustling past the others to the edge of the stall. Then, stepping up

---

30. *Actually, sheep are very good at doing this. Just try going "Yoo hoo!" over the fence to a field of them next time you're in the country and you'll see just what I mean.*

onto its lowest bar he raised his head and regarded Aries with eyes as round as cattle cakes.

"Golden ram, you have made of da escape?" he said in disbelief as Aries clattered down the stairs, scattering scraps of wood behind him. "Why den come you here?"

"Because no sheep should be kept away from the fields!" said Aries. "I've come to set everyone free!"

The word galvanised the sheep like a lightning storm. Suddenly alert, they bobbed and jostled, pushing against each other, eager for a better view of Aries as he turned towards Martha's and Toby's stall.

The hefty bolt on its gate reminded him of the one on the door of the harpies' enclosure, and he'd certainly seen Alex open that often enough to know what to do. Taking it in his mouth, he slammed it back. For a moment everyone held his or her breath as Toby stepped forwards and nudged open the gate before wobbling out on long gangly legs, beaming.

At which the cellar erupted into a cacophony of bleats and shrieks of delight. Horns crashed against bars. Hooves clattered against the stone floor. Everywhere, the sheep bounced up and down like woolly seesaws, their tails spinning with delight.

For a moment, Aries stood. Glowing inside, he felt the sort of happiness that he hadn't known for years, not since he'd worn his fleece.

Turning to Olaf's stall he was surprised to see a look of admiration on the Icelandic's face. He paused, watching as from the opposite side of the bars, Olaf lowered his horns slowly, which in sheep-speak means an apology.

"Misjudge you I did, golden ram," he said over the din. "And sorry I am."

Aries lowered his head in response, which is sheep for 'thank you' and 'you did have a point' and 'let's put it all behind us' and lots of other things like that. However, as I've told you before, this story doesn't have time for sloppy bits and standing around going, "Ooh, bless!" and neither do we.

A moment later Aries had released Olaf and the two of them, together with Martha, started freeing everyone else. Sheep surged out of stalls and milled together in a flossy tide, nuzzling relatives and friends, brushing horns and flanks amiably.

Of course, needless to say, in all this sheepy excitement, no one noticed Alex and Hex step through the broken door into the cellar.

Alex stopped and stared down, surprised.

And small wonder.

After all, he knew that the Aries of only a few days ago wouldn't even have stopped long enough to smile at an ordinary sheep, never mind risk his own safe escape for them. He smiled in surprise.

Hex didn't.

Not that snakes tend to smile very much anyway, but as he quickly unwrapped himself from Alex's neck and lunged out onto the banister, his brow was furrowed with worry as he scanned the merriment below. And much as I hate to be a spoilsport, he did have a point. After all, they were still in a sorceress's house, weren't they?

"Will you lot be quiet!" he hissed, whizzing towards them like a long, thin and rather rubbery bobsleigh.

Except that since no one could hear him, no one did what he asked.

Instead, spotting the upturned tin bath of the night before, Aries stamped on it with all four hooves, flattening it into a tray. He booted it over the floor so that it rattled wildly. Delighted, the others copied, snapping paddles in two and butting the dark machines hanging on the walls before sweeping the counters clear with their horns, sending electrodes and pots of oily grey liquids spinning to the floor.

"I sssaid ssstop!" yelled Hex, looping his tail around the banister and swinging his body out over their heads.

Finally a few of the sheep saw him and froze, shocked to see the sorceress's familiar back amongst them. Backing away, they bumped into the others, and a nervous hush fell over the herd.

Seeing the sheep's faces, not to mention hearing the splash of nervous wee on the floor, Alex hurried down and raised his hands to calm the sheep.

"Hex is with us now," he explained quickly, lifting the snake from the banister and wrapping him around his neck again. "And he's right. This place gives me the creeps. Come on!"

Now, it's never easy to hurry harried sheep up a staircase, but with a mixture of coaxing, flank-patting and hoicking the most reluctant by their horns, Alex ushered the flock out of the cellar and drove them clattering back down the underground passage towards the main house.

Aries ran with Alex at the back. "Where shall we take them?"

Before Alex could answer, Hex swung down, and bouncing against Alex's chest, frowned at Aries. "You didn't consssider that before you let them all out?" hissed Hex, his eyes glittering.

"I knew Alex would come up with something," said Aries loyally.

Alex frowned. "Hex, is there safe grazing near here?" he said.

"In central London?" Hex's mouth bunched up in disbelief. "There'sss a park at the end of the road. We'll herd them there."

"Will they be safe?"

Hex nodded. "Don't worry. The park keeper will call the police the minute a hoof touches his grassss."

And he was absolutely right because this particular park keeper prided himself on his prize-winning Californian roses, blooms that had already suffered one attack of vandalism that week leaving three holes, littered with razor-edged feathers and goat fur, where his Belles of Los Angeles used to grow.

Excited bleating bounced off the walls as the sheep surged ahead, their hooves rattling over the flagstones to freedom. Which was rather unfortunate since such a sheepy rumpus of delight made it quite impossible to hear anything else like, for example, the unpleasant *clacketty-slapping* sound now echoing from the other direction.

✣XXVI✣
FLOCK, SHOCK AND PERIL

Up ahead the first few sheep vanished through the doorway into the garden room. Yet no sooner had they disappeared from sight than their woolly rumps reappeared, reversing back into the passage again and crashing into the other in a muffle of shrieks and insults.

Hex lifted his head like a scaly periscope. "I don't like the look of thisss," he muttered ominously.

Neither did Alex. To be honest he didn't much like the look of Hex's face either. Drained of its steely shimmer it now looked as if the snake had been dipped in flour. So it was with a rising sense of dread that he began wading through the sea of fuzzy backs, aware that the bleating was dying away around him as a cold fear rippled over the flock.

In the new silence, a different sound became audible. Thumping, dull and regular, and it was coming from the direction of the garden.

Hex gulped.

Pushing past the last few sheep, Alex stepped into the garden room, quickly edged around the wall and, biting his lip, peeped through the window.

And gulped too.

The garden heaved with mannequins. No longer posed and rigid to show off the sorceress's clothes, they were marching from side to side in long, horrifying rows. Alex felt the breath almost stop inside his chest, watching as they turned in unison and began stamping in the other direction, as jerky as robots. They were everywhere – lining the high garden walls, blocking the gate, encircling the swimming pool — filling every patch of lawn like a regiment of eerie sentries and completely obstructing their escape route.

A sudden whoop made Alex jump. Turning his head, he saw Fred skipping joyfully from the direction of the horrible temple-styled crypt, waving his chubby arms over his head as he wove through the shifting rows.

"What is it?" said Aries, clopping over to join them.

Alex looked back at Aries. Trying not to make a noise, the ram was tippyhoofing, hunched down and knock-kneed, across the flagstones, and if

Alex hadn't been so leaden with fear he might have laughed.

"What it isss," said Hex acidly, "isss your fault!" He dangled down from Alex's neck and pressed his cold grey snout against Aries' muzzle. "All that racket you made in the cellar! Fred mussst have heard you. He'sss only gone and triggered Mistress'sss enchanted mannequinsss!"

"Enchanted?" stammered Alex, as Fred skipped over to the one dressed in Nelson's clothes, standing a couple of lines back, towing a small, wheeled cannon. He remembered creeping past him last night. "You didn't mention that before!"

"I didn't like to," muttered Hex, wrapping himself around the boy's neck again. "We had enough to worry about trying to free muttonbrain. But the fact isss that Mistressss hasss alwaysss usssed them asss her sssecurity sssystem. When she goesss out she givesss her ssstaff the passssword."

Alex, Aries and Hex watched as the Cyclops leaned up against Nelson and tucked his right arm into his jacket to copy the Admiral. Looking up at him, his rubbery face broke into a clownish grin, revealing two stumpy grey teeth. At which the Admiral raised his lace-cuffed hand above his head and stuck his nose in the air.

"England expects every mannequin to do its duty!" he cried in a snooty English accent.

Aries frowned and looked up at Hex. "Who does he think he is?"

"Britain'sss greatessst naval hero," snipped Hex. "But then, they all think they're sssomeone."

Alex stared at him dumbfounded. "They do?"

"The mistressss wasss lonely," explained Hex. "Giving each one the perssssonality of the people whossse clothesss they wear made for plenty of guesssts for her Christmasss cocktail partiesss and soireesss on gloomy Tuesssday afternoonsss."

Which explained Marie Antoinette's dainty steps, Alex now supposed, and the way Captain Smith was wheeling around with a telescope to his eye. He shivered, aware that every mannequin was a souvenir of someone's horrible death.

"Ssstatues, too," muttered Hex, jabbing his head towards the statue of the girl with the rose basket. Who was, at that moment, stepping down from her plinth, her chiselled features twitching into a sneer. "Though they were more for garden partiesss," he added quietly.

Alex bit his lip, looking away from the stone girl's sneer to the other side of the lawn, feeling his stomach lurch to see that the dolphin statue had begun moving too, flapping its flippers and snapping its bottlenose like garden shears.

"What are we going to do?" said Aries.

Behind them, the sheep spilled out into the room behind them, bleating and turning in terrified circles, knocking over giant pots of dahlias and paddling in the water.

"I'll have to think," said Alex.

"Think?" muttered Aries. "I'm not sure we have time for that!"

Meanwhile, the Cyclops made three big jumps through gaps in the moving rows to stand in front of Marie Antoinette.

"Left left, right!" he cried gleefully, sidestepping as she swished past.

She glanced down and wrinkled her nose at his salute.

Undeterred, he clicked his heels.

"Fred Fred's Army!" he announced and threw his bottom out in a deep clumsy bow.

Army? Alex felt his mind whirring. He stepped back from the window, blinking, as the queen plucked a pomander of flowers from her drawstring bag and held it to her nose.

"That's it!" he burst out.

"Balls of flowers?" said Aries. Bemused, he

looked up at Alex's suddenly bright face.

"No!" Alex turned away into the chaos of sheep behind them. "An *army*, of course! Don't you see? It's the only way to beat that lot!"

"You don't sssay?" said Hex, his eyes as round as ball bearings. "Well, jussst hold on while I sssee if I can find one for hire in the phone book!"

Except that Alex wasn't listening. He was too busy, pacing through the milling sheep, thinking.

"Listen to me!" he said.

But the sheep stumbled on, stupefied by fear.

Slamming his foot down on the floor he tried again. "I said *everyone*!" he demanded.

Shocked by his tone, the sheep bolted upright and turned to face him. Half-chewed dahlias fell out of mouths onto the floor.

"Right, we've got a job to do here," said Alex firmly. "And every one of you will play your part. You, with the ringlets," he said, pointing to three silky Wensleydales, "line up, over here, now!" The sheep shuffled grimly across the room, and stood shoulder-to-shoulder, flanks trembling. "Next, you four with the brown fleeces! Well, come on!"

Quickly, Alex arranged the seven sheep into a row before calling for seven more. Muttering nervously amongst themselves, the sheep did what he asked.

Edging a rather arthritic Bighorn onto the end of the next row, he looked up, sweating.

"Olaf and Martha!" he said. "I need you two to check the cellar for anyone who's run back. Aries, chivvy the others out of the passageway."

And whilst everyone is so busy, I'll explain.

There aren't many moments in life where being a zookeeper *and* the son of an ancient Greek soldier is a useful combination, but this was definitely one of them.

Being a zookeeper meant that Alex knew that sheep simply scattered in panic unless a shepherd took control, and that what one did, they'd all copy[31].

Being a soldier's son he remembered his father telling him of how he'd arranged his men into fighting units, or phalanxes, with the men in tight rows and those around the outside holding up their shields to protect the group. As long as the men stayed together, they could flatten anything in their path. Not that Alex had soldiers, of course, or anything as useful as shields. But he did have sheep's bottoms. And, on the upside, he had sixty-six of them, each one attached to a powerful kick.

---

31. *He also knew they were likely to eat your washing if you left it out on rocks to dry, but that isn't relevant here.*

"You are the first phalanx," he said to the quivery bottoms and upturned faces of the three rows of sheep organised in front of him. "You at the front, kick on my command. You in the middle, guide the group. You at the back, slam any attacks to the rear!"

Clever, eh?

And I suppose if there was anything lucky about this dreadful situation, it was that wealthy sorceresses have big houses. I mean, could you dragoon sixty-odd sheep in the front room of your house? Well, quite. But five minutes later, Alex had built two more phalanxes. Aries and Olaf stood either side of him, whilst, despite his squeaky protests of being tough enough to fight, Toby had been bundled under an ornate bench and barricaded by cushions.

"Phalanx one, you charge left towards the olive trees," said Alex, walking around the groups of sheep, inspecting their lines. "Phalanx two, you charge right towards the pool. Phalanx three, in front of me and straight up the middle. Ready?"

Despite their nervousness, the sheep were calmer now, and looked up at him with bright eager eyes, poised and alert, like a flock guided by a sheepdog.

"On my command, we march! Remember that you absolutely must stay together!" he instructed, only just ignoring the sensible voice in his mind that pointed out that sheep rarely did, but scattered instead like flossy confetti. "One sheep on its own can be grabbed. Hold fast, and we'll crush them."

He looked over at Aries and Olaf. "The doors!"

Quickly, each ram took hold of a door and folded it back on itself, opening up the wall of the room to the garden and the colonnade of pillars beyond.

Alex took a deep breath, feeling his heart pounding. After all, it's hard to abandon a lifetime of sensible thinking when you're in a terrible situation, and suddenly he felt grimly certain that his idea was crazy, the sort of half-baked notion that Aries would come up with. Out of habit he quickly guessed at their chance of success. But, on discovering his answer to be barely more than zero, he stopped. After all, there were no other options. This was their only chance to get out, to find Rose and Hazel.

It had to work.

On hearing the swoosh of doors, Fred, who'd been busy peering down the mouth of Nelson's cannon, shot upright and stared, his eye goggling in astonishment.

"Attention!" he shrieked.

Around him, the mannequins stopped, spun towards the house and regarded it with eyes as dead as buttons. For a moment the two strange armies stood and faced one another. Silk skirts and feathered headdresses rustled in the breeze.

"March!" cried Alex.

Slowly, the sheep began to move in their appointed directions. Guided by the sheep in the middle rows, they wobbled like woolly tanks over the lawn, presenting their bottoms to the enemy.

"*Mon Dieu!*" squealed Marie Antoinette, fluttering her fingers to her face, appalled at the view.

Around her the mannequins sniggered, a sound like plastic boxes being scrunched.

"Attack, attack!" yelled Fred, leaping up onto the funnel of the cannon.

Now the mannequins lurched forwards. Boots creaked and spurs jangled. Bangles clattered down moulded arms. Old silk rustled like brown paper. In their midst, Fred rose, frowning like a furious troll, riding on the cannon.

"Take aim!" he cried.

The mannequins raised their arms, brandishing spears and swords, rifles, nets and ice axes. Not to mention some rather vicious-looking handbags.

Behind the third phalanx, Alex reached down, touching Olaf and Aries' horns, who walked either side.

"Everyone keep marching!" he commanded.

The sheep pushed on as the mannequins closed in, looming over the blocks of sheep. Shivering, Alex met the blank eyes of a mannequin dressed in a cream kaftan, a golden headdress twinkling on her black bobbed wig. We'd have recognised her as Cleopatra. Alex didn't. He only recognised her as dangerous and rather dusty. But her row was close now. And closer. Close enough to smell the must on antique clothes. Close enough to touch. Close enough to…

"Kick!" roared Alex.

Like a reflex, the front row of every phalanx bucked and kicked out hard. Shrieks and squeals tore through the garden as hooves made contact with plastic, sending heads and arms and legs spinning into the air to scatter in the flower beds.

Mindless as plastic zombies, the next row of mannequins stepped forwards.

"Kick!" commanded Alex.

Again, the outside sheep tipped forwards, slamming the figures in front of them. The garden exploded in another cacophony of screams and crumpling plastic. Over by the swimming pool, Marilyn Monroe doubled over. Gasping through pouted lips, she pitched into the water in a flutter of white skirt. Over by the olive trees, a queen's head rolled away through the trees, striking out four Arctic explorers and a man in puffball trousers.

Alex turned back and came eye to, well, eye, with Fred.

"Kick!" he commanded.

This time, the hooves of the third phalanx slammed Nelson over backwards, snapping him in two over his cannon. From the grass, the Admiral waved his good arm helplessly in the air, bewildered by falling plastic body parts.

"Nelly Nelly!" roared Fred. He leaped down off the cannon and poked the Admiral's crumpled head. Looking up, he glared at Alex. Slowly he unfastened Nelson's starburst medal and pinned it to his own chest.

"Fred Fred kill Alex and scummy scummy woollies!"

Smiling nastily[32], he looked at the boy and reached into his pocket, drawing out a long match. He dragged it down the side of the cannon and lit the fuse.

"Oh no you don't!" shouted Alex.

---

32. *His unpleasant smile wasn't down to his mood, although that was also rather vile. No, it was simply that even the bonniest smile looks horrible on a Cyclops's lumpy face.*

Leaping around the side of the phalanx, he threw his weight behind the the breech[33] of the cannon and spun it round to face the lines of approaching mannequins. There was a resounding boom as the cannon ball tore through them and when the black cloud of smoke cleared, Alex saw twenty or more of them, smashed to pieces, jerking on the grass.

His heart soared.

The plan was working!

"What what?" squealed Fred.

Stumbling towards Alex, soot-faced and dazed from the cannon blast, he flung out his arms to grab him. At which Aries exchanged a rapid glance with Olaf and together they charged, each hooking a horn each through Fred's belt to carry him over to the snapping dolphin. With a single coordinated toss of their heads, they launched the Cyclops into the dolphin's mouth. Squeaking with delight, the dolphin began swinging him from side to side, boxing the Cyclops's ears with his stone flippers and

---

33. Since Nelson's mannequin has seen better days, it's lucky I am
a technical expert and can tell you that a cannon's breech is its
round bottom, not its rumbly-rumbly-here-comes-the-cannon-
ball-wheee end.

making a sound like a cauliflower being repeatedly thumped.

"Well done!" shouted Alex.

He scanned the garden to see that more than half of the mannequins now lay groaning on the lawn.

Commanding the sheep to kick again, Alex glanced over at the gate to see three mannequins guarding it wearing padded orange suits, what appeared to be fishbowls on their heads and silver boots, who we'd recognise to be astronauts.

As the squeals of plastic rang through the garden again, Alex gently unwound the snake from his shoulders.

"Hex," he said. "I need you to open those gates."

The snake nodded and slithered through the stomping feet to the safety of the tulip borders that lined the drive to the gate. In a flash of silver, he was gone and Alex turned back to the fray, hoping the snake would be all right. After all, venom has no effect on a mannequin and for once in his snakey life, Hex was vulnerable.

Again and again, the sheep phalanxes bucked and moved forwards. Olaf and Aries joined the front of the third phalanx, adding their formidable kicks to the others, bleating furiously.

Alex laughed as a blizzard of snow-booted legs

fell around him. It was going to be all right.

Which was when he heard a yelp, and, panicked, he turned to see one of the spacemen pointing to something, or rather someone, in the bushes.

"Aries," he shouted. "Hex needs help!"

Peeling away from the group, Aries saw all three spacemen peering into the border. One of them twitched his silver-gloved fingers, reaching for the small hammer on his belt as he bent down for a closer look. Seconds later Aries' head made contact with the shiny target and launched the rocket man into a new orbit. Then, swinging round, he gave the other two their own personal 'lift-offs' over the wall.

Whereupon Hex shot up the gatepost, nodded his thanks to Aries and began tapping buttons with his nose.

Aries turned back, ready to attack again and stopped.

Because there wasn't a single mannequin standing.

Instead, the lawn looked like a massacre in a doll factory. Every patch of grass was strewn with crumpled body parts. Fingers fluttered uselessly. Legs kicked their feet in the air. Wigs floated in the swimming pool like furry water lilies.

"We did it!" yelled Alex.

He leaped up and punched the air.

All at once, the sheep surged round him, cheering. They stamped their hooves and licked him with rough tongues, bustling against him in delight. Aries galloped back to Olaf and the rams knocked horns in a victory clash. And Hex, swaying and curling in a mamba-samba, rode the top of the ironwork gate as it slowly opened to freedom.

As Alex looked over the scene of triumph, he was oddly reminded of his father at **the Battle of Marathon** and of how he'd beaten thousands of Persians with only a few hundred Greeks. And although it was true that the Athenians hadn't celebrated by eating roses, rolling around on clumps of dahlias and jumping up and down on plastic body parts, Alex finally knew how his father must have felt to fight even when logic told him the odds were against him – to fight and win.

A moment later he'd scooped Toby up from the garden room and walked back out into the sunshine.

Aries trotted up to him, wreathed in smiles.

"Well done, Alex!" he said. He looked up into the boy's face and nudged him gently in the ribs. "Alexander the Great!" he added.

Alex smiled, and for once he didn't even feel silly at blushing because inside he was glowing with pride.

But there was no time to lose.

Stepping deftly over the muddle of body parts he led the flock to the gate and lifted up his arm for Hex to slither down.

The open road lay ahead of them.

Alex turned and looked into Hex's sparkling eyes. "Which way?"

❖XXVII❖
SHOWSTOPPER!

Medea stood draped in the darkness of the wings of the Leicester Square Luxe, watching Hazel rehearse her welcome speech one last time. The stage in front of the cinema screen had been dressed to look like a rodeo with stacks of hay bales, hung ropes and saddles. Dwarfed by a neon sign of a silhouetted rider on a bucking bronco, and talking in whispers to the closed theatre curtains, the young singer looked deliciously vulnerable and just thinking about what was to happen later on released a swarm of butterflies [34] behind Medea's ribs. As usual she had no idea of how her curse would work or how Hazel would actually die, but as she looked around the stage, her mind popped with exquisite possibilities.

That tangle of electrical cables looped along the front of the stage looked promising. So did the

---

34. Or, in her case, death's-head moths.

buckets of water ready for the star's bouquets, which had been left far too close to the panel of lighting controls. Overhead, a galaxy of glittering mirrors twisted on wires, ready to be spotlit and send splashes of light dancing around the stage, while just in front of that gloriously deep drop into the orchestra pit, the stage shone, smooth and slippery. A cold tingle of pleasure wrapped itself around the sorceress's heart like an octopus tentacle and she clasped her hands gleefully to her chest, knowing that the young star's performance would be truly unforgettable.

Unforgettable was one word that Rose might have used to describe her day.

However, it wouldn't have been top of her list. Words like unbelievable, mind-twisting and heart-stoppingly terrifying[35] would all have been much higher up.

After bursting in on Medea and Hazel that morning, Rose felt sure that she would be in serious trouble. And yet, the sorceress had carried on as if nothing had happened, simply promising Rose a 'little chat' over their post-show meal together, all about how important it was to follow her instructions.

---

35. *All right, I know, that's three words.*

Rose shivered.

Perhaps the sorceress intended to convince her that she'd imagined the whole thing?

Or, bewitch her into forgetting anything *inconvenient*?

Either way, Rose didn't intend to stick around to find out. But for Hazel she wouldn't even be sitting in the theatre now. Yet despite the clammy fear that had made her skin freeze back at the hotel, she'd known that she couldn't simply abandon her new friend to whatever horrible fate Medea had planned. And even if she'd felt like running away, she couldn't have, because she'd been immediately escorted out of the hotel here by Pandemic, which was why she was now here, pinned down by his bony elbow, in one of the red velvet seats of the VIP section.

Around her, famous actors chatted with pop stars, laughing and hugging each other. People that she'd only ever seen in magazines and on television were standing right in front of her. But Rose didn't feel remotely star-struck. Instead, as Hazel's band took their places in the orchestra pit, all she felt was a clawing sicklike fear in the pit of her stomach, knowing that something horrible was going to happen.

Clutching the arms of her cinema seat, her mind flicked back to the terrible image of the pink coffin she'd seen projected behind the singer on the wall at the hotel. And of Medea crouched at the singer's feet, frantically stitching. Something about the pink dress, her mind insisted, something about that wonderful dress would harm Hazel.

Hazel's three bodyguards, each dressed in black suits and pink cummerbunds, lined up in front of the stage and for one ridiculous, fleeting moment Rose wondered whether she ought to just go up there and tell them straight. She looked from one to the other, at their stern, unsmiling faces and wondered which man might be most likely to listen. The first, thickset and muscled, with his big bumpy nose that looked like a clump of broccoli? The next, tall and lean, with a military buzz cut? Or the last? With his broad shoulders, thin neck and bald head, he looked like a skittle. And a bad-tempered one, at that.

"Excuse me," she imagined herself saying. "I have to tell you that Hazel's dress is dangerous." She sank back in her seat and sighed heavily. Even to her, it sounded completely nuts.

Sinking further still into her whirl of worry she didn't notice the lights dimming above her, or the curtains swish back. In fact, it was only when Hazel's band started to play the opening bars of the film's title song and everyone around her began clapping that she looked up to see Steven Speedbug, the film's director, striding across the stage. And, as he stopped to take a bow, the altogether more shadowy figure stalking up the aisle.

A moment later Medea took the seat beside her.

There are many wonderful sights in our capital city of London but a flock of sheep hurtling behind a boy draped in a venomous snake down Piccadilly is not traditionally one of them. However, far too excited to settle for a lunch of even the juiciest roses, the sheep had insisted on coming with Alex and Aries to help find Rose and save Hazel. Knowing that the best chance they had to do this was to disrupt and stop the show, Alex had quickly come up with a plan, a simple one: act like sheep and don't talk. Now, with Hex whispering in Alex's ear like a GPS[36], they surged as a furious grey tide through the centre of town.

Office workers stared open-mouthed from their glass-fronted buildings as the flock poured over traffic islands and spilled across pavements, bringing buses to wheezing standstills and sending shoppers sprinting down stairwells to the Underground.

---

36. *Global positioning snake.*

With a deafening cacophony of blaring horns and sheep-related insults rising behind them, the sheep streamed past the swanky Ritz Hotel, snatching mouthfuls of red geraniums from its window boxes and alarming diners who dropped teacups on the black-and-white tiles floor of the Palm Court. They thundered on past the jewellers, causing a goldsmith to bite into a dazzling tiara instead of his custard cream biscuit, whilst at Fortnum & Mason's the manager did a spectacular war dance in his highly polished shoes, just thinking about all that dung on his prestigious entrance carpet.

On an unstoppable river of hooves, snorts and woolly bottoms, the sheep pounded past the statue of Eros, beneath the flashing neon advertisements wrapped around the tall buildings of Piccadilly Circus and finally swung towards Leicester Square.

"There it isss!" shouted Hex.

Alex looked to see a tall cream-stone building with an ornate ironwork canopy above which the word 'LUXE' was spelt out in pink light bulbs. Huge banners of a pretty girl in a white, wide-brimmed hat hung down from its roof. Life-sized cut-outs of the same girl dressed in pink-chequered shirts, jeans and leather boots stood at the top of the steps up to a row of doors above.

"That's her?" said Alex.

The snake nodded.

Ahead of them a crowd of Hazel's fans stood chatting in front of the theatre, milling over the swathe of pink carpet, which today had replaced the traditional red one. But not for long. At the sound of muffled hooves, they spun round. Wide-eyed, their yelps of surprise quickly turned into shrieks of panic as they fled squealing, flinging fan rosettes and cowboy hats into the air behind them.

On seeing the chaos outside, theatre staff lunged for the row of doors, trying desperately to slam them closed against the onslaught. But they were too late. Seconds later the sheep stormed the foyer, scattering the staff like human skittles.

"This way!" shouted Alex, spotting a sign which read '*Rodeo Love* Premiere: Screen Six'.

The sheep swirled after him, flying across the foyer like a giant woolly arrow. Sending kiosks of Hazel Praline T-shirts and DVDs flying and journalists diving behind the popcorn counters, they flooded after him through the archway leading to the screens. At the far end of the poster-lined hallway, the number six glowed over a set of doors and, snatching up a life-sized cut-out of Hazel, Alex led the sheep towards it.

Hazel Praline walked on stage to a cheering crowd. Dappled with swirling dots of mirror light, she glittered like a pink diamond.

"Hello, London!"

As the twang of country guitars rang out, Rose squirmed furiously beneath Pandemic's grip, desperate to do something, anything, to stop the show. But the more she tried to twist free, the tighter his fingers clenched around her arm.

Hazel walked to the front of the stage, gracefully stepping over a rather untidy cluster of electrical cables, and began singing.

Love in the rain an' I've no umbrella,
Falling down like rhinestones an' glitterin' like tears.

Suddenly the doors at the back of the theatre slammed open. Shocked, Hazel dropped her microphone and, squinting against the spotlights, tried to see what was happening. As her band strummed to a stop, a pounding drone of hooves filled the darkness. Rose gasped to see both aisles filled with moving shadowy bulks. A second later the lights snapped on and the bulks became sheep. Some had Hazel Praline banners shredded in their horns; others had pink rosettes stuck to their rumps;

all had their heads down as they stormed towards the stage.

Either side, people clambered up onto their seats, clutching one another, squealing as the odd curious sheep broke off from the flock, stuck its nose into an open handbag or snatched an expensive coat to chew.

And yet as Rose watched the chaos, she had the weirdest feeling that the sheep were somehow organised into two groups: the ones in the right aisle following an ivory-coloured ram with rippled horns, the ones in the left a tight-fleeced ewe with a bumpy-faced lamb beside her.

Beside her, the sorceress leaped to her feet, and startled, two small grey-faced sheep squealed in alarm and ran faster. Almost, Rose thought, as if they recognised her.

"How in Hades did they get free?" growled Medea.

Get free? Rose sat bolt upright in her seat, her mind spinning, realising that the disruption was no freaky coincidence.

Medea turned back, pausing briefly to smile at the people in the row ahead who were now giving her strange looks, and glared at Pandemic. "The pipes, you fool!"

As Pandemic frantically patted each pocket in turn, the first sheep reached the area in front of the stage and began milling around wildly. Bustling into the rows of seats, they nuzzled the audience and stuffed their muzzles into bags of wine gums. All round, the theatre rang with shrieks and yelps and the soft thud of rolled up programmes walloping woolly rumps.

Stopping the show!

Two rows further down, Rose saw Mitch Praline leap into the thundering sheep and run with them, his arms spread wide[37]. "It's okay, honey!" he shouted, glancing up at Hazel, who stood watching him round-eyed from the stage.

Waving his hat in the air, he began cornering some sheep by the fire doors at the front of the theatre. Of course, back before her rise to stardom, Hazel had loved helping her dad out on the ranch and now, seeing what he was trying to do, she unhooked one of the looped white ropes from the stage dressing and threw it to him.

"You guys!" she called her bodyguards over quickly. "Go help m'daddy!"

Immediately, the men ran to join Mitch, standing behind him with their arms linked like a human

---

37. *After all, you don't spend most of your life as a Texan rancher without some things becoming second nature.*

fence, stepping towards the five or six sheep he'd split off from the others.

Of course, as the Pralines might have told you, handling awkward animals is much easier on a Texan ranch. Women there rarely scream because their sparkly shoes have squelched into something warm and wet. And there are no action-hero actors making nuisances of themselves by wielding evening jackets like matadors' capes. Consequently, despite Mitch's efforts, the theatre now descended into utter bedlam.

In fact, it was just like that film about the great white shark when someone spots a dorsal fin in the water and the swimmers go bananas, charging onto the beach for safety and tripping over one another in the surf.

Apart from the beach, of course.

And the surf.

Oh, all right, and the shark.

People flew out of their seats, squealing and flapping into the aisles, making for the exits.

"Finally!" snarled Medea, as Pandemic plucked a wooden arch of pipes from his coat. She scowled as a flurry of ice-cream pots and programmes rained down on her head, discarded by the audience members sprinting past the end of the row and fixed him with a vicious stare. "Freeze the flock!"

Freeze them, thought Rose, fleetingly wondering how they might possibly stop a herd of sheep in their tracks. Smiling coldly, Pandemic brought the pipes to his lips.

With both hands.

Seizing her chance, she leaped to her feet and kicked his shin hard. As he buckled over, she swept the pipes out of his hand, sending them spinning into the path of the running sheep where they smashed under thundering hooves. Swiftly ducking out of Medea's reach, she grabbed her rucksack and scrambled over the back of her seat, stepping onto the empty seat of the row behind, and then over again, leaving Medea lunging hopelessly after her. Then, quickly apologising to the few people remaining whom she trod on, squashed or tripped over, she reached the other aisle.

Which was when she spotted Alex, at the back of the stampede, deftly fending off the furious manager of the Luxe using one of Hazel's cut-outs as a makeshift shield. Beside him, Aries, looking decidedly greener than she remembered, bellowed at the three attendants cowering behind the manager and sent them racing away. Immediately realising that they were behind this wonderful disruption, she punched the air in triumph.

"Alex!" she shouted, stepping into the buffeting sheep to reach him.

He glanced over his shoulder and smiled. "You're all right!" he yelled, before blocking a thump from the manager with Hazel's cardboard head.

Lurching backwards, the manager clutched his throbbing hand, collided with a plump old lady in a silver dress and stole, and vanished in a muffle of fake fur and chubby ankles.

Alex ran up to Rose and threw his arms round her.

"I'm so glad to see you!" she exclaimed, reaching down with the other to rub Aries' brow. "And you!"

It was a lovely group hug moment, apart from the alarming hissing sound that now whistled in her ear, the sort of alarming hissing sound that snakes make when they are being squashed. Drawing back, Rose jumped to see Hex, his eyes glittering with outrage.

"It's all right," said Alex. "He's a friend."

Now, Hex's face broke into a wide grin, touched[38].

Rose looked at Alex and nodded towards the stage, where Hazel was now on her hands and knees shouting instructions to the bodyguards above a

---

38. *Which was rather charming, except for the fangs*

flossy sea of sheep. "You caused all this? So, you know what Medea's up to?"

"'Fraid so," replied Alex. He grabbed hold of Rose's hand and pulled her with him after the sheep. "Come on!"

Together, using the cut-out to force their way through, the four of them jostled their way towards the stage, pushing against the bulldozing crowd that was intent on moving in the opposite direction. Overhead the cinema sound system crackled into life and a polished voice told everyone to stay calm and seated. Not that anyone did, of course, and as Rose looked at the crush of people wedged in uncomfortably in the narrow aisles, she began to feel a glimmer of hope. After all, she reasoned as she sidestepped a cluster of sheep sharing seat stuffing like candy floss, with no audience, no music and nowhere to sit, there couldn't be a show, could there?

No.

Meaning that in just a few minutes Hazel would be offstage, out of that dress and away from danger.

Well, actually, no, again.

Because as much as I hate to be a spoilsport, I do have to remind you that we still have a deadly sorceress in our midst. The sort, say, whose face might at that precise second be lit up by a spume of silver stars exploding over her head, wholly unnoticed by the people dashing past.

Or Rose and the others.

Shame, really.

Meanwhile, on the patch of carpet below the stage, Mitch had managed to string up a makeshift roped corral and had penned in six sheep. Above him, Hazel shouted sheep-catching instructions to her bodyguards whilst wrestling another hay bale from the set dressing to throw down. Turning, she stopped to peer out over the auditorium.

"Where are those pretty stars comin' from?" she said.

"Ssstars?" Hex's voice was deadly serious.

Shooting up from Alex's shoulders, like a walking stick tossed by a tap dancer, he scanned the cinema, high over the sea of bobbing heads.

"What's happening?" demanded Alex.

"Medea!" hissed Hex, twisting into a panicky figure of eight. "She'sss cassssting a ssspell."

Horrified, Rose and Alex strained to catch a glimpse of the sorceress. Craning their necks to peer past the mayhem in the aisles, they saw her turning on the spot in the gap in front of her seat, twirling her arms above her head.

"But she looks like she's dancing!" said Rose, confused.

"Magic needsss movement!" explained Hex. "It generatesss the energy to make the ssspell work!"

For a moment Rose stared, fascinated.

"But why?" Aries rattled his hooves furiously. "The fleece curse doesn't need her help!"

"No," hissed Hex. "But no one'sss ever tried to ssstop it before, have they? Now—"

Hex's voice was lost beneath the sound of a soft *whump*. Turning, they saw one of the corralled sheep lying on its side, its legs stuck out, its face a mask of shock.

Rose clasped a hand to her mouth. "It's not—?" She stopped, unable to say the word.

"No." Alex shook his head quickly. "It's still breathing. It's just been stunned."

"Stunned?" spluttered Aries.

Behind them, a second sheep jerked rigid and keeled over. Then a third star-jumped in the air, froze and landed like a woolly starfish.

"Ssslumber-bound," replied Hex. "It'sss her sssheep-ssssleep ssspell."

"Her what?" said Rose.

"It'sss how ssshe captured them from the fieldsss in the firsssst place!" He grimaced as sheep dropped in the aisles, the orchestra pit and vanished suddenly between rows of seats. "It'sss one of her mossst basssic ssspells"

And Hex was right.

Sorceresses, you see, can't use their best magic in public. Partly because spells take time, special ingredients, fire and ancient tools, but mostly because you simply can't turn someone into a wart frog without passers-by badgering you about it.

Around them the thumps grew closer together as more and more sheep fell, turning the theatre into something that was beginning to resemble a storehouse for merry-go-round sheep-shaped rides. Trapped in the corral, Mitch, together with Hazel's bodyguards, vanished under an avalanche of toppling sheep.

"They'll all be asleep soon!" muttered Aries.

Rose looked around her and realised that people were no longer panicking. Instead of running they stood in the aisles. They chatted and pointed instead of screaming.

Relief brightened their faces.

Relief that finally the chaos was all over.

Relief that everything would soon go back to normal.

"We've got to break the spell!" said Rose desperately.

"Then ssstop her moving!" answered Hex.

Obviously, this was excellent advice if you didn't happen to be trapped in a cinema whose aisles were jammed by human and sheep sardines at the time.

Unless you were with the strongest ram in history, of course.

"Aries!" said Alex. "You can get through to her!"

There was no reply.

He looked down to see the ram, a deep sigh flapping his lips, his eyes drooping slowly closed.

"Not him as well!" squealed Rose.

"Aries!" yelled Alex. He bent down and lifted the ram's ear. "Wake up!"

Aries jumped to attention. "Whatisit?" he spluttered.

"Ssstand ssstill!" commanded Hex, slithering down Alex's arm onto the ram's brow where he promptly began wrapping himself tightly around Aries' ears, twisting from side to side to make a squirmy turban.

"The sspell's a dark lullaby," he explained, looking up at Alex and Rose between loops. "Only creaturesss with cloven hoovesss can hear it. We have to block hisss hearing before it takesss effect."

Drowsily, Aries watched the snake weave from side to side above his eyes. But a few seconds later, after Hex had slithered back under his own loops to whisper down the ram's ear, Aries was fully alert and knew exactly what he must do. Bustling into an empty row of seats to reach the aisle that led to Medea's seat, and protected from the sorceress's dangerous words by his own personal mamba-muffler, he took a deep breath and ran.

Meanwhile, Alex and Rose turned back towards the stage and, bracing themselves behind the cut-out of Hazel, began forcing their way forwards against the buffeting crowd until they reached a patch of clear seats that would take them to the front of the stage.

Three rows behind them, Aries reached the aisle, stomped out, turned and lowered his head, arranging his horns in front of the vast wall of tightly packed people stumbling towards him and pushed.

Hard.

Force powered up his legs and along his broad back, sending quivers through the straining tendons in his neck and wild shivers down his flanks. Sweat poured off his brow. But in his heart, fury rose like blistering lava in a volcano.

Fury at how Medea was still mistreating the sheep forced him one big step forwards, scooping an elegant old lady off her feet and into his horns.

Fury at what she'd done with his fleece catalysed

another three steps that bundled two men and a boy scout into his encompassing horns.

Fury about all the innocent people she'd killed for her miserable sport fired him into a slow clop, gathering two squealing usherettes and a Dorset ewe as he thrust on.

But feeling a seething rage at what she'd tried to do to his friends sent him shooting forwards. Like a monster snowplough plunging through a drift, he caused people and sheep to spill out of his horns, toppling either side into the empty banks of seats, as he powered up the aisle to draw level with Medea.

Oblivious, the sorceress continued to twirl, her eyes closed in a rapture of spite, her hands spinning wildly in front of her.

Beside her, Pandemic's deep snores rattled the air. Being half-goat, of course, and owning the most splendid pair of cloven hooves himself, he too had fallen prey to her spell.

Exchanging a look with Aries, Hex released his hold on the ram's ears and looped round and round on Aries' back. Then, using the coils like a giant spring, he threw himself into the air, flying, just as his grandfather had taught him to bounce over mangrove swamps of Africa, and whipped around the sorceress's frantic wrists.

Medea snapped her eyes open and squealed with frustration before meeting Aries' furious glare.

But only for a moment.

Spinning round, he kicked out his back legs with the force of a small truck and pitched Medea off her feet. Shrieking, she shot up towards the ceiling, her arms bound in front of her, and for a moment she seemed to hang like a furious exclamation mark before arcing over to dive head first into a stockpile of snoozing sheep. There was a *whump*, several surprised gasps and then nothing. Aries stretched up his head, delighted to see only the sorceress's feet sticking out of a now muttering, waking heap of sheep, and Hex sliding away into the shadows.

And then the first scream ripped through the auditorium.

Horrified, Rose and Alex looked up from hurdling over seat backs to see Hazel tugging furiously at the skirt of her dress. It was stapled firm to the stage by a vicious-looking shard of mirror. At the same instant two flashes of silver fell from the area above the stage, stabbing the wooden boards with the ferocity of thrown knives.

"Come on!" shouted Alex.

Rose leaped over the next two sets of seats and, drawing level with the stage, looked up.

Suspended from scaffolding, the mirrors that had previously made such pretty twinkles around the stage now swung crazily back and forth like enchanted pendulums, swishing higher and higher each time until they snapped their threads.

And dropped.

Momentarily frozen, Rose realised that this was the way the curse would kill Hazel. Her heart hammered in her ears, thumping against the swish of mirrors falling faster now in a sudden shimmering shower that tacked Hazel's skirt to the stage like silver stitches sewn by an invisible hand.

Beside her, Alex dragged the cut-out of Hazel over his head and, as she reached out to help him, she met Hazel's terrified eyes.

"I'm coming too," she said, sliding beneath the cardboard beside him.

Together they sprinted up the stage steps and threw themselves into the sparkling storm of mirrors. Each seizing one of Hazel's arms they yanked her, yelling, off her feet. Behind them the fabric ripped, like a chorus of tiny screams, as all three of them flew backwards towards the cinema screen. In the split second before all the lights went out, Rose glimpsed the remains of the dress billow up from the floor after them, as menacing as a monstrous pink jellyfish. Then everything was in darkness. A darkness spliced by splintering wood as every last mirror fell in a torrent of slashing glass.

❋XXVII❋
So Long, Farewell, Auf Wiedersehen, Good-Baaaah

Blanketed in darkness, their ears still jangling, Alex, Hazel and Rose huddled beneath the cardboard.

"Are you two all right?" whispered Alex.

"I think so," replied Rose. "Hazel?"

There was a soft moan. "Sure had better days," she sighed.

"And sssso have I," hissed Hex from the inky blackness of the orchestra pit. "I think I've got ssscale-chafe. Where'sss the ram?"

In reply there was a loud twanging noise coupled with the sound of horns entangled with musical strings.

"I'm here, too," he muttered. "Although in my haste to return I appear to have got my hoof stuck in some sort of funny-shaped lyre."

"Guitar," corrected Rose.

"Ex-guitar," added Hazel before breaking in a wobbly laugh that sounded close to crying.

At that moment the cinema flooded with light and, blinking, Rose wrapped her arm around Hazel's shoulder before turning to look at the stage.

She gasped.

Like an alien moonscape of gleaming rocks, mirrors stabbed every few centimetres of stage, splicing the wooden boards. As she watched them spangle in the light, Rose felt her heart begin to thump hard behind her ribs, realising just how vicious the curse had been.

If she and Alex had been only a few seconds later...

Shaking her head, she pushed the thought away.

Beside her, Hazel glanced up and burst into deep gulping sobs before burying her face in her knees, smudged with stage dust.

"C'mon," said Alex. He looked at Rose from beneath the cardboard cut-out. "Let's get this thing off us!"

Together Rose and Alex gingerly felt for some shard-free patches with their fingers and slid the cardboard, clattering, to the floor behind them, before helping Hazel to her feet.

Then, quickly glancing over to where the sorceress had crash-landed, and seeing no sign of her, Alex jumped down into the orchestra pit to disentangle

Aries from the guitar and tuck Hex back into his jumper.

But Rose simply stood, staring out over the ruined auditorium, feeling rather like one of those marathon runners who cross the line and promptly burst into tears. Her mind jumbled with astonishment that they'd actually saved Hazel, nerve-trembling shock at just how close it had been and a fizzing dollop of relief.

The sudden clatter of footsteps snapped her out of her thoughts and she looked sideways to see Mitch Praline racing up the steps two at a time.

"Haze, honey!" he cried, striding over the stage, smashing mirrors beneath his boots, to throw his arms around his daughter.

The young singer sank gratefully into her father's embrace, looking more like a child, her spectacular pink dress no more than a dirt-streaked bodice attached to a miniskirt of frayed rags. Rose sighed, remembering her own father's bear hugs and how they always put anything right and wished with all her heart that he were there, too. Then, blinking back a sudden prickle of tears, she heard Alex calling her name. Meeting her gaze, he nodded towards the police who were now running into the auditorium.

"We have to go," he said.

There is no finer police force than HM London Constabulary, and that late afternoon the officers set about sorting the scene of destruction with great relish.

They comforted women with popcorn in their hair and men whose trousers were covered with hoof-prints. They helped the dishevelled manager of the Luxe to his feet and offered him a cup of hot sweet tea. They called an ambulance for Hazel and saw her off, wrapped in a tartan blanket, gently led away by her father. And they flipped open their notebooks and took down witness statements that would later be filed at the station under 'mass hysteria'. (This being a fancy term that police officers use when faced with people who insist that they have seen a green ram wearing a venomous snake on his head in a London cinema. Or a man with horns on his head sprinting out of the fire doors the second the lights flicked back on.)

But policemen are just like the rest of us when it comes to a celebrity. And never more so than when that celebrity is young and pretty, and happens to be waving a sore, but attractive, knee about. Consequently, several younger male officers attended upon the sorceress, swarming about her like navy blue bees around a dahlia.

And she wasn't happy about it.

"A butt from a ram, you say, Madam?" said one

officer with a sparkle in his smile. "You'll need a hospital check-up."

"I will not!" snapped Medea.

Whereupon a second officer, wearing a concerned expression on his chubby face that made him look like an anxious goldfish, stepped forwards. "My mum sprained her knee," he added gravely. "Knocked down by a llama at a petting zoo, she was. Turned nasty. The sprain, I mean, although the llama was pretty bad-tempered too."

By now, of course, Medea's temper could easily have topped the most livid of llamas. Shaking with frustration and unspent rage, her white fingers twitched in her lap, itching for magical revenge.

"You're in shock, Miss," said the first officer.

Which was precisely the sort of astute observation for which the British police are famed the world over. However, the reason for Medea's state of mind wasn't one that any police constable, anywhere, was ever likely to guess.

You see, Medea had not been crossed for hundreds and hundreds of years. Not since Jason ditched her for Glauce had she been so wrong-footed and humiliated.

And mad.

For it to be at the hands of a couple of children, a ram and a rabble of grubby sheep was almost intolerable. And so, whilst the police officers continued to soothe and coax, she carried on scowling and thinking about snails. Specifically, the little brown garden one she planned to turn Alex into before stamping on him with her good leg, dunking Aries back into super-strength bacteria and giving Rose some much needed crystal clear instruction in how to behave [39].

If only the police would get out of her way so that she could find them.

"Tango sierra ambulance assistance requested," said the policeman with the bright smile.

"But I don't want one!" insisted Medea.

"Calm down, dear!" offered the chubby officer. "Everything will be—"

But whatever solace the officer was predicting was lost in a loud, "Oof!" as Medea punched him squarely in the face. Reeling, he toppled backwards and vanished in a blur of boots and trousers, over the next row of seats.

"Madam!" The smiling officer's voice was stern.

---

39. *What? You were expecting a scrunched Rose snail, too? Ah, no. You see, Medea hadn't spent hundreds of years on Earth without developing a great deal of patience, and having found such a super student in Rose, she wasn't about to turn her into a mollusc. That's the good news. In fact, she still liked her. That's the bad. Sorry.*

He puffed his chest up in outrage. "There's no need for that!"

But Medea disagreed and walloped him too.

However, please note: it is never, I repeat *never*, a good idea to punch a policeman and it's an even more terrible idea to punch two in a row. They simply don't like it. And, worse, they'll put you in a police cell to prove it. Which was why ten minutes later Medea was led out in handcuffs, scowling and raging, to a waiting police car.

Whereupon I'd just like to say, "Hooray!"

HOORAY!

Thank you.

Meanwhile Alex, Rose and Aries had slipped out of the door leading backstage and hurried down corridors cluttered with theatre props to leave the building by the stage door. This led them into a quiet alleyway and, from there, back into the bustling crowds of Leicester Square where they discovered the flock being ushered by the RSPCA into a corner of the square's lush gardens, temporarily penned off by the crowd barriers from the premiere. Whilst Alex went to find out where the sheep would be taken to, Aries watched them spill onto the grass, feeling his heart lift as they demolished rose bushes, weed in the fountain and waggled their bottoms at a snooty-looking statue of a man in funny trousers [40].

But it was seeing Toby, sniffing the grass beneath his hooves, round-eyed at the novelty of it that brought a tear to Aries' eye. A tear quickly blinked away as Alex returned to tell them the good news. That, since the police hadn't received any reports about a missing flock, the sheep would be taken to The Funky Farm Experience, a petting zoo run by a doting family, set in acres of green pastures with cosy straw-filled barns to sleep in at night [41].

In the time before the trucks arrived, Alex and Aries said goodbye to everyone.

Several times.

"Amazing!" muttered one RSPCA man, as a Greyface Dartmoor knelt down behind the barrier allowing the dark-haired boy to remove the popcorn boxes from its horns.

"Quite astonishing," added another, watching an Icelandic ram nuzzle the girl with the wild red hair.

"Extraordinary," added a third, as the green ram tilted its head towards a bumpy-faced ewe,

---

40. *Actually Shakespeare, in his puffball pants. (No, honestly, that is their proper name. Trust you to mention pants again!)*

41. *Junction 6 off the A23. Follow the signs to Brighton. Open 10 to 5 each day and all bank holidays (except Christmas Day).*

almost as if she were talking to him.

But as the trucks rumbled into the square, Rose led Aries away and quickly hid him behind a large hawthorn bush (where his new green colour blended in perfectly) to avoid any awkward questions about why he wasn't boarding the trucks too.

Minutes later, as the sunset streaked the London sky with gold, the trucks were ready to leave.

It was a scene everyone would remember.

After all, it's not every day that you see Leicester Square overrun by sheep.

Even fewer when you see a world-famous fashion designer being led away in handcuffs to a waiting police car.

And hardly any at all when that same designer is driven past cattle trucks that start to bounce under the stamping hooves of sixty-six sheep in a deafening roar of bleats that sound suspiciously like cheering.

By twenty past ten that evening, Alex and Aries had told the girls about all the terrible things Medea had done with the fleece, Hazel[42] (who was just back from the hospital) had burst into tears several more times, Rose had hugged everyone until they felt better and the little group had returned to the British Museum. Now, whilst Medea paced up and down the concrete floor of her police cell across town, Rose stroked Aries' head, watching the others examine the newly repaired caryatid. Flown back from Greece that same afternoon, the statue now stood on her original plinth, in front of the curtain in Room 18. Having only just finished repositioning her, the curators had left their scaffolding up on either side, which was lucky really, since it'd make it much easier for Alex and, especially, Aries to clamber back up to the portal.

Of course, the museum had closed to the public three hours before, but as I'm sure you won't be surprised to hear, Rose's mother was still working in its basement, so that once again Rose had the run of the exhibition rooms.

Looping out from Alex's shoulders, Hex twisted round the caryatid's back, hissing appreciatively.

"She's done a remarkable job," said Alex, running his finger over the barely visible join in the caryatid's

---

42. *What, you're surprised she was there? What with her being a world-class mega pop star and everything? Well, don't forget she would have been at her own world-class mega pop star's funeral, but for Alex, Aries, Hex and Rose, and she wasn't about to miss saying goodbye to three of her four newest and most special friends.*

neck. "I just hope it's a seamless mend."

"It will be," sighed Rose. "Mum's besotted by old relics, remember?"

Alex did, and hearing the sadness in her voice, he felt his heart tighten. Turning, he noticed the same resigned expression on Rose's face that he'd seen the first time that she'd spoken about her mother. Of course, he knew that she was sad they were leaving, but now he realised something else: that after they'd gone, her life would go back to normal, to being stuck in the museum, alone and waiting around for her mother, day after day.

Unless…

He walked over and picked up Rose's rucksack, which lay slumped at her feet.

"Aren't you forgetting something?" he said, handing it to her.

Rose's eyes widened in excitement. "The Scroll!"

He watched as she quickly unbuckled the straps, rummaged inside and plucked out the Scroll, thinking for a moment before lifting it to her lips.

"Scroll," she began, her voice little more than a whisper, "if my father is still living, please tell me where he is."

(Which, when you think about it, was a rather

clever way to phrase the question. After all, who wants to be led through the jungle to a heap of jaguar-chewed bones?)

The Scroll fidgeted. It fluttered its ends. It twitched. It rippled. It made a wet, rattling sound as though it was blowing a papery raspberry. And then it became absolutely silent.

"Scroll?" urged Alex, trying to ignore the little voice in his head warning that it might be delaying bad news.

"Shhh!" The Scroll rustled irritably. "I'm trying to think!"

"Great," sighed Aries and sank gloomily onto his haunches. "Get comfortable, everybody. It's going to be a long night!"

And indeed, several minutes dragged past, slow as treacle dribbling off a spoon. Finally, unable to stand it any longer, Rose lifted the Scroll with her trembling hand.

"Please?" her voice wavered.

Instantly the Scroll sprang open. "Minus nought point eight three three!" it announced with a flourish.

"What?" Rose's voice was barely audible.

"Minus fifty-seven point two!" added the Scroll, flapping its edges in excitement.

The others looked at each other blankly.

"Maybe it's a code?" suggested Alex. "One where numbers stand for letters of the alphabet. You know, one stands for 'A'—"

"And fifty-ssseven?" muttered Hex.

Aries tutted loudly. "Clearly the Scroll's as useless as ever! When it's not waffling on in mysterious verse it's reciting pointless numbers."

"Hang on a minute!" said Hazel quietly, pulling her smartphone from her bag. The others watched as she began tapping the screen. "Somethin' 'bout those numbers with all their minuses and points sounds jus' a bit familiar to me."

Everyone waited, watching.

"I thought so!" she cried. "I knew they were the sorta things my pilot talks about when we're tour-plannin'. They're coordinates!"

"Coordinates?" said Alex blankly.

"Numbers," said Rose. "They pinpoint places on a map."

"Look," said Hazel, holding out the glowing screen.

The others looked to see a single red dot glowing on an illuminated map of a wide river surrounded by green jungle.

"It's showin' a point way up in the north-east Amazon," added Hazel. "The Amazon,

Rose! Didn't you say—"

"He's alive!" squealed Rose, leaping up and punching the air.

Euphoric, she threw her arms around Alex and Hazel. Aries jammed his head in between them whilst Hex flicked his tongue into the air, tasting the happiness and looping round their feet.

"Oh, Hazel!" cried Rose, her eyes glittering with tears. "Thank you! You're wonderful!"

At which the Scroll cleared its throat pointedly.

"And so are you!" added Rose, tickling the Scroll in the palm of her hand so that it squealed with laughter. "You papery marvel!"

Cradling the Scroll she began pacing across the room, thinking out loud. "So, I need to find someone who'll take me to look for him. Someone from the Royal Geographical Society, maybe? I mean, they funded his trip in the first place." A frown crossed her face. "Except they gave up looking for him months ago."

"Hang those ol' boys," said Hazel. "I got a plane, don't I?"

Rose stared at her. "You mean…?"

"Sure," nodded Hazel. "Least I can do after today, ain't it? Besides, I reckon I'm in need of a vacation after this tour!"

"Oh!" squealed Rose, which was really the only sensible thing to say, and everyone jumped up and down a bit more and hugged each other again. For the longest time the friends embraced again, or at least Alex and Rose and Hazel did whilst Aries gave everyone an affectionate prod with his horns and Hex weaved between their ankles.

But finally when they all stepped apart again, pink-faced and happy, there was an awkward silence. One of those bumpy bits of quiet that happen when everyone knows there's a goodbye coming and nobody wants to be the one to say it.

Finally, Alex stepped back and picked Hex up from the floor, looping him over his shoulders and began walking, with Aries, towards the ramp to the scaffolding.

At the top, he lifted the curtain and turned.

"Goodbye," he smiled, and letting Aries walk through in front of him, stepped inside and let the curtain fall.

There was a moment's silence, loaded with a sparkly anticipation that something special was about to happen, before the cloth rumpled up messily and Aries stuck his head back out.

"I'll miss you, Rose," he said, blinking back his own tears.

Rose sniffed and blew him a kiss. "And I'll miss you, too," she whispered. "I never met proper heroes before."

Aries stepped back inside, blushing.

The two girls watched the cloth fall back, rippling in a cold breeze before lying flat against the wall. For a moment the room thrummed with a deafening quiet, suddenly yawning with new emptiness.

"C'mon, little lady," said Hazel, linking arms with Rose. "We got us some plannin' to do."

Nodding, Rose swallowed her tears and together the two girls walked out of Room 18, leaving its secrets behind them, into the Grand Hall where the first splashes of moonlight were painting the floor silver.

"Do you think they'll throw a party for us?" said Aries, nudging the boy's hand. "With Elysian thistles, I mean, and dandelions and some fresh swags of nettles?" He slapped his lips. "Ooh, and some wine for you?"

"Maybe," said Alex uncertainly, stepping through the portal.

Behind them, the huge stone door thundered closed, sending a rumble around the walls of the cavern.

"Maybe?" Aries looked up at him, puzzled.

"What I mean," said Alex gently, "is that we didn't complete our quest, did we?" He rubbed Aries' brow. "We don't have the fleece, Aries."

Aries turned away and studied his hooves quietly as Alex tucked the Scroll back into his bag and started down the shale-strewn slope towards the Styx. He was halfway to the riverbank when he felt the sharp jab of Aries' horns.

"But we thwarted her, didn't we?" said Aries brightly. "I mean, we saved Hazel, we freed the sheep. Alex, we stopped a sorceress!"

"True," said Alex slowly.

"And that's more than Jason or Herakles or any of those other tunicked twerps managed, isn't it?"

"Well, yes," said Alex. "I suppose so!"

At which Aries shot past him, skittering over the rocks, down to the water. "I mean, did you hear what Rose called us?" he cried over his shoulder.

"Proper heroes," replied Alex.

"That's right," said Aries, scuffling to a stop. "Hey, do you think Athena will commission statues of us? To stand with the other ones in the pavilion?" He lifted up a front hoof and stuck it out nobly in front of him. "What do you reckon?"

"What'sss he doing?" muttered Hex in Alex's ear.

"Striking a hero's pose, " smiled Alex, watching Aries spin round to stick out a back hoof instead.

As Aries continued to model for the imagined sculptor, Alex picked his way gingerly down the bank and began thinking back over the last few days.

Perhaps Rose was right, he reflected.

After all, who would have thought that he, Alex Knossos, potter and zoo keeper, could fight harpies and fauns and Cyclopes or persuade a sorceress's snake intent on killing him to change sides, or rally an army of frightened sheep into action?

"A hero's **krater** filled with olives would be nice!" added Aries. "At the big unveiling, I mean!"

Or that Aries could accept that his fleece was lost forever? That he was no longer obsessed about how he appeared on the outside, but had become a different and better ram on the inside?

Despite the chill wind lifting off the Styx, Alex felt a warm glow around his heart, thinking about Rose's words. More than that, for the first time in his life (and death) he understood the difference between the sort of person who lops the heads off monsters for the sake of it and the sort of person who finds the courage deep inside themselves to fight for their friends. The difference between one who's born looking fabulous and the one who learns to behave that way.

The difference between a Greek hero and a *proper* one.

Not that he was about to share that thought with Aries.

Not yet, anyway.

After all, there's only so much swaggering and bleating you can put up with on the dusty road back to the Underworld.

THE END

ALL GREEK TO YOU?

Just ask the all-knowing Scroll if you've forgotten who's who, what's what and what's not...

Agora

Agora is the Greek word for market place. We still use the word to describe a phobia, or fear, of wide, open spaces: agoraphobia.

Apollonius of Rhodes

Or Old Baloney of Rhodes as Aries prefers to calls him, since he was the ancient Greek poet who wrote about Jason and the Argonauts' adventure and, as we now know, got it all wrong.

Argo

This was Jason's ship and was named after Argus, the man who built it.

Atalanta

Atalanta was the only female member of Jason's Argonauts. She was the fastest runner in ancient Greece and used this to challenge men who wanted to marry her and whom she didn't fancy. She knew that she could beat them easily and then execute them, which was great fun and saved loads of money on wedding parties.

Alexander the Great

Alexander the Great was the son of King Philip of Macedon, a country to the north of Greece. After his father died, Alexander led the army and conquered a third of the world including the Persian Empire and Egypt. During the twelve years of his campaigns, he founded seventy cities and never lost a battle. He always rode his favourite horse, Bucephalus. Regarded as one of the cleverest military leaders ever to live, his strategies are still taught to army leaders today. He died at the age of thirty-two. Personally, I think Alexander the Absolutely Amazing would have been a better name.

The Argonauts

These were the sailors who travelled with Jason. 'Naut' comes from the Greek word for sailor so Argo-nauts, are sailors on the *Argo*. Lucky their ship wasn't called the *Coco* really, otherwise they'd be Coconauts.

Athena

The goddess of wisdom, war and crafts. With all that battling, brain-strain and button-making to deal with, no wonder she liked to throw a good party.

Barque

A barque is a small boat, rather like a gondola; a funeral barque is a small boat used to carry coffins over water and should not be confused with the sound a dog makes when it sees a hearse.

The Battle of Marathon

The first time the Persians invaded Greece was in 490 BC at the Battle of Marathon. There were tens of thousands more Persians than Athenians. However, by clever use of phalanxes, the Athenians drove the Persians back to their boats. Unfamiliar with the terrain, many Persians drowned in the surrounding marshlands. The Athenians then marched quickly back to Athens and defeated the Persians when they made their second attempt, this time to seize the city. Score – Athens 2: Persia 0.

Centaurs

Creatures with the head, chest and arms of a man and the body and legs of a horse, these chatty trotters can be found in the Underworld's Centaur Parcs.

The Ceryneian Hind

The Ceryneian Hind was a female deer with golden antlers and hooves made of brass. Faster than a flying arrow, she could have beaten any horse in the Grand National but would have been disqualified for eating the hedges.

Charon

Charon was the skeleton boatman who escorted the dead over the River Styx. For the price of one **obol**, this bony ferryman, dressed in a hooded cloak, would take shades over the water from the Land of the Living on to the path to the Underworld. A gloomy sort, he seldom made small talk on the journey, which was hardly surprising after centuries spent in a murky cave with rising damp seeping up his shinbones.

Charybdis

A ferocious whirlpool that sucked sailors round and down into a horrible watery death, rather like being flushed down the world's biggest toilet. She stayed close to Scylla, offering sailors a thoughtful choice of how they'd like to get to the Underworld.

Chiton

This was a common sort of clothing in ancient Greece worn by men and women. Made from rectangles of cloth, the chiton draped from the shoulders like a tunic and was often worn with a belt. Why not impress your friends by making your own? Simply wrap your duvet cover around you and pin the top edge at each shoulder. Instant Greek chic! (Although, do remember that traditional Greek chitons, unlike your duvet cover, were rarely stripy and absolutely never had pictures of superheroes or pop stars on them.)

Circe

Circe was Medea's aunt. Unlike normal aunts, who come round for tea and cakes every so often, Circe taught Medea how to be a sorceress. Turning sailors into pigs and harnessing dragons to chariots were amongst the many skills Circe shared with her niece, which set her on the road to bad behaviour but cheered up many a wet Wednesday.

The Elgin Marbles

In the early 1800s a Scottish nobleman called Lord Elgin brought lots of bits of the Parthenon back to Britain. These are now in the British Museum and include the carved panels that used to hang beneath the roof of the Parthenon, decorated with **centaurs** fighting men on one side and an ancient procession on the other. A lot of people think that the marbles should be returned to Greece. A lot of people think they should stay in the British Museum. What do you think?

The Fates

The ancient Greeks believed that three old women decided what would happen to you in your life. These were the three Fates. One old lady began spinning a skein of thread on the day you were born. A second measured it out day by day whilst a third snipped it with silver scissors on the day of your death. This job made her very busy and bad-tempered on battle days, when she could be found saying all manner of rude words and complaining about missing her favourite television programme.

Fire-Breathing Bulls

One of Jason's three tasks on Kolkis was to yoke, or harness, the fire-breathing bulls in order to plough a field and sow the dragons' teeth as King Aeetes demanded.

I suppose he was lucky it wasn't a competition for matador skills. One flick of the cape and it'd be smoking trousers all round.

Glauce

The princess who would have been the second Mrs Jason but for you-know-who turning her burning love into a burning wedding dress instead.

Greaves

Greaves are the bronze shin-plates that Greek soldiers wore to protect them from swords, horse kicks and stinging nettles.

Harpies

Birds with the heads and shoulders of women, these creatures were famous for snatching food away from people and never being invited on picnics.

Hector

A prince of Troy who was popped off by Achilles during the Battle of Troy, according to Homer in his epic poem, *The Iliad*.

Herakles

One of Jason's Argonauts, Herakles was the strongest man on Earth. He began his monster-mashing career early when he throttled the two giant snakes that the goddess Hera had released into his cradle. Without his later antics there wouldn't have been much point going to the Underworld Zoo since it was largely down to his handiwork in performing his **Twelve Labours** that Alex had so many creatures to care for.

Homer

No, not the yellow one with a skateboarding son, but the ancient Greek poet famous for giving us the story of the Battle of Troy in his epic poem, *The Iliad*.

Hoplite

A Greek foot soldier. Hoplites were armed with spears and shields and attacked the opposing army in their **phalanx** formation.

The Hydra

This reptilian monster with hundreds of heads lived in a swamp and spent her days mooching about blowing mud bubbles. Then Herakles arrived. Chopping off each of her heads, he was horrified to see two more grow back on each stump. However, he finally killed the monster with the help of his nephew, who seared each neck stump with a fiery club so that no new heads could grow back.

Jason

The Prince of Iolkus, robbed of the throne by his wicked Uncle Pelias who snuck in and made himself king. Brought up by a centaur, Jason later sailed to Kolkis to steal the Golden Fleece.

Krater

Despite sounding like the smoky hole you find on top of a volcano, a krater was a large clay pot used for mixing wine and water to serve to guests at parties. Like an ancient Greek punch bowl, drinks were drawn from it. Or, in Aries' case, slurped.

The Lion of Nemea

A ferocious big cat strangled by Herakles, who then snaffled its impenetrable pelt to complete his strongman's outfit.

Man-Eating Horses

The clue's in the name. These four terrifying horses belonged to the giant Diomedes and with their huge appetites and horrible diet put the 'mare' into nightmare.

Medea

The sorceress of Kolkis who helped Jason steal the fleece from the sacred grove and became his first wife.

Medusa

An old lady with hair that was made of real snakes. As if this wasn't bad enough, anyone who looked at her was immediately turned into stone, which made it very difficult to get a good hairdresser.

Midas

Midas was the king who was given the golden touch so that everything he put his hand on turned into gold. The gift became a curse when he hugged his daughter who promptly became a gleaming statue. However, on the bright side she did make a delightful garden feature.

The Minotaur

The Minotaur was a monster with the head and shoulders of a bull and the body of a man. This made finding clothes very difficult and so he was usually to be found pacing about in his maze, beneath the palace at Knossos, in just a pair of big underpants. Every so often young men and women were pushed screaming into his lair for him to eat. This went on until **Theseus** took the place of one of the men and stomped into the maze with a sword and ball of wool. He slew the Minotaur with his sword and then found his way back out of the maze by following the wool he had unwound along the passages.

Narcissus

Narcissus was an extremely handsome man who fell in love with his own reflection in a forest pool and spent his life gazing wide-eyed at it. He was so besotted by his own loveliness that he couldn't leave it. He stayed by the pool until he died. I know. How silly was that? But, as I said, he was good-looking, not smart.

Obol

An ancient Greek coin. Although the word 'obol' sounds like 'oboe', you'll find that however hard you blow, you can't get a decent tune out of it.

Oracles

Oracles, for those of you who've never had their palms read on Brighton Pier, were widely respected Greek women, whom people consulted to find out what was going to happen. A sort of ancient Greek fortune teller, they leaned over steaming pots to see into the future. Of course, it's not the leaning over steaming pots bit that's important, otherwise all dinner ladies would be oracles and they're not, because when they look into pots all they see is custard.

Parthenon

Athena's temple still stands high on its rock in Athens today. However, during its long lifetime it has been blown up by people from Venice who stored gunpowder under its roof, had bits taken away by Lord Elgin and endured years of traffic pollution, acid rain and curious tourists stomping all over it. So, I'm afraid it doesn't look quite as snazzy as it used to and Athena would not be amused.

Pegasus

A beautiful white horse with wings so that it could fly. And you thought seagull doo-doo was bad...

Perseus

Another have-a-go hero, Athena's nephew, Perseus, killed **Medusa** by reflecting her face back at her in his shiny shield and turning her to stone.

Phalanx

A rectangular formation of soldiers, or hoplites, who marched behind a wall of shields with their spears high and ready to fight the enemy.

Prow

Part of the bow, the prow is the very front of a ship, the bit above the waterline. Oddly enough, Jason was killed by the *Argo's* prow. It happened many years after the voyage when he took a nap under the beached *Argo*, only to be dispatched first class to the Underworld when its prow dropped off due to rampant wood rot. (Of course, I think we can guess who magicked the rot into it, can't we?)

Queen Persephone

Pronounced pur-sef-pho-knee (otherwise it sounds like a mobile someone called Percy might text on) Persephone was a teenager minding her own business on Earth, when one day King Hades suddenly burst through the ground of the field where she was gathering flowers and dragged her down to the Underworld to be his wife. Her mother, Demeter, the goddess of grain, was distraught and travelled down to the Underworld to demand King Hades return her daughter. However, anyone who'd eaten food in the Underworld may not return, and Persephone had eaten six pomegranate seeds. Hades ruled that Persephone must spend six months, for the six seeds eaten, in the Underworld each year, but could live with her mother on Earth during the other six. Of course, during those months, Demeter was delighted, the sun shone and harvests flourished giving the Greeks spring and summer. But for the six that her daughter resided in the Underworld the Earth was cold and rain-swept giving the Greeks autumn and winter.

River Styx

The Styx is the river that separates the Underworld from the Earth and the dead from the living and, as you might expect, it's not terribly cheerful. It's not the sort of place that you'd choose to picnic in or pitch a tent. The river doesn't babble or tinkle, nor does it weave prettily beneath rustic bridges and there are absolutely no fluffy-wuffy duckies. Instead, the water roils and twists, lurching black and menacing beneath rock that skitters with eyeless cave spiders.

Sconces

Sconces are iron candleholders. Written down the word looks like 'scones'. However, jam and cream doesn't improve the flavour of sconces and they really hurt your teeth when you bite into one.

Scylla

This sea monster had six heads, tentacles for legs and a ring of dogs' heads around her waist that wouldn't win best of anything at Crufts. She lived next to Charybdis, the whirlpool, so that sailors who tried to sail between her and Charybdis either sailed too close to Scylla and were devoured, or sailed too close to Charybdis and were drowned.

Shades

This is the correct name for the ancient Greek ghosts

who dwell in the Underworld, making Alex and Aries a pair of shades. However, only Aries would be much good at blocking out the sun.

The Spartan Army

Sparta was an area of ancient Greece famous for its ferocious army. Boys joined when they were seven years old and, if they survived the brutal military training, served until they were thirty. Girls didn't join the army, but were scarily tough and would punch you on the nose for nothing.

Stymphalian Birds

Man-eating birds with beaks made out of bronze. You wouldn't want one of these sharing a cage with your budgie.

Tartarus

This was the darkest, most horrible part of the Underworld, containing a prison where the wickedest ghosts were held.

Theseus

One of Jason's Argonauts, this prince killed the half-man half-bull Minotaur in his maze armed with just a sword and a ball of wool.

Trireme

A trireme was an ancient Greek ship with three rows of oars on each side with one man per oar. They were streamlined and fast and used as warships in sea battles. The tri of trireme means three, like the tri in tricycle.

However, tricycles were not nearly as useful in crossing the oceans and left everyone very wet and bad-tempered.

The Twelve Labours of Herakles

Pronounced hair-a-klees, the Romans called this hero Hercules. By either name his stepmother, Hera, hated him because he was the son of one of her husband, Zeus's, many girlfriends. To punish Herakles, she sent him into a mad destructive rage during which he killed his wife and children. When he came round he was horrified and stricken by grief. The god, Apollo, gave him the chance to cleanse his conscience by performing certain labours, or tasks, for King Eurystheus. A bit like Jason's three tasks on Kolkis, Herakles' labours were believed to be impossible. Worse, Herakles had twelve of them and they comprised a mixture of killing, capturing, stealing and er, spring cleaning.

He killed the **Lion of Nemea** (and wore his lion-skin pelt), the **Hydra** and the **Stymphalian birds**.

He captured the **Ceryneian Hind**, the Erymanthian Boar (a wild pig with bristles and tusks), the Bull of Crete and the three-headed dog, Cerberus, who guarded the entrance to the Underworld.

He stole the four **man-eating horses** (and fed Diomedes, their owner, to them), a flock of sheep from under a monster's nose and the golden apples from Zeus's back garden. He also stole the girdle of the queen of the

Amazons and, believe me, she wasn't happy about it when she couldn't get her frock on.

His tidying job was to clean the Augean stables, a horse block even filthier than Medea's cellar, which had been left festering for several years. However, rather than scrub them by hand, he diverted a river to *whoosh* through them and flush them clean. Neat, eh?

And finally, just in case you were wondering:

The Legend of the Golden Fleece

Long, long ago in ancient Greece, a hero named Jason sailed across the sea with his band of Argonauts in search of the Golden Fleece, in order to win back the throne his wicked uncle, Pelias, had stolen from Jason's father.

With its ringlets of glittering gold, the fleece was truly the greatest treasure on Earth. Once it had belonged to Aries, the flying ram, but he was sacrificed and his coat given to King Aeetes of Kolkis.

To protect it, he hung it on the topmost branches of an oak in the palace's dark forest and left it guarded by a man-eating snake. Eighteen metres long, a writhing, slithering heap of coils and teeth, Drako, was said never to sleep. Instead he watched the fleece, day and night, night and day, the ruby lights of his eyes blazing through the forest gloom, poised to slice through its creepers and shred would-be burglars into bundles of bones.

After a long and dangerous voyage, Jason and his men sailed into Kolkis Harbour. Jason presented himself to King Aeetes and told him that he had come for the fleece. King Aeetes could not refuse Jason – that would be seen as rude – and so he told Jason that he could have the fleece, if he could perform three special challenges. The challenges were, of course, impossible and Aeetes was sure that Jason would die in trying to achieve them.

However, Aeetes had reckoned without Medea, his daughter, a powerful sorceress. The moment she saw Jason she melted, falling helplessly in love, and vowed to use her dark magic to help him.

The king told Jason to yoke two fire-breathing bulls; Medea created a salve to protect Jason's skin from the flames.

The king told Jason to plough a field with the yoked bulls; Medea hypnotised the animals so they followed his every command.

The king told Jason to plant dragons' teeth and when those dragons' teeth sprang out of the soil as skeletons dressed in armour, it was Medea who told Jason to throw a rock into their midst, confusing the bone men into fighting and destroying each other.

The king was furious at the thought of losing his fleece and in fury, he ordered his generals to kill Jason at the feast that evening. But Medea overheard him and crept down to her secret rooms to mix a potion of herbs and magic. Then she led Jason into the enchanted forest, sprinkled the mixture over Drako's snout, sending the snake into a dark, blissful sleep, so that a moment later, Jason scaled the serpent's slumbering coils, snatched the fleece and sailed home on the Argo with his new bride by his side.

And everyone lived happily ever after.

THE END

Oh no they didn't.

Because as we know now, even though Mr Printer typed a big fat **THE END** at the end of Jason's story, what he should have typed was **THE BEGINNING**. In fact, since Jason dumped Medea, resulting in her staying on Earth with the fleece and causing all manner of misery, writing **THE END** was the biggest, fibbiest myth of them all because the most important story, Aries' story, was yet to start. To be honest, I expect the printer only typed **THE END** so that he could lock up early and go home for his dinner.

About the author

Julia was born in Stafford, but has also lived in Australia, Stockport and Oxford. Unfortunately, since she was a toddler at the time, she can't remember much about Australia, other than that she's pretty sure that the spiders were nearly as big as she was and that there were shark-watchers on the beaches. She's certain this is why *Jaws* remains her favourite film.

Julia has had lots of jobs, including keeping a photographic library of petrol stations for an oil-company, deciding what colour packets sausages look their best in and teaching eight-year olds. As Miss Wills her favourite lesson was history since it was here that she and the children first discovered the Ancient Greeks, their fabulous monsters and the problem with wearing a chiton on a windy day.

She now lives in Warwickshire with her partner Jim and Bosworth the dog, who is half-cocker-spaniel, half-poodle (and all teddy bear). She enjoys planting her garden with roses and violas – the flowers, not the instruments, as they tend to twang in the breeze and there's nothing like a furious orchestra stomping across your lawn to retrieve them to spoil the grass.